1 MONTH OF
FREE
READING

at

www.ForgottenBooks.com

By purchasing this book you are eligible for one month membership to ForgottenBooks.com, giving you unlimited access to our entire collection of over 700,000 titles via our web site and mobile apps.

To claim your free month visit:

www.forgottenbooks.com/free208725

ISBN 978-0-483-63133-5
PIBN 10208725

This book is a reproduction of an important historical work. Forgotten Books uses
state-of-the-art technology to digitally reconstruct the work, preserving the original format
whilst repairing imperfections present in the aged copy. In rare cases, an imperfection in
the original, such as a blemish or missing page, may be replicated in our edition. We do,
however, repair the vast majority of imperfections successfully; any imperfections that
remain are intentionally left to preserve the state of such historical works.

THE IMMORTALS

CINQ MARS

(Vol. I.)

By ALFRED DE VIGNY

CROWNED BY THE FRENCH ACADEMY

With a Preface by CHARLES DE MAZADE, of the French Academy, and illustrations by A. DUVIVIER

Alfred de Vigny.

[From the Original Drawing by Goujean.]

Published by MAISON MAZARIN

PARIS—NUMBER SIX RUE LAMARCK

Alfred de Vigny.

[From the Original Drawing by Couraux.]

THE IMMORTALS

CINQ MARS

(Vol. I.)

By ALFRED DE VIGNY

CROWNED BY THE FRENCH ACADEMY

With a Preface by CHARLES DE MAZADE, *of the French Academy, and Illustrations by* A. DUVIVIER

Published by MAISON MAZARIN
PARIS: NUMBER SIX RUE LAMARCK

ALFRED DE VIGNY

THE reputation of Alfred de Vigny has endured extraordinary vicissitudes in France. First he was lauded as the precursor of French romantic poetry and stately prose; then he sank in semi-oblivion, became the curiosity of criticism, died in retirement, and was neglected for a long time, until the last ten years or so produced a marked revolution of taste in France. The supremacy of Victor Hugo has been, if not questioned, at least mitigated; other poets have recovered from their obscurity. Lamartine shines now like a lamp relighted; and the pure, brilliant, and profoundly original genius of Alfred de Vigny now takes, for the first time, its proper place as one of the main illuminating forces of the nineteenth century.

It was not until one hundred years after this poet's birth that it became clearly recognized that he is one of the most important of all the great writers of France, and he is distinguished not only in fiction, but also in poetry and the drama. He is a follower of André Chénier, Lamartine, and Victor Hugo, a lyric sun, a philosophic poet, later, perhaps in consequence of the Revolution of 1830, becoming a "Symbolist." He has been held to occupy a middle ground between De Musset and

PREFACE

Chénier, but he has also something suggestive of Madame de Staël, and, artistically, he has much in common with Chateaubriand, though he is more coldly impersonal and probably much more sincere in his philosophy. If Sainte-Beuve, however, calls the poet in his *Nouveaux Lundis* a "beautiful angel, who has been drinking vinegar," then the modern reader needs a strong caution against malice and raillery, if not jealousy and perfidy, although the article on De Vigny abounds otherwise with excessive critical cleverness.

At times, indeed, under the cruel deceptions of love, he seemed to lose faith in his idealism; his pessimism, nevertheless, always remained noble, restrained, sympathetic, manifesting itself not in appeals for condolence, but in pitying care for all who were near and dear to him. Yet his lofty prose and poetry, interpenetrated with the stern despair of pessimistic idealism, will always be unintelligible to the many. As a poet, De Vigny appeals to the chosen few alone. In his dramas his genius is more emancipated from himself, in his novels most of all. It is by these that he is most widely known, and by these that he exercised the greatest influence on the literary life of his generation.

Alfred-Victor, Count de Vigny, was born in Loches, Touraine, March 27, 1797. His father was an army officer, wounded in the Seven Years' War. Alfred, after having been well educated, also selected a military career and received a commission in the "Mousquetaires Rouges," in 1814, when barely seventeen. He served until 1827, "twelve long years of peace," then re-

PREFACE

signed. Already in 1822 appeared a volume of *Poëmes* which was hardly noticed, although containing poetry since become important to the evolution of French verse: *La Neige, le Cor, le Deluge, Elva, la Frégate,* etc., again collected in *Poëmes antiques et modernes* (1826). Other poems were published after his death in *Les Destinées* (1864).

Under the influence of Walter Scott, he wrote a historical romance in 1826, *Cinq-Mars, ou une Conjuration sans Louis XIII.* It met with the most brilliant and decided success and was crowned by the Academy. *Cinq-Mars* will always be remembered as the earliest romantic novel in France and the greatest and most dramatic picture of Richelieu now extant. De Vigny was a convinced Anglophile, well acquainted with the writings of Shakespeare and Milton, Byron, Wordsworth, Shelley, Matthew Arnold, and Leopardi. He also married an English lady in 1825—Lydia Bunbury.

Other prose works are *Stello* (1832), in the manner of Sterne and Diderot, and *Servitude et Grandeur militaire* (1835), the language of which is as caustic as that of Merimée. As a dramatist, De Vigny produced a translation of *Othello—Le More de Venice* (1829); also *La Maréchale d'Ancre* (1832); both met with moderate success only. But a decided "hit" was *Chatterton* (1835), an adaption from his prose-work *Stello, ou les Diables bleus*; it at once established his reputation on the stage; the applause was most prodigious, and in the annals of the French theatre can only be compared with that of *Le Cid*. It was a great victory for the Romantic School, and the type of Chatterton, the

PREFACE

slighted poet, "the marvellous boy, the sleepless soul that perished in his pride," became contagious as erstwhile did the type of Werther.

For twenty years before his death Alfred de Vigny wrote nothing. He lived in retirement, almost a recluse, in La Charente, rarely visiting Paris. Admitted into L'Académie Française in 1845, he describes in his *Journal d'un Poëte* his academic visits and the reception held out to him by the members of L'Institut. This work appeared posthumously in 1867.

He died in Paris, September 17, 1863.

de l'Académic Française.

TRUTH IN ART

HE study of social progress is to-day not less needed in literature than is the analysis of the human heart. We live in an age of universal investigation, and of exploration of the sources of all movements. France, for example, loves at the same time history and the drama, because the one explores the vast destinies of humanity, and the other the individual lot of man. These embrace the whole of life. But it is the province of religion, of philosophy, of pure poetry only, to go beyond life, beyond time, into eternity.

Of late years (perhaps as a result of our political changes) art has borrowed from history more than ever. All of us have our eyes fixed on our chronicles, as though, having reached manhood while going on toward greater things, we had stopped a moment to cast up the account of our youth and its errors. We have had to double the interest by adding to it recollection.

As France has carried farther than other nations this love of facts, and as I had chosen a recent and well-remembered epoch, it seemed to me that I ought not to imitate those foreigners who in their pictures barely show in the horizon the men who dominate their history. I placed ours in the foreground of the scene; I made them leading actors in this tragedy, wherever I endeavored to represent the three kinds of ambition by which we are influenced, and with them the beauty of self-sacrifice to a noble ideal. A treatise on the fall of the feudal system; on the position, at home and abroad, of France in the seventeenth century; on foreign alliances; on the justice of parliaments or of secret commissions, or on accusations of sorcery, would not perhaps have been read. But the romance was read.

I do not mean to defend this last form of historical composition, being convinced that the real greatness of a work lies in the substance of the author's ideas and sentiments, and not in the literary form in which they are dressed. The choice of a certain epoch necessitates a certain treatment—to another epoch it would be unsuitable; these are mere secrets of the workshop of thought which there is no need of disclosing. What is the use of theorizing as to wherein lies the charm that moves us? We hear the tones of the harp, but its graceful form conceals from us its frame of iron. Nevertheless, since I have been convinced that this book possesses vitality, I can not help throwing out some reflections on the liberty which the imagination should employ in weaving into its tapestry all the leading figures of an age, and, to give more consistency to their acts, in making the reality of fact give way to the idea which each of them should represent in the eyes of posterity; in short, on the difference which I find between Truth in art and the True in fact.

Just as we descend into our consciences to judge of actions which our minds can not weigh, can we not also search in ourselves for the feeling which gives birth to forms of thought, always vague and cloudy? We shall find in our troubled hearts, where discord reigns, two needs which seem at variance, but which merge, as I think, in a common source—the love of the true, and the love of the fabulous.

On the day when man told the story of his life to man, history was born. Of what use is the memory of facts, if not to serve as an example of good or of evil? But the examples which the slow train of events presents to us are scattered and incomplete. They lack always a tangible and visible coherence leading straight on to a moral conclusion. The acts of the human race on the world's stage have doubtless a coherent unity, but the meaning of the vast tragedy enacted will be visible only to the eye of God, until the end, which will reveal it perhaps to the last man. All systems of philosophy have sought in vain to explain it, ceaselessly rolling up their rock, which, never reaching the top, falls back upon them—each raising its frail structure on the ruins of the others, only to see it fall in its turn.

I think, then, that man, after having satisfied his first longing for facts, wanted something fuller—some grouping, some adaptation to his capacity and experience, of the links of this vast chain of events which his sight could not take in. Thus he hoped to find in the historic recital examples which might support the moral truths of which he was conscious. Few single careers could satisfy this longing, being only incomplete parts of the elusive whole of the history of the world; one was a quarter, as it were, the other a half of the proof; imagination did the rest and completed them. From this, without doubt, sprang the fable. Man created it thus, because it was not given him to see more than himself and nature, which surrounds him; but he created it true with a truth all its own.

This Truth, so beautiful, so intellectual, which I feel, I see, and long to define, the name of which I here venture to distinguish from that of the True, that I may the better make myself understood, is the soul of all the arts. It is the selection of the characteristic token in all the beauties and the grandeurs of the visible True; but it is not the thing itself, it is something better: it is an ideal combination of its principal forms, a luminous tint made up of its brightest colors, an intoxicating balm of its purest perfumes, a delicious elixir of its best juices, a perfect harmony of its sweetest sounds—in short, it is a concentration of all its good qualities. For this Truth, and nothing else, should strive those works of art which are a moral representation of life—dramatic works. To attain it, the first step is undoubtedly to learn all that is true in fact of every period, to become deeply imbued with its general character and with its details; this involves only a cheap tribute of attention, of patience, and of memory. But then one must fix upon some chosen centre, and group everything around it; this is the work of im-

agination, and of that sublime common-sense which is
genius itself.

Of what use were the arts if they were only the reproduction and the imitation of life? Good heavens!
we see only too clearly about us the sad and disen-
chanting reality—the insupportable lukewarmness of
feeble characters, of shallow virtues and vices, of
irresolute loves, of tempered hates, of wavering friend-
ships, of unsettled beliefs, of constancy which has its
height and its depth, of opinions which evaporate.
Let us dream that once upon a time have lived men
stronger and greater, who were more determined for
good or for evil; that does us good. If the paleness of
your True is to follow us into art, we shall close at
once the theatre and the book, to avoid meeting it a
second time. What is wanted of works which revive
the ghosts of human beings is, I repeat, the philosophical spectacle of man deeply wrought upon by the
passions of his character and of his epoch; it is, in
short, the artistic Truth of that man and that epoch,
but both raised to a higher and ideal power, which
concentrates all their forces. You recognize this
Truth in works of the imagination just as you cry out
at the resemblance of a portrait of which you have
never seen the original; for true talent paints life
rather than the living.

To banish finally the scruples on this point of the
consciences of some persons, timorous in literary matters, whom I have seen affected with a personal sorrow
on viewing the rashness with which the imagination
sports with the most weighty characters of history, I

will hazard the assertion that, not throughout this work, I dare not say that, but in many of these pages, and those perhaps not of the least merit, history is a romance of which the people are the authors. The human mind, I believe, cares for the True only in the general character of an epoch. What it values most of all is the sum total of events and the advance of civilization, which carries individuals along with it; but, indifferent to details, it cares less to have them real than noble or, rather, grand and complete.

Examine closely the origin of certain deeds, of certain heroic expressions, which are born one knows not how; you will see them leap out ready-made from hearsay and the murmurs of the crowd, without having in themselves more than a shadow of truth, and, nevertheless, they will remain historical forever. As if by way of pleasantry, and to put a joke upon posterity, the public voice invents sublime utterances to mark, during their lives and under their very eyes, men who, confused, avow themselves as best they may, as not deserving of so much glory* and as not being able to sup-

---

* In our time has not a Russian General denied the fire of Moscow, which we have made heroic, and which will remain so? Has not a French General denied that utterance on the field of Waterloo which will immortalize it? And if I were not withheld by my respect for a sacred event, I might recall that a priest has felt it to be his duty to disavow in public a sublime speech which will remain the noblest that has ever been pronounced on a scaffold: "Son of Saint Louis, rise to heaven!" When I learned not long ago its real author, I was overcome by the destruction of my illusion, but before long I was consoled by a thought that does honor to humanity in my eyes. I feel that France has consecrated this speech, because she felt the need of reestablishing herself in her own eyes, of blinding herself to her awful error, and of believing that then and there an honest man was found who dared to speak aloud.

port so high renown. In vain; their disclaimers are not received. Let them cry out, let them write, let them print, let them sign—they are not listened to. These utterances are inscribed in bronze; the poor fellows remain historical and sublime in spite of themselves. And I do not find that all this is done in the ages of barbarism alone; it is still going on, and it molds the history of yesterday to the taste of public opinion —a Muse tyrannical and capricious, which preserves the general purport and scorns detail.

Which of you knows not of such transformation? Do you not see with your own eyes the chrysalis fact assume by degrees the wings of fiction? Half formed by the necessities of the time, a fact is hidden in the ground obscure and incomplete, rough, misshapen, like a block of marble not yet rough-hewn. The first who unearth it, and take it in hand, would wish it differently shaped, and pass it, already a little rounded, into other hands; others polish it as they pass it along; in a short time it is exhibited transformed into an immortal statue. We disclaim it; witnesses who have seen and heard pile refutations upon explanations; the learned investigate, pore over books, and write. No one listens to them any more than to the humble heroes who disown it; the torrent rolls on and bears with it the whole thing under the form which it has pleased it to give to these individual actions. What was needed for all this work? A nothing, a word; sometimes the caprice of a journalist out of work. And are we the losers by it? No. The adopted fact is always better composed than the real one, and it is even adopted only because it is better. The human race feels a need that its destinies should afford it a series of lessons; more careless than we think of the reality of facts, it strives to perfect the event in order to give it a great moral significance, feeling sure that the succession of scenes which it plays upon earth is not a comedy, and that since it advances, it marches toward an end, of which the explanation must be sought beyond what is visible.

For my part, I acknowledge my gratitude to the voice of the people for this achievement; for often in the finest life are found strange blemishes and inconsistencies which pain me when I see them. If a man seems to me a perfect model of a grand and noble character, and if some one comes and tells me of a mean trait which disfigures him, I am saddened by it, even though I do not know him, as by a misfortune which affects me in person; and I could almost wish that he had died before the change in his character.

Thus, when the Muse (and I give that name to art as a whole, to everything which belongs to the domain of imagination, almost in the same way as the ancients gave the name of Music to all education), when the Muse has related, in her impassioned manner, the adventures of a character whom I know to have lived; and when she reshapes his experiences into conformity with the strongest idea of vice or virtue which can be conceived of him—filling the gaps, veiling the incongruities of his life, and giving him that perfect unity of conduct which we like to see represented even in evil—

if, in addition to this, she preserves the only thing essential to the instruction of the world, the spirit of the epoch, I know no reason why we should be more exacting with her than with this voice of the people which every day makes every fact undergo so great changes.

The ancients carried this liberty even into history; they wanted to see in it only the general march, and broad movements of peoples and nations; and on these great movements, brought to view in courses very distinct and very clear, they placed a few colossal figures—symbols of noble character and of lofty purpose.

One might almost reckon mathematically that, having undergone the double composition of public opinion and of the author, their history reaches us at third hand and is thus separated by two stages from the original fact.

It is because in their eyes history too was a work of art; and in consequence of not having realized that such is its real nature, the whole Christian world still lacks an historical monument like those which dominate antiquity and consecrate the memory of its destinies—as its pyramids, its obelisks, its pylons, and its porticos still dominate the earth which was known to them, and thereby commemorate the grandeur of antiquity.

If, then, we find everywhere evidence of this inclination to desert the positive, to bring the ideal even into historic annals, I believe that with greater reason we should be completely indifferent to historical reality in judging the dramatic works, whether poems, romances, or tragedies, which borrow from history celebrated characters. Art ought never to be considered except in its relations with its ideal beauty. Let it be said that what is *true in fact* is secondary merely; it is only an illusion the more with which it adorns itself—one of our prejudices which it respects. It can do without it, for the Truth by which it must live is the truth of observation of human nature, and not authenticity of fact. The names of the characters have nothing to do with the matter. The idea is everything; the proper name is only the example and the proof of the idea.

So much the better for the memory of those who are chosen to represent philosophical or moral ideas; but, once again, that is not the question. The imagination can produce just as fine things without them; it is a power wholly creative; the imaginary beings which it animates are endowed with life as truly as the real beings which it brings to life again. We believe in Othello as we do in Richard III., whose tomb is in Westminster; in Lovelace and Clarissa as in Paul and Virginia, whose tombs are in the Isle of France. It is with the same eye that we must watch the performance of its characters, and demand of the Muse only her artistic Truth, more lofty than the True— whether collecting the traits of a character dispersed among a thousand entire individuals, she composes from them a type whose name alone is imaginary; or whether she goes to their tomb to seek and to touch with her galvanic current the dead whose great deeds are known, forces them to arise again, and drags them dazzled to the light of day, where, in the circle which this fairy has traced, they re-assume unwillingly their passions of other days, and begin again in the sight of their descendants the sad drama of life.

Alfred de Vigny.

1827.

CONTENTS

VOLUME I

CHAPTER I

THE ADIEU 1

PAGE

CHAPTER II

THE STREET 30

CHAPTER III

THE GOOD PRIEST 44

CHAPTER IV

THE TRIAL 60

CHAPTER V

THE MARTYRDOM 74

CHAPTER VI

THE DREAM 87

CHAPTER VII

THE CABINET 99

CHAPTER VIII

THE INTERVIEW 129

CONTENTS

CHAPTER IX

THE SIEGE 146

CHAPTER X

THE RECOMPENSE 163

CHAPTER XI

THE BLUNDERS 179

CHAPTER XII

THE NIGHT-WATCH 194

CHAPTER XIII

THE SPANIARD 216

CHAPTER XIV

THE RIOT 230

CHAPTER XV

THE ALCOVE 251

CHAPTER XVI

THE CONFUSION 270

CHAPTER XVII

THE TOILETTE 281

ILLUSTRATIONS

FACING PAGE

Alfred de Vigny (*portrait*) . . . . . . *Frontispiece*

The silent traveller kissed his mother's hand 20

"Ah, who can resist your Eminence?" 112

"I come here to kill him!" 208

CINQ-MARS

CHAPTER I

THE ADIEU

Fare thee well! and if forever,
Still forever fare thee well!
                    LORD BYRON.

D O you know that charming part of our country which has been called the garden of France—that spot where, amid verdant plains watered by wide streams, one inhales the purest air of heaven?

If you have travelled through fair Touraine in summer, you have no doubt followed with enchantment the peaceful Loire; you have regretted the impossibility of determining upon which of its banks you would choose to dwell with your beloved. On its right bank one sees valleys dotted with white houses surrounded by woods, hills yellow with vines or white with the blossoms of the cherry-tree, walls covered with honeysuckles, rose-gardens, from which pointed roofs rise suddenly. Everything reminds the traveller either of the fertility of the land or of the antiquity of its monuments; and everything interests him in the work of its busy inhabitants.

1   [1]

ALFRED DE VIGNY

Nothing has proved useless to them; it seems as if in their love for so beautiful a country—the only province of France never occupied by foreigners—they have determined not to lose the least part of its soil, the smallest grain of its sand. Do you fancy that this ruined tower is inhabited only by hideous night-birds? No; at the sound of your horse's hoofs, the smiling face of a young girl peeps out from the ivy, whitened with the dust from the road. If you climb a hillside covered with vines, a light column of smoke shows you that there is a chimney at your feet; for the very rock is inhabited, and families of vine-dressers breathe in its caverns, sheltered at night by the kindly earth which they laboriously cultivate during the day. The good people of Touraine are as simple as their life, gentle as the air they breathe, and strong as the powerful earth they dig. Their countenances, like their characters, have something of the frankness of the true people of St.-Louis; their chestnut locks are still long and curve around their ears, as in the stone statues of our old kings; their language is the purest French, with neither slowness, haste, nor accent—the cradle of the language is there, close to the cradle of the monarchy.

But the left bank of the stream has a more serious aspect; in the distance you see Chambord, which, with its blue domes and little cupolas, appears like some great city of the Orient; there is Chanteloup, raising its graceful pagoda in the air. Near these a simpler building attracts the eyes of the traveller by its magnificent situation and imposing size; it is the château of Chaumont. Built upon the highest hill of the shore, it frames the broad summit with its lofty walls and its enormous towers; high slate steeples increase their loftiness, and give to the building that conventual air, that religious form of all our old châteaux, which casts an aspect of gravity over the landscape of most of our provinces. Black and tufted trees surround this ancient mansion, resembling from afar the plumes that encircled the hat of King Henry. At the foot of the hill, connected with the château by a narrow path, lies a pretty village, whose white houses seem to have sprung from the golden sand; a chapel stands half-way up the hill; the lords descended and the villagers ascended to its altar—the region of equality, situated like a neutral spot between poverty and riches, which have been too often opposed to each other in bitter conflict.

Here, one morning in the month of June, 1639, the bell of the château having, as usual, rung at midday, the dinner-hour of the family, occurrences of an unusual kind were passing in this ancient dwelling. The numerous domestics observed that in repeating the morning prayers before the assembled household, the Maréchale d'Effiat had spoken with a broken voice and with tears in her eyes, and that she had appeared in a deeper mourning than was customary. The people of the household and the Italians of the Duchesse de Mantua, who had at that time retired for a while to Chaumont, saw with surprise that sudden preparations were being made for departure. The old domestic of the Maréchal d'Effiat (who had been dead six months)

[3]

had taken again to his travelling-boots, which he had sworn to abandon forever. This brave fellow, named Grandchamp, had followed the chief of the family everywhere in the wars, and in his financial work; he had been his equerry in the former, and his secretary in the latter. He had recently returned from Germany, to inform the mother and the children of the death of the Maréchal, whose last sighs he had heard at Luzzelstein. He was one of those faithful servants who are become too rare in France; who suffer with the misfortunes of the family, and rejoice with their joys; who approve of early marriages, that they may have young masters to educate; who scold the children and often the fathers; who risk death for them; who serve without wages in revolutions; who toil for their support; and who in prosperous times follow them everywhere, or exclaim at their return, "Behold our vines!" He had a severe and remarkable face, a coppery complexion, and silver-gray hair, in which, however, some few locks, black as his heavy eyebrows, made him appear harsh at first; but a gentle countenance softened this first impression. At present his voice was loud. He busied himself much that day in hastening the dinner, and ordered about all the servants, who were in mourning like himself.

"Come," said he, "make haste to serve the dinner, while Germain, Louis, and Etienne saddle their horses; Monsieur Henri and I must be far away by eight o'clock this evening. And you, gentlemen, Italians, have you warned your young Princess? I wager that she is gone to read with her ladies at the end of the

park, or on the banks of the lake. She always comes
in after the first course, and makes every one rise from
the table."

"Ah, my good Grandchamp," said in a low voice a
young maid servant who was passing, "do not speak of
the Duchess; she is very sorrowful, and I believe that
she will remain in her apartment. Santa Maria! what
a shame to travel to-day! to depart on a Friday, the
thirteenth of the month, and the day of Saint Gervais
and of Saint-Protais—the day of two martyrs! I have
been telling my beads all the morning for Monsieur de
Cinq-Mars; and I could not help thinking of these
things. And my mistress thinks of them too, although
she is a great lady; so you need not laugh!"

With these words the young Italian glided like a
bird across the large dining-room, and disappeared
down a corridor, startled at seeing the great doors of
the salon opened.

Grandchamp had hardly heard what she had said,
and seemed to have been occupied only with the preparations for dinner; he fulfilled the important duties
of major-domo, and cast severe looks at the domestics
to see whether they were all at their posts, placing
himself behind the chair of the eldest son of the house.
Then all the inhabitants of the mansion entered the
salon. Eleven persons seated themselves at table.
The Maréchale came in last, giving her arm to a handsome old man, magnificently dressed, whom she placed
upon her left hand. She seated herself in a large
gilded armchair at the middle of one side of the table,
which was oblong in form. Another seat, rather more

ornamented, was at her right, but it remained empty. The young Marquis d'Effiat, seated in front of his mother, was to assist her in doing the honors of the table. He was not more than twenty years old, and his countenance was insignificant; much gravity and distinguished manners proclaimed, however, a social nature, but nothing more. His young sister of fourteen, two gentlemen of the province, three young Italian noblemen of the suite of Marie de Gonzaga (Duchesse de Mantua), a lady-in-waiting, the governess of the young daughter of the Maréchale, and an abbé of the neighborhood, old and very deaf, composed the assembly. A seat at the right of the elder son still remained vacant.

The Maréchale, before seating herself, made the sign of the cross, and repeated the *Bénédicité* aloud; every one responded by making the complete sign, or upon the breast alone. This custom was preserved in many families in France up to the Revolution of 1789; some still practise it, but more in the provinces than in Paris, and not without some hesitation and some preliminary words upon the weather, accompanied by a deprecatory smile when a stranger is present—for it is too true that virtue also has its blush.

The Maréchale possessed an imposing figure, and her large blue eyes were remarkably beautiful. She did not appear to have yet attained her forty-fifth year; but, oppressed with sorrow, she walked slowly and spoke with difficulty, closing her eyes, and allowing her head to droop for a moment upon her breast, after she had been obliged to raise her voice. At such efforts ner uand pressed to her bosom showed that she experienced sharp pain. She saw therefore with satisfaction that the person who was seated at her left, having at the beginning engrossed the conversation, without having been requested by any one to talk, persisted with an imperturbable coolness in engrossing it to the end of the dinner. This was the old Maréchal de Bassompierre; he had preserved with his white locks an air of youth and vivacity curious to see. His noble and polished manners showed a certain gallantry, antiquated like his costume—for he wore a ruff in the fashion of Henri IV, and the slashed sleeves fashionable in the former reign, an absurdity which was unpardonable in the eyes of the beaux of the court. This would not have appeared more singular than anything else at present; but it is admitted that in every age we laugh at the costume of our fathers, and, except the Orientals, I know of no people who have not this fault.

One of the Italian gentlemen had hardly finished asking the Maréchal what he thought of the way in which the Cardinal treated the daughter of the Duc de Mantua, when he exclaimed, in his familiar language:

"Heavens, man! what are you talking about? what do I comprehend of this new system under which France is living? We old companions-in-arms of his late Majesty can ill understand the language spoken by the new court, and that in its turn does not comprehend ours. But what do I say? We speak no language in this sad country, for all the world is silent before the Cardinal; this haughty little vassal looks upon us as merely old family portraits, which occasionally he shortens by the head; but happily the motto always remains. Is it not true, my dear Puy-Laurens?"

This guest was about the same age as the Maréchal, but, being more grave and cautious, he answered in vague and few words, and made a sign to his contemporary in order to induce him to observe the unpleasant emotions which he had caused the mistress of the house by reminding her of the recent death of her husband and in speaking thus of the minister, his friend. But it was in vain, for Bassompierre, pleased with the sign of half-approval, emptied at one draught a great goblet of wine—a remedy which he lauds in his Memoirs as infallible against the plague and against reserve; and leaning back to receive another glass from his esquire, he settled himself more firmly than ever upon his chair, and in his favorite ideas.

"Yes, we are in the way here; I said so the other day to my dear Duc de Guise, whom they have ruined. They count the minutes that we have to live, and shake the hour-glass to hasten the descent of its sands. When Monsieur le Cardinal-Duc observes in a corner three or four of our tall figures, who never quitted the side of the late King, he feels that he is unable to move those statues of iron, and that to do it would require the hand of a great man; he passes quickly by, and dares not meddle with us, who fear him not. He believes that we are always conspiring; and they say at this very moment that there is talk of putting me in the Bastille."

"Eh! Monsieur le Maréchal, why do you delay your departure?" said the Italian. "I know of no place, except Flanders, where you can find shelter."

"Ah, Monsieur! you do not know me. So far from flying, I sought out the King before his departure, and told him that I did so in order to save people the trouble of looking for me; and that if I knew when he wished to send me, I would go myself without being taken. He was as kind as I expected him to be, and said to me, 'What, my old friend, could you have thought that I desired to send you there? You know well that I love you.'"

"Ah, my dear Maréchal, let me compliment you," said Madame d'Effiat, in a soft voice. "I recognize the benevolence of the King in these words; he remembers the affection which the King, his father, had toward you. It appears to me that he always accorded to you all that you desired for your friends," she added, with animation, in order to put him into the track of praise, and to beguile him from the discontent which he had so loudly declared.

"Assuredly, Madame," answered he; "no one is more willing to recognize his virtues than François de Bassompierre. I shall be faithful to him to the end, because I gave myself, body and fortune, to his father at a ball; and I swear that, with my consent at least, none of my family shall ever fail in their duties toward the King of France. Although the Bestcins are foreigners and Lorrains, a shake of the hand from Henri IV gained us forever. My greatest grief has been to see my brother die in the service of Spain;

and I have just written to my nephew to say that I shall disinherit him if he has passed over to the Emperor, as report says he has."

One of the gentlemen guests who had as yet been silent, and who was remarkable for the profusion of knots, ribbons, and tags which covered his dress, and for the black *cordon* of the Order of St.-Michael which decorated his neck, bowed, observing that it was thus all faithful subjects ought to speak.

"I' faith, Monsieur de Launay, you deceive yourself very much," said the Maréchal, to whom the recollection of his ancestors now occurred; "persons of our blood are subjects only at our own pleasure, for God has caused us to be born as much lords of our lands as the King is of his.   When I came to France, I came at my ease, accompanied by my gentlemen and pages. I perceive, however, that the farther we go, the more we lose sight of this idea, especially at the court.   But here is a young man who arrives very opportunely to hear me."

The door indeed opened, and a young man of fine form entered.   He was pale; his hair was brown, his eyes were black, his expression was sad and reckless. This was Henri d'Effiat, Marquis de Cinq-Mars (a name taken from an estate of his family).   His dress and his short cloak were black; a collar of lace fell from his neck halfway down his breast; his stout, small, and very wide-spurred boots made so much noise upon the flags of the salon that his approach was heard at a distance.   He walked directly toward the Maréchale, bowed low, and kissed her hand.

"Well, Henri," she said, "are your horses ready? At what hour do you depart?"

"Immediately after dinner, Madame, if you will allow me," said he to his mother, with the ceremonious respect of the times; and passing behind her, he saluted M. de Bassompierre before seating himself at the left of his eldest brother.

"Well," said the Maréchal, continuing to eat with an excellent appetite, "you are about to depart, my son; you are going to the court—a slippery place nowadays. I am sorry for your sake that it is not now what it used to be. In former times, the court was simply the drawing-room of the King, in which he received his natural friends: nobles of great family, his peers, who visited him to show their devotion and their friendship, lost their money with him, and accompanied him in his pleasure parties, but never received anything from him, except permission to bring their vassals with them, to break their heads in his service. The honors a man of quality received did not enrich him, for he paid for them out of his purse. I sold an estate for every grade I received; the title of colonel-general of the Swiss cost me four hundred thousand crowns, and at the baptism of the present King I had to buy a costume that cost me a hundred thousand francs."

"Ah!" said the mistress of the house, smiling, "you must acknowledge for once that you were not obliged to do that. We have all heard of your splendid dress of pearls; but I should be much vexed were it still the custom to wear such."

"Oh, Madame la Marquise, do not fear, those times of magnificence never will return. We committed follies, no doubt, but they proved our independence; it is clear that it would then have been hard to convert from their allegiance to the King adherents who were attached to him by love alone, and whose coronets contained as many diamonds as his own locked-up crown. It is also certain that ambition could not then attack all classes, since such expenses could come only from rich hands, and since gold comes only from mines. Those great houses, which are being so furiously assailed, were not ambitious, and frequently, desiring no employment from the Government, maintained their places at court by their own weight, existed upon their own foundation, and might say, as one of them did say, 'The Prince condescends not; I am Rohan.' It was the same with every noble family, to which its own nobility sufficed; the King himself expressed it in writing to one of my friends: 'Money is not a common thing between gentlemen like you and me.'"

"But, Monsieur le Maréchal," coldly, and with extreme politeness, interrupted M. de Launay, who perhaps intended to anger him, "this independence has produced as many civil wars and revolts as those of Monsieur de Montmorency."

"Monsieur! I can not consent to hear these things spoken," said the fiery Maréchal, leaping up in his armchair. "Those revolts and wars had nothing to do with the fundamental laws of the State, and could no more have overturned the throne than a duel could have done so. Of all the great party-chiefs, there was not one who would not have laid his victory at the feet of the King, had he succeeded, knowing well that all the other lords who were as great as himself would have abandoned the enemy of the legitimate sovereign. Arms were taken against a faction, and not against the sovereign authority; and, this destroyed, everything went on again in the old way. But what have you done in crushing us? You have crushed the arm of the throne, and have not put anything in its place. Yes, I no longer doubt that the Cardinal-Duke will wholly accomplish his design; the great nobility will leave and lose their lands, and, ceasing to be great proprietors, they will cease to be a great power. The court is already no more than a palace where people beg; by and by it will become an antechamber, when it will be composed only of those who constitute the suite of the King. Great names will begin by ennobling vile offices; but, by a terrible reaction, those offices will end by rendering great names vile. Estranged from their homes, the nobility will be dependent upon the employments which they shall have received; and if the people, over whom they will no longer have any influence, choose to revolt——"

"How gloomy you are to-day, Maréchal!" interrupted the Marquise; "I hope that neither I nor my children will ever see that time. I no longer perceive your cheerful disposition, now that you talk like a politician. I expected to hear you give advice to my son. Henri, what troubles you? You seem very absent."

Cinq-Mars, with eyes fixed upon the great bay-window of the dining-room, looked sorrowfully upon the magnificent landscape. The sun shone in full splendor, and colored the sands of the Loire, the trees, and the lawns with gold and emerald. The sky was azure, the waves were of a transparent yellow, the islets of a vivid green; behind their rounded outlines rose the great sails of the merchant-vessels, like a fleet in ambuscade.

"O Nature, Nature!" he mused; "beautiful Nature, farewell! Soon will my heart cease to be of simplicity enough to feel your charm, soon you will no longer please my eyes. This heart is already burned by a deep passion; and the mention of the interests of men stirs it with hitherto unknown agitation. I must, however, enter this labyrinth; I may, perchance, lose myself there, but for Marie——"

At this moment, aroused by the words of his mother, and fearing to exhibit a childish regret at leaving his beautiful country and his family, he said:

"I am thinking, Madame, of the road which I shall take to Perpignan, and also of that which shall bring me back to you."

"Do not forget to take that of Poitiers, and to go to Loudun to see your old tutor, our good Abbé Quillet; he will give you useful advice about the court. He is on very good terms with the Duc de Bouillon; and besides, though he may not be very necessary to you, it is a mark of deference which you owe him."

"Is it, then, to the siege of Perpignan that you are going, my boy?" asked the old Maréchal, who began to think that he had been silent a long time. "Ah!

it is well for you. Plague upon it! a siege! 'tis an excellent opening. I would have given much had I been able to assist the late King at a siege, upon my arrival in his court; it would have been better to be disembowelled then than at a tourney, as I was. But we were at peace; and I was compelled to go and shoot the Turks with the Rosworm of the Hungarians, in order that I might not afflict my family by my idleness. For the rest, may his Majesty receive you as kindly as his father received me! It is true that the King is good and brave; but they have unfortunately taught him that cold Spanish etiquette which arrests all the impulses of the heart. He restrains himself and others by an immovable presence and an icy look; as for me, I confess that I am always waiting for the moment of thaw, but in vain. We were accustomed to other manners from the witty and simple-hearted Henri; and we were at least free to tell him that we loved him."

Cinq-Mars, with eyes fixed upon those of Bassompierre, as if to force himself to attend to his discourse, asked him what was the manner of the late king in conversation.

"Lively and frank," said he. "Some time after my arrival in France, I played with him and with the Duchesse de Beaufort at Fontainebleau; for he wished, he said, to win my gold-pieces, my fine Portugal money. He asked me the reason why I came into this country. 'Truly, Sire,' said I, frankly, 'I came with no intention of enlisting myself in your service, but only to pass some time at your court, and afterward at that of

Spain; out you have charmed me so much that, instead of going farther, if you desire my service, I will devote myself to you till death.' Then he embraced me, and assured me that I could not find a better master, or one who would love me more. Alas! I have found it so. And for my part, I sacrificed everything to him, even my love; and I would have done more, had it been possible to do more than renounce Mademoiselle de Montmorency."

The good Maréchal had tears in his eyes; but the young Marquis d'Effiat and the Italians, looking at one another, could not help smiling to think that at present the Princesse de Condé was far from young and pretty. Cinq-Mars noticed this interchange of glances, and smiled also, but bitterly.

"Is it true then," he thought, "that the affections meet the same fate as the fashions, and that the lapse of a few years can throw the same ridicule upon a costume and upon love? Happy is he who does not outlive his youth and his illusions, and who carries his treasures with him to the grave!"

Bu tagain, with effort breaking the melancholy course of his thoughts, and wishing that the good Maréchal should read nothing unpleasant upon the countenances of his hosts, he said:

"People spoke, then, with much freedom to King Henri? Possibly, however, he found it necessary to assume that tone at the beginning of his reign; but when he was master did he change it?"

"Never! no, never, to his last day, did our great King cease to be the same. He did not blush to be a

man, and he spoke to men with force and sensibility.¹
Ah! I fancy I see him now, embracing the Duc de
Guise in his carriage, on the very day of his death;
he had just made one of his lively pleasantries to me,
and the Duke said to him, 'You are, in my opinion,
one of the most agreeable men in the world, and destiny
ordained us for each other. For, had you been but
an ordinary man, I should have taken you into my
service at whatever price; but since heaven ordained
that you should be born a great King, it is inevitable
that I belong to you.' Oh, great man!" cried Bassompierre, with tears in his eyes, and perhaps a little excited by the frequent bumpers he had drunk, "you
said well, 'When you have lost me you will learn my
value.'"

During this interlude, the guests at the table had
assumed various attitudes, according to their position
in public affairs. One of the Italians pretended to
chat and laugh in a subdued manner with the young
daughter of the Maréchale; the other talked to the
deaf old Abbé, who, with one hand behind his ear that
he might hear, was the only one who appeared attentive. Cinq-Mars had sunk back into his melancholy
abstraction, after throwing a glance at the Maréchal,
as one looks aside after throwing a tennis-ball until its
return; his elder brother did the honors of the table
with the same calm. Puy-Laurens observed the mistress of the house with attention; he was devoted to the
Duc d'Orléans, and feared the Cardinal. As for the
Maréchale, she had an anxious and afflicted air. Careless words had often recalled the death of her husband

or the departure of her son; and, oftener still, she had feared lest Bassompierre should compromise himself. She had touched him many times, glancing at the same time toward M. de Launay, of whom she knew little, and whom she had reason to believe devoted to the prime minister; but to a man of his character, such warnings were useless. He appeared not to notice them; but, on the contrary, crushing that gentleman with his bold glance and the sound of his voice, he affected to turn himself toward him, and to direct all his conversation to him. M. de Launay assumed an air of indifference and of assenting politeness, which he preserved until the moment when the folding-doors opened, and "Mademoiselle la Duchesse de Mantua" was announced.

The conversation which we have transcribed so lengthily passed, in reality, with rapidity; and the repast was only half over when the arrival of Marie de Gonzaga caused the company to rise. She was small, but very well made, and although her eyes and hair were black, her complexion was as dazzling as the beauty of her skin. The Maréchale arose to acknowledge her rank, and kissed her on the forehead, in recognition of her goodness and her charming age.

"We have waited a long time for you to-day, dear Marie," she said, placing the Duchess beside her; "fortunately, you remain with me to replace one of my children, who is about to depart."

The young Duchess blushed, lowered her head and her eyes, in order that no one might see their redness, and said, timidly:

"Madame, that may well be, since you have taken toward me the place of a mother;" and a glance thrown at Cinq-Mars, at the other end of the table, made him turn pale.

This arrival changed the conversation; it ceased to be general, and each guest conversed in a low voice with his neighbor. The Maréchal alone continued to utter a few sentences concerning the magnificence of the old court, his wars in Turkey, the tournaments, and the avarice of the new court; but, to his great regret, no one made any reply, and the company were about to leave the table, when, as the clock struck two, five horses appeared in the courtyard. Four were mounted by servants, cloaked and armed; the other horse, black and spirited, was held by old Grandchamp—it was his master's steed.

"Ah!" exclaimed Bassompierre; "see, our battle-horses are saddled and bridled. Come, young man, we must say, with our old Marot:

> "'Adieu la cour, adieu les dames!
> Adieu les filles et les femmes!
> Adieu vous dy pour quelque temps;
> Adieu vos plaisans passe-temps!
> Adieu le bal, adieu la dance;
> Adieu mesure, adieu cadance,
> Tabourins, Hautbois, Violons,
> Puisqu'à la guerre nous allons!'"*

These old verses and the air of the Maréchal made all the guests laugh, except three persons.

"Heavens!" he continued, "it seems to me as if,

* In this quotation the Old French form has been preserved.

like him, I were only seventeen years old; he will return to us covered with embroidery. Madame, we must keep his chair vacant for him."

The Maréchale suddenly grew pale, and left the table in tears; every one rose with her; she took only two steps, and sank into another chair. Her sons and her daughter and the young Duchess gathered anxiously around her, and heard her say, amid the sighs and tears which she strove to restrain:

"Pardon, my friends! it is foolish of me—childish; but I am weak at present, and am not mistress of myself. We were thirteen at table; and you, my dear Duchess, were the cause of it. But it is very wrong of me to show so much weakness before him. Farewell, my child; give me your forehead to kiss, and may God conduct you! Be worthy of your name and of your father."

Then, as Homer says, "smiling under tears," she raised herself, pushed her son from her, and said:

"Come, let me see you on horseback, fair sir!"

The silent traveller kissed the hands of his mother, and made a low bow to her; he bowed also to the Duchess, without raising his eyes. Then, embracing his elder brother, pressing the hand of the Maréchal, and kissing the forehead of his young sister almost simultaneously, he went forth, and was on horseback in an instant. Every one went to the windows which overlooked the court, except Madame d'Effiat, who was still seated and suffering.

"He sets off at full gallop. That is a good sign," said the Maréchal, laughing.

The silent traveller kissed his mother's hand.

[*From the Original Drawing by A. Duvivier.*]

... the well she

... we

... and left the

... she took only

... Her sons and

... Duchess gathered anx-

... the sighs

... medish of me—childish;

... am not mistress of my-

... and you, my dear

... it is very wrong of

... Farewell,

The silent traveller kissed his mother's hand.

conduct you ...

[From the Original Drawing by A. Duvivier.]

father."

Then, as Her ...

raised herself, ...

"Come, let ...

The silent ... ther,

and made a low ... to the

Duchess, without ...

his elder brother, ...

and kissing the forehead of h ... almost

simultaneously, he went forth ... on horseback

in an instant. Every one went to the windows which

overlooked the court, ...

was still seated and suffering

"He sets off at full gallop. What is a ...

said the Maréchal, laughing

"Oh, heavens!" cried the young Princess, retiring from the bay-window.

"What is the matter?" said the mother.

"Nothing, nothing!" said M. de Launay. "Your son's horse stumbled under the gateway; but he soon pulled him up. See, he salutes us from the road."

"Another ominous presage!" said the Marquise, upon retiring to her apartments.

Every one imitated her by being silent or speaking low.

The day was sad, and in the evening the supper was silent at the château of Chaumont.

At ten o'clock that evening, the old Maréchal, conducted by his valet, retired to the northern tower near the gateway, and opposite the river. The heat was extreme; he opened the window, and, enveloping himself in his great silk robe, placed a heavy candlestick upon the table and desired to be left alone. His window looked out upon the plain, which the moon, in her first quarter, indistinctly lighted; the sky was charged with thick clouds, and all things disposed the mind to melancholy. Although Bassompierre had nothing of the dreamer in his character, the tone which the conversation had taken at dinner returned to his memory, and he reconsidered his life, the sad changes which the new reign had wrought in it, a reign which seemed to have breathed upon him a wind of misfortune—the death of a cherished sister; the irregularities of the heir of his name; the loss of his lands and of his favor; the recent fate of his friend, the Maréchal d'Effiat, whose chambers he now occupied. All these thoughts drew from him an involuntary sigh, and he went to the window to breathe.

At that moment he fancied he heard the tramp of a troop of horse at the side of the wood; but the wind rising made him think that he had been mistaken, and, as the noise suddenly ceased, he forgot it. He still watched for some time all the lights of the château, which were successively extinguished, after winding among the windows of the staircases and rambling about the courtyards and the stables. Then, leaning back in his great tapestried armchair, his elbow resting on the table, he abandoned himself to his reflections. After a while, drawing from his breast a medallion which hung concealed, suspended by a black ribbon, he said:

"Come, my good old master, talk with me as you have so often talked; come, great King, forget your court for the smile of a true friend; come, great man, consult me concerning ambitious Austria; come, inconstant chevalier, speak to me of the lightness of thy love, and of the fidelity of thine inconstancy; come, heroie soldier, complain to me again that I obscure you in combat. Ah, had I only done it in Paris! Had I only received thy wound? With thy blood the world has lost the benefits of thine interrupted reign——"

The tears of the Maréchal obscured the glass that covered the large medallion, and he was effacing them with respectful kisses, when, his door being roughly opened, he quickly drew his sword.

"Who goes there?" he cried, in his surprise, which was much increased when he saw M. de Launay, who, hat in hand, advanced toward him, and said to him, with embarrassment:

"Monsieur, it is with a heart pierced with grief that I am forced to tell you that the King has commanded me to arrest you. A carriage awaits you at the gate, attended by thirty of the Cardinal-Duke's musketeers."

Bassompierre had not risen: and he still held the medallion in his right hand, and the sword in the other. He tendered it disdainfully to this man, saying:

"Monsieur, I know that I have lived too long, and it is that of which I was thinking; in the name of the great Henri, I restore this sword peacefully to his son. Follow me."

He accompanied these words with a look so firm that De Launay was depressed, and followed him with drooping head, as if he had himself been arrested by the noble old man, who, seizing a flambeau, issued from the court and found all the doors opened by horse-guards, who had terrified the people of the château in the name of the King, and commanded silence. The carriage was ready, and departed rapidly, followed by many horses. The Maréchal, seated beside M. de Launay, was about to fall asleep, rocked by the movement of the vehicle, when a voice cried to the driver, "Stop!" and, as he continued, a pistol-shot followed. The horses stopped.

"I declare, Monsieur, that this is done without my participation," said Bassompierre. Then, putting his head out at the door, he saw that they were in a little wood, and that the road was too narrow to allow the

horses to pass to either the right or the left of the carriage—a great advantage for the aggressors, since the
musketeers could not advance. He tried to see what
was going on when a cavalier, having in his hand a long
sword, with which he parried the strokes of the guard,
approached the door, crying:

"Come, come, Monsieur le Maréchal!"

"What! is that you, you madcap, Henri, who are
playing these pranks? Gentlemen, let him alone; he
is a mere boy."

And, as De Launay called to the musketeers to cease,
Bassompierre recognized the cavalier.

"And how the devil came you here?" cried Bassompierre. "I thought you were at Tours, or even farther,
if you had done your duty; but here you are returned
to make a fool of yourself."

"Truly, it was not for you I returned, but for a secret
affair," said Cinq-Mars, in a lower tone; "but, as I
take it, they are about to introduce you to the Bastille,
and I am sure you will not betray me, for that delightful edifice is the very Temple of Discretion. Yet had
you thought fit," he continued, aloud, "I should have
released you from these gentlemen in the wood here,
which is so dense that their horses would not have been
able to stir. A peasant informed me of the insult passed
upon us, more than upon you, by this violation of my
father's house."

"It is the King's order, my boy, and we must respect
his will; reserve your ardor for his service, though I
thank you with all my heart. Now farewell, and let me
proceed on my agreeable journey."

De Launay interposed, "I may inform you, Monsieur de Cinq-Mars, that I have been desired by the King himself to assure Monsieur le Maréchal, that he is deeply afflicted at the step he has found it necessary to take, and that it is solely from an apprehension that Monsieur le Maréchal may be led into evil that his Majesty requests him to remain for a few days in the Bastille."*

Bassompierre turned his head toward Cinq-Mars with a hearty laugh. "You see, my friend, how we young men are placed under guardianship; so take care of yourself.' '

"I will go, then," said Henri; "this is the last time I shall play the knight-errant for any one against his will;" and, reëntering the wood as the carriage dashed off at full speed, he proceeded by narrow paths toward the castle, followed at a short distance by Grandchamp and his small escort.

On arriving at the foot of the western tower, he reined in his horse. He did not alight, but, approaching so near the wall that he could rest his foot upon an abutment, he stood up, and raised the blind of a window on the ground-floor, made in the form of a portcullis, such as is still seen on some ancient buildings.

It was now past midnight, and the moon was hidden behind the clouds. No one but a member of the family could have found his way through darkness so profound. The towers and the roof formed one dark mass, which stood out in indistinct relief against the sky, hardly less dark; no light shone throughout the

*He remained there twelve years.

château, wherein all inmates seemed buried in slumber. Cinq-Mars, enveloped in a large cloak, his face hidden under the broad brim of his hat, awaited in suspense a reply to his signal.

It came; a soft voice was heard from within:

"Is that you, Monsieur Cinq-Mars?"

"Alas, who else should it be? Who else would return like a criminal to his paternal house, without entering it, without bidding one more adieu to his mother? Who else would return to complain of the present, without a hope for the future, but I?"

The gentle voice replied, but its tones were agitated, and evidently accompanied with tears: "Alas! Henri, of what do you complain? Have I not already done more, far more than I ought? It is not my fault, but my misfortune, that my father was a sovereign prince. Can one choose one's birthplace or one's rank, and say for example, 'I will be a shepherdess?' How unhappy is the lot of princesses! From the cradle, the sentiments of the heart are prohibited to them; and when they have advanced beyond childhood, they are ceded like a town, and must not even weep. Since I have known you, what have I not done to bring my future life within the reach of happiness, in removing it far from a throne? For two years I have struggled in vain, at once against my evil fortune, that separates me from you, and against you, who estrange me from the duty I owe to my family. I have sought to spread a belief that I was dead; I have almost longed for revolutions. I should have blessed a change which deprived me of my rank, as I thanked Heaven when my father was dethroned; but the court wonders at my absence; the Queen requires me to attend her. Our dreams are at an end, Henri; we have already slumbered too long. Let us awake, be courageous, and think no more of those dear two years—forget all in the one recollection of our great resolve. Have but one thought; be ambitious for—be ambitious—for my sake."

"Must we, then, indeed, forget all, Marie?" murmured Cinq-Mars.

She hesitated.

"Yes, forget all—that I myself have forgotten." Then, after a moment's pause, she continued with earnestness: "Yes, forget our happy days together, our long evenings, even our walks by the lake and through the wood; but keep the future ever in mind. Go, Henri; your father was Maréchal. Be you more; be you Constable, Prince. Go; you are young, noble, rich, brave, beloved——"

"Beloved forever?" said Henri.

"Forever; for life and for eternity."

Cinq-Mars, tremulously extending his hand to the window, exclaimed:

"I swear, Marie, by the Virgin, whose name you bear, that you shall be mine, or my head shall fall on the scaffold!"

"Oh, Heaven! what is it you say?" she cried, seizing his hand in her own. "Swear to me that you will share in no guilty deeds; that you will never forget that the King of France is your master. Love him above all, next to her who will sacrifice all for you, who will await you amid suffering and sorrow. Take this little gold cross and wear it upon your heart; it has often been wet with my tears, and those tears will flow still more bitterly if ever you are faithless to the King. Give me the ring I see on your finger. Oh, heavens, my hand and yours are red with blood!"

"Oh, only a scratch. Did you hear nothing, an hour ago?"

"No; but listen. Do you hear anything now?"

"No, Marie, nothing but some bird of night on the tower."

"I heard whispering near us, I am sure. But whence comes this blood? Tell me, and then depart."

"Yes, I will go, while the clouds are still dark above us. Farewell, sweet soul; in my hour of danger I will invoke thee as a guardian angel. Love has infused the burning poison of ambition into my soul, and for the first time I feel that ambition may be ennobled by its aim. Farewell! I go to accomplish my destiny."

"And forget not mine."

"Can they ever be separated?"

"Never!" exclaimed Marie, "but by death."

"I fear absence still more," said Cinq-Mars.

"Farewell! I tremble; farewell!" repeated the beloved voice, and the window was slowly drawn down, the clasped hands not parting till the last moment.

The black horse had all the while been pawing the earth, tossing his head with impatience, and whinnying. Cinq-Mars, as agitated and restless as his steed, gave it the rein; and the whole party was soon near the city of Tours, which the bells of St. Gatien had announced from afar. To the disappointment of old Grandchamp, Cinq-Mars would not enter the town, but proceeded on his way, and five days later he entered, with his escort, the old city of Loudun in Poitou, after an uneventful journey.

CHAPTER II

THE STREET

Je m'avancais d'un pas pénible et mal assuré vers le but de ce convoi tragique.—NODIER, *Smarra*.

THE reign of which we are about to paint a few years—a reign of feebleness, which was like an eclipse of the crown between the splendors of Henri IV and those of Louis le Grand—afflicts the eyes which contemplate it with dark stains of blood, and these were not all the work of one man, but were caused by great and grave bodies. It is melancholy to observe that in this age, still full of disorder, the clergy, like a nation, had its populace, as it had its nobility, its ignorant and its criminal prelates, as well as those who were learned and virtuous. Since that time, its remnant of barbarism has been refined away by the long reign of Louis XIV, and its corruptions have been washed out in the blood of the martyrs whom it offered up to the revolution of 1793.

We felt it necessary to pause for a moment to express this reflection before entering upon the recital of the facts presented by the history of this period, and to intimate that, notwithstanding this consolatory reflection, we have found it incumbent upon us to pass over many details too odious to occupy a place in our pages, sighing in spirit at those guilty acts which it was necessary to record, as in relating the life of a virtuous old man, we should lament over the impetuosities of his passionate youth, or over the corrupt tendencies of his riper age.

When the cavalcade entered the narrow streets of Loudun, they heard strange noises all around them. The streets were filled with agitated masses; the bells of the church and of the convent were ringing furiously, as if the town was in flames; and the whole population, without paying any attention to the travellers, was pressing tumultuously toward a large edifice that adjoined the church. Here and there dense crowds were collected, listening in silence to some voice that seemed raised in exhortation, or engaged in emphatic reading; then, furious cries, mingled with pious exclamations, arose from the crowd, which, dispersing, showed the travellers that the orator was some Capuchin or Franciscan friar, who, holding a wooden crucifix in one hand, pointed with the other to the large building which was attracting such universal interest.

"Jésu Maria!" exclaimed an old woman, "who would ever have thought that the Evil Spirit would choose our old town for his abode?"

"Ay, or that the pious Ursulines should be possessed?" said another.

"They say that the demon who torments the Superior is called Legion," cried a third.

"One demon, say you?" interrupted a nun; "there were seven in her poor body, whereunto, doubtless, she had attached too much importance, by reason of its great beauty, though now 'tis but the receptacle of evil spirits. The prior of the Carmelites yesterday expelled the demon Eazas through her mouth; and the reverend Father Lactantius has driven out in like manner the demon Beherit. But the other five will not depart, and when the holy exorcists (whom Heaven support!) summoned them in Latin to withdraw, they replied insolently that they would not go till they had proved their power, to the conviction even of the Huguenots and heretics, who, misbelieving wretches! seem to doubt it. The demon Elimi, the worst of them all, as you know, has threatened to take off Monsieur de Laubardemont's skull-cap to-day, and to dangle it in the air at *Miserere*."

"Holy Virgin!" rejoined the first speaker, "I'm all of a tremble! And to think that many times I have got this magician Urbain to say masses for me!"

"For myself," exclaimed a girl, crossing herself; "I too confessed to him ten months ago! No doubt I should have been possessed myself, but for the relic of Saint-Geneviève I luckily had about me, and——"

"Luckily, indeed, Martine," interposed a fat gossip; "for—no offence!—you, as I remember, were long enough with the handsome sorcerer."

"Pshaw!" said a young soldier, who had joined the group, smoking his pipe, "don't you know that pretty Martine was dispossessed a month ago."

The girl blushed, and drew the hood of her black cloak over her face. The elder gossips cast a glance of indignation at the reckless trooper, and finding themselves now close to the door of the building, and thus sure of making their way in among the first when it should be thrown open, sat down upon the stone bench at the side, and, talking of the latest wonders, raised the expectations of all as to the delight they were about to have in being spectators of something marvellous—an apparition, perhaps, but at the very least, an administration of the torture.

"Is it true, aunt," asked Martine of the eldest gossip, "that you have heard the demons speak?"

"Yes, child, true as I see you; many and many can say the same; and it was to convince you of it I brought you with me here, that you may see the power of the Evil One."

"What kind of voice has he?" continued the girl, glad to encourage a conversation which diverted from herself the invidious attention procured her by the soldier's raillery.

"Oh, he speaks with a voice like that of the Superior herself, to whom Our Lady be gracious! Poor young woman! I was with her yesterday a long time; it was sad to see her tearing her breast, turning her arms and her legs first one way and then another, and then, all of a sudden, twisting them together behind her back. When the holy Father Lactantius pronounced the name of Urbain Grandier, foam came out of her mouth, and she talked Latin for all the world as if she were reading the Bible. Of course, I did not understand what she said, and all I can remember of it now is, '*Urbanus Magicus rosas diabolica*,' which they tell me means that the magician Urbain had bewitched her with some roses the Devil had given him; and so it must have been, for while Father Lactantius spoke, out of her ears and neck came a quantity of flame-colored roses, all smelling of sulphur so strongly that the Judge-Advocate called out for every one present to stop their noses and eyes, for that the demons were about to come out."

"Ah, look there now!" exclaimed with shrill voices and a triumphant air the whole bevy of assembled women, turning toward the crowd, and more particularly toward a group of men attired in black, among whom was standing the young soldier who had cut his joke just before so unceremoniously.

"Listen to the noisy old idiots!" exclaimed the soldier. "They think they're at the witches' Sabbath, but I don't see their broomsticks."

"Young man, young man!" said a citizen, with a sad air, "jest not upon such subjects in the open air, or, in such a time as this, the wind may become gushing flames and destroy you."

"Pooh! I laugh at your exorcists!" returned the soldier; "my name is Grand-Ferré, and I've got here a better exorciser than any of you can show."

And significantly grasping the handle of his rapier in one hand, with the other he twisted up his blond moustache, as he looked fiercely around; but meeting no glance which returned the defiance of his own, he slowly withdrew, left foot foremost, and strolled along the dark, narrow streets with all the reckless nonchalance of a young soldier who has just donned his uniform, and a profound contempt for all who wear not a military coat.

In the meantime eight or ten of the more substantial and rational inhabitants traversed in a body, slowly and silently, the agitated throng; they seemed overwhelmed with amazement and distress at the agitation and excitement they witnessed everywhere, and as each new instance of the popular frenzy appeared, they exchanged glances of wonder and apprehension. Their mute depression communicated itself to the working-people, and to the peasants who had flocked in from the adjacent country, and who all sought a guide for their opinions in the faces of the principal townsmen, also for the most part proprietors of the surrounding districts. They saw that something calamitous was on foot, and resorted accordingly to the only remedy open to the ignorant and the beguiled—apathetic resignation.

Yet, in the character of the French peasant is a certain scoffing finesse of which he makes effective use, sometimes with his equals, and almost invariably with his superiors. He puts questions to power as embarrassing as are those which infancy puts to mature age. He affects excessive humility, in order to confuse him whom he addresses with the very height of his isolated elevation. He exaggerates the awkwardness of his manner and the rudeness of his speech, as a means of covering his real thoughts under the appearance of mere uncouthness; yet, despite all his self-command, there is something in his air, certain fierce expressions which betray him to the close observer, who discerns in his sardonic smile, and in the marked emphasis with which he leans on his long staff, the hopes that secretly nourish his soul, and the aid upon which he ultimately relies.

ALFRED DE VIGNY

One of the oldest of the peasants whom we have indicated came on vigorously, followed by ten or twelve young men, his sons and nephews, all wearing the broad-brimmed hat and the blue frock or blouse of the ancient Gauls, which the peasants of France still wear over their other garments, as peculiarly adapted to their humid climate and their laborious habits.

When the old man had reached the group of personages of whom we have just spoken, he took off his hat —an example immediately followed by his whole family—and showed a face tanned with exposure to the weather, a forehead bald and wrinkled with age, and long, white hair. His shoulders were bent with years and labor, but he was still a hale and sturdy man. He was received with an air of welcome, and even of respect, by one of the gravest of the grave group he had approached, who, without uncovering, however, extended to him his hand.

"What! good Father Guillaume Leroux!" said he, "and have you, too, left our farm of La Chenaïe to visit the town, when it's not market-day? Why, 'tis as if your oxen were to unharness themselves and go hunting, leaving their work to see a poor rabbit run down!"

"Faith, Monsieur le Comte du Lude," replied the farmer, "for that matter, sometimes the rabbit runs across our path of itself; but, in truth, I've a notion that some of the people here want to make fools of us, and so I've come to see about it."

"Enough of that, my friend," returned the Count; "here is Monsieur Fournier, the Advocate, who assuredly will not deceive you, for he resigned his office of Attorney-General last night, that he might henceforth devote his eloquence to the service of his own noble thoughts. You will hear him, perhaps, to-day, though truly, I dread his appearing for his own sake as much as I desire it for that of the accused."

"I care not for myself," said Fournier; "truth is with me a passion, and I would have it taught in all times and all places."

He that spoke was a young man, whose face, pallid in the extreme, was full of the noblest expression. His blond hair, his light-blue eyes, his thinness, the delicacy of his frame, made him at first sight seem younger than he was; but his thoughtful and earnest countenance indicated that mental superiority and that precocious maturity of soul which are developed by deep study in youth, combined with natural energy of character. He was attired wholly in black, with a short cloak in the fashion of the day, and carried under his left arm a roll of documents, which, when speaking, he would take in the right hand and grasp convulsively, as a warrior in his anger grasps the pommel of his sword. At one moment it seemed as if he were about to unfurl the scroll, and from it hurl lightning upon those whom he pursued with looks of fiery indignation—three Capuchins and a Franciscan, who had just passed.

"Père Guillaume," pursued M. du Lude, "how is it you have brought with you only your sons, and they armed with their staves?"

"Faith, Monsieur, I have no desire that our girls should learn to dance of the nuns; and, moreover, just now the lads with their staves may bestir themselves to better purpose than their sisters would."

"Take my advice, my old friend," said the Count, "and don't bestir yourselves at all; rather stand quietly aside to view the procession which you see approaching, and remember that you are seventy years old."

"Ah!" murmured the old man, drawing up his twelve sons in double military rank, "I fought under good King Henriot, and can play at sword and pistol as well as the worthy *ligueurs;*" and shaking his head he leaned against a post, his knotty staff between his crossed legs, his hands clasped on its thick butt-end, and his white, bearded chin resting on his hands. Then, half closing his eyes, he appeared lost in recollections of his youth.

The bystanders observed with interest his dress, slashed in the fashion of Henri IV, and his resemblance to the Béarnese monarch in the latter years of his life, though the King's hair had been prevented by the assassin's blade from acquiring the whiteness which that of the old peasant had peacefully attained. A furious pealing of the bells, however, attracted the general attention to the end of the great street, down which was seen filing a long procession, whose banners and glittering pikes rose above the heads of the crowd, which successively and in silence opened a way for the at once absurd and terrible train.

First, two and two, came a body of archers, with pointed beards and large plumed hats, armed with long halberds, who, ranging in a single file on each side of the middle of the street, formed an avenue along which marched in solemn order a procession of Gray Penitents—men attired in long, gray robes, the hoods of which entirely covered their heads; masks of the same stuff terminated below their chins in points, like beards, each having three holes for the eyes and nose. Even at the present day we see these costumes at funerals, more especially in the Pyrenees. The Penitents of Loudun carried enormous wax candles, and their slow, uniform movement, and their eyes, which seemed to glitter under their masks, gave them the appearance of phantoms.

The people expressed their various feelings in an undertone:

"There's many a rascal hidden under those masks," said a citizen.

"Ay, and with a face uglier than the mask itself," added a young man.

"They make me afraid," tremulously exclaimed a girl.

"I'm only afraid for my purse," said the first speaker.

"Ah, heaven! there are our holy brethren, the Penitents," cried an old woman, throwing back her hood, the better to look at them. "See the banner they bear! Ah, neighbors, 'tis a joyful thing to have it among us! Beyond a doubt it will save us; see, it shows the devil in flames, and a monk fastening a chain round his neck, to keep him in hell. Ah, here come the judges—noble gentlemen! dear gentlemen! Look at their red robes; how beautiful! Blessed be the Virgin, they've been well chosen!"

"Every man of them is a personal enemy of the

Curé," whispered the Count du Lude to the advocate Fournier, who took a note of the information.

"Don't you know them, neighbors?" pursued the shrill, sharp voice of the old woman, as she elbowed one and pinched another of those near her to attract their attention to the objects of her admiration; "see, there's excellent Monsieur Mignon, whispering to Messieurs the Counsellors of the Court of Poitiers; Heaven bless them all, say I!"

"Yes, there are Roatin, Richard, and Chevalier— the very men who tried to have him dismissed a year ago," continued M. du Lude, in undertones, to the young advocate, who, surrounded and hidden from public observation by the group of dark-clad citizens, was writing down his observations in a note-book under his cloak.

"Here; look, look!" screamed the woman. "Make way! here's Monsieur Barré, the Curé of Saint-Jacques at Chinon."

"A saint!" murmured one bystander.

"A hypocrite!" exclaimed a manly voice.

"See how thin he is with fasting!"

"See how pale he is with remorse!"

"He's the man to drive away devils!"

"Yes, but not till he's done with them for his own purposes."

The dialogue was interrupted by the general exclamation, "How beautiful she is!"

The Superior of the Ursulines advanced, followed by all her nuns. Her white veil was raised; in order that the people might see the features of the possessed ones, it had been ordered that it should be thus with her and six of the sisterhood. Her attire had no distinguishing feature, except a large rosary extending from her neck nearly to her feet, from which hung a gold cross; but the dazzling pallor of her face, rendered still more conspicuous by the dark hue of her *capuchon*, at once fixed the general gaze upon her. Her brilliant, dark eyes, which bore the impress of some deep and burning passion, were crowned with eyebrows so perfectly arched that Nature herself seemed to have taken as much pains to form them as the Circassian women to pencil theirs artistically; but between them a slight fold revealed the powerful agitation within. In her movements, however, and throughout her whole bearing, she affected perfect calm; her steps were slow and measured, and her beautiful hands were crossed on her bosom, as white and motionless as those of the marble statues joined in eternal prayer.

"See, aunt," ejaculated Martine, "see how Sister Agnes and Sister Claire are weeping, next to the Superior!"

"Ay, niece, they weep because they are the prey of the demon."

"Or rather," interposed the same manly voice that spoke before, "because they repent of having mocked Heaven."

A deep silence now pervaded the multitude; not a word was heard, not a movement, hardly a breath. Every one seemed paralyzed by some sudden enchantment, when, following the nuns, among four Penitents who held him in chains, appeared the Curé of the

Church of Ste.-Croix, attired in his pastor's robe. His was a noble, fine face, with grandeur in its whole expression, and gentleness in every feature. Affecting no scornful indifference to his position, he looked calmly and kindly around, as if he sought on his dark path the affectionate glances of those who loved him. Nor did he seek in vain; here and there he encountered those glances, and joyfully returned them. He even heard sobs, and he saw hands extended toward him, many of which grasped weapons. But no gesture of his encouraged these mute offers of aid; he lowered his eyes and went on, careful not to compromise those who so trusted in him, or to involve them in his own misfortunes. This was Urbain Grandier.

Suddenly the procession stopped, at a sign from the man who walked apart, and who seemed to command its progress. He was tall, thin, sallow; he wore a long black robe, with a cap of the same material and color; he had the face of a Don Basilio, with the eye of Nero. He motioned the guards to surround him more closely, when he saw with affright the dark group we have mentioned, and the strong-limbed and resolute peasants who seemed in attendance upon them. Then, advancing somewhat before the Canons and Capuchins who were with him, he pronounced, in a shrill voice, this singular decree:

"We, Sieur de Laubardemont, referendary, being delegated and invested with discretionary power in the matter of the trial of the magician Urbain Grandier, upon the various articles of accusation brought against him, assisted by the reverend Fathers Mignon, canon, Barré, curé of St. Jacques at Chinon, Father

Lactantius, and all the other judges appointed to try the said magician, have decreed as follows:

" *Primo:* the factitious assembly of proprietors, noble citizens of this town and its environs, is dissolved, as tending to popular sedition; its proceedings are declared null, and its letter to the King, against us, the judges, which has been intercepted, shall be publicly burned in the market-place as calumniating the good Ursulines and the reverend fathers and judges.

" *Secundo:* it is forbidden to say, publicly or in private, that the said nuns are not possessed by the Evil Spirit, or to doubt of the power of the exorcists, under pain of a fine of twenty thousand livres, and corporal punishment.

"Let the bailiffs and sheriffs obey this. Given the eighteenth of June, in the year of grace 1639.'

Before he had well finished reading the decree, the discordant blare of trumpets, bursting forth at a pre-arranged signal, drowned, to a certain extent, the murmurs that followed its proclamation, amid which Laubardemont urged forward the procession, which entered the great building already referred to—an ancient convent, whose interior had crumbled away, its walls now forming one vast hall, well adapted for the purpose to which it was about to be applied. Laubardemont did not deem himself safe until he was within the building and had heard the heavy, double doors creak on their hinges as, closing, they excluded the furious crowd without.

CHAPTER III

THE GOOD PRIEST

L'homme de paix me parla ainsi.—VICAIRE SAVOYARD.

OW that the diabolical procession is in the arena destined for its spectacle, and is arranging its sanguinary representation, let us see what Cinq-Mars had been doing amid the agitated throng. He was naturally endowed with great tact, and he felt that it would be no easy matter for him to attain his object of seeing the Abbé Quillet, at a time when public excitement was at its height. He therefore remained on horseback with his four servants in a small, dark street that led into the main thoroughfare, whence he could see all that passed. No one at first paid any attention to him; but when public curiosity had no other aliment, he became an object of general interest. Weary of so many strange scenes, the inhabitants looked upon him with some exasperation, and whispered to one another, asking whether this was another exorcist come among them. Feeling that it was time to take a decided course, he advanced with his attendants, hat in hand, toward the group in black of whom we have spoken, and addressing him who appeared its chief member, said, "Monsieur, where can I find Monsieur l'Abbé Quillet?"

At this name, all regarded him with an air of terror, as if he had pronounced that of Lucifer. Yet no anger was shown; on the contrary, it seemed that the question had favorably changed for him the minds of all who heard him. Moreover, chance had served him well in his choice; the Comte du Lude came up to his horse, and saluting him, said, "Dismount, Monsieur, and I will give you some useful information concerning him."

After speaking a while in whispers, the two gentlemen separated with all the ceremonious courtesy of the time. Cinq-Mars remounted his black horse, and passing through numerous narrow streets, was soon out of the crowd with his retinue.

"How happy I am!" he soliloquized, as he went his way; "I shall, at all events, for a moment see the good and kind clergyman who brought me up; even now I recall his features, his calm air, his voice so full of gentleness."

As these tender thoughts filled his mind, he found himself in the small, dark street which had been indicated to him; it was so narrow that the knee-pieces of his boots touched the wall on each side. At the end of the street he came to a one-storied wooden house, and in his eagerness knocked at the door with repeated strokes.

"Who is there?" cried a furious voice within; and at the same moment, the door opening revealed a little short, fat man, with a very red face, dressed in black, with a large white ruff, and riding-boots which engulfed his short legs in their vast depths. In his hands were a pair of horse-pistols.

"I will sell my life dearly!" he cried; "and——"

"Softly, Abbé, softly," said his pupil, taking his arm; "we are friends."

"Ah, my son, is it you?" said the good man, letting fall his pistols, which were picked up by a domestic, also armed to the teeth. "What do you here? The abomination has entered the town, and I only await the night to depart. Make haste within, my dear boy, with your people. I took you for the archers of Laubardemont, and, faith, I intended to take a part somewhat out of my line. You see the horses in the courtyard there; they will convey me to Italy, where I shall rejoin our friend, the Duc de Bouillon. Jean! Jean! hasten and close the great gate after Monsieur's domestics, and recommend them not to make too much noise, although for that matter we have no habitation near us."

Grandchamp obeyed the intrepid little Abbé, who then embraced Cinq-Mars four consecutive times, raising himself on the points of his boots, so as to attain the middle of his pupil's breast. He then hurried him into a small room, which looked like a deserted granary; and seating him beside himself upon a black leather trunk, he said, warmly:

"Well, my son, whither go you? How came Madame la Maréchale to allow you to come here? Do you not see what they are doing against an unhappy man, whose death alone will content them? Alas, merciful Heaven! is this the first spectacle my dear pupil is to see? And you at that delightful period of life when friendship, love, confidence, should alone encompass you; when all around you should give you a favorable opinion of your species, at your very entry into the great world! How unfortunate! alas, why did you come?"

When the good Abbé had followed up this lamentation by pressing affectionately both hands of the young traveller in his own, so red and wrinkled, the latter answered:

"Can you not guess, my dear Abbé, that I came to Loudun because you are here? As to the spectacle you speak of, it appears to me simply ridiculous; and I swear that I do not a whit the less on its account love that human race of which your virtues and your good lessons have given me an excellent idea. As to the five or six mad women who——"

"Let us not lose time; I will explain to you all that matter; but answer me, whither go you, and for what?"

"I am going to Perpignan, where the Cardinal-Duke is to present me to the King."

At this the worthy but hasty Abbé rose from his box, and walked, or rather ran, to and fro, stamping. "The Cardinal! the Cardinal!" he repeated, almost choking, his face becoming scarlet, and the tears rising to his eyes; "My poor child! they will destroy him! Ah, *mon Dieu!* what part would they have him play there? What would they do with him? Ah, who will protect thee, my son, in that dangerous place?" he continued, reseating himself, and again taking his pupil's hands in his own with a paternal solicitude, as he endeavored to read his thoughts in his countenance.

"Why, I do not exactly know," said Cinq-Mars, looking up at the ceiling; "but I suppose it will be the

Cardinal de Richelieu, who was the friend of my father."

"Ah, my dear Henri, you make me tremble; he will ruin you unless you become his docile instrument. Alas, why can not I go with you? Why must I act the young man of twenty in this unfortunate affair? Alas, I should be perilous to you; I must, on the contrary, conceal myself. But you will have Monsieur de Thou near you, my son, will you not?" said he, trying to re-assure himself; "he was your friend in childhood, though somewhat older than yourself. Heed his counsels, my child, he is a wise young man of mature reflection and solid ideas."

"Oh, yes, my dear Abbé, you may depend upon my tender attachment for him; I never have ceased to love him."

"But you have ceased to write to him, have you not?" asked the good Abbé, half smilingly.

"I beg your pardon, my dear Abbé, I wrote to him once, and again yesterday, to inform him that the Cardinal has invited me to court."

"How! has he himself desired your presence?"

Cinq-Mars hereupon showed the letter of the Cardinal-Duke to his mother, and his old preceptor grew gradually calmer.

"Ah, well!" said he to himself, "this is not so bad, perhaps, after all. It looks promising; a captain of the guards at twenty—that sounds well!" and the worthy Abbé's face became all smiles.

The young man, delighted to see these smiles, which so harmonized with his own thoughts, fell upon the

neck of the Abbé and embraced him, as if the good man
had thus assured to him a futurity of pleasure, glory,
and love.

But the good Abbé, with difficulty disengaging himself from this warm embrace, resumed his walk, his
reflections, and his gravity. He coughed often and
shook his head; and Cinq-Mars, not venturing to pursue the conversation, watched him, and became sad as
he saw him become serious.

The old man at last sat down, and in a mournful tone
addressed his pupil:

"My friend, my son, I have for a moment yielded
like a father to your hopes; but I must tell you, and it
is not to afflict you, that they appear to me excessive
and unnatural. If the Cardinal's sole aim were to show
attachment and gratitude toward your family, he would
not have carried his favors so far; no, the extreme probability is that he has designs upon you. From what
has been told him, he thinks you adapted to play some
part, as yet impossible for us to divine, but which he
himself has traced out in the deepest recesses of his
mind. He wishes to educate you for this; he wishes to
drill you into it. Allow me the expression in consideration of its accuracy, and think seriously of it when the
time shall come. But I am inclined to believe that, as
matters are, you would do well to follow up this vein in
the great mine of State; in this way high fortunes have
begun. You must only take heed not to be blinded and
led at will. Let not favors dazzle you, my poor child,
and let not elevation turn your head. Be not so indignant at the suggestion; the thing has happened to older

4   [49]

men than yourself. Write to me often, as well as to your mother; see Monsieur de Thou, and together we will try to keep you in good counsel. Now, my son, be kind enough to close that window through which the wind comes upon my head, and I will tell you what has been going on here."

Henri, trusting that the moral part of the discourse was over, and anticipating nothing in the second part but a narrative more or less interesting, closed the old casement, festooned with cobwebs, and resumed his seat without speaking.

"Now that I reflect further," continued the Abbé, "I think it will not perhaps be unprofitable for you to have passed through this place, although it be a sad experience you shall have acquired; but it will supply what I may not have formerly told you of the wickedness of men. I hope, moreover, that the result will not be fatal, and that the letter we have written to the King will arrive in time."

"I heard that it had been intercepted," interposed Cinq-Mars.

"Then all is over," said the Abbé Quillet; "the Curé is lost. But listen. God forbid, my son, that I, your old tutor, should seek to assail my own work, and attempt to weaken your faith! Preserve ever and everywhere that simple creed of which your noble family has given you the example, which our fathers possessed in a still higher degree than we, and of which the greatest captains of our time are not ashamed. Always, while you wear a sword, remember that you hold it for the service of God. But at the same time, when you are

among men, avoid being deceived by the hypocrite.
He will encompass you, my son; he will assail you on
the vulnerable side of your ingenuous heart, in addressing your religion; and seeing the extravagance of
his affected zeal, you will fancy yourself lukewarm as
compared with him. You will think that your conscience cries out against you; but it will not be the
voice of conscience that you hear. And what cries
would not that conscience send forth, how fiercely
would it not rise upon you, did you contribute to the
destruction of innocence by invoking Heaven itself as
a false witness against it?"

"Oh, my father! can such things be possible?" exclaimed Henri d'Effiat, clasping his hands.

"It is but too true," continued the Abbé; "you saw
a partial execution of it this morning. God grant you
may not witness still greater horrors! But listen! whatever you may see, whatever crime they dare to commit,
I conjure you, in the name of your mother and of all
that you hold dear, say not a word; make not a gesture
that may indicate any opinion whatever. I know the
impetuous character that you derive from the Maréchal,
your father; curb it, or you are lost. These little ebullitions of passion give but slight satisfaction, and bring
about great misfortunes. I have observed you give way
to them too much. Oh, did you but know the advantage that a calm temper gives one over men! The ancients stamped it on the forehead of the divinity as his
finest attribute, since it shows that he is superior to our
fears and to our hopes, to our pleasures and to our
pains.. Therefore, my dear child, remain passive in the

scenes you are about to witness; but see them you must. Be present at this sad trial; for me, I must suffer the consequences of my schoolboy folly. I will relate it to you; it will prove to you that with a bald head one may be as much a child as with your fine chestnut curls."

And the excellent old Abbé, taking his pupil's head affectionately between his hands, continued :

"Like other people, my dear son, I was curious to see the devils of the Ursulines; and knowing that they professed to speak all languages, I was so imprudent as to cease speaking Latin and to question them in Greek. The Superior is very pretty, but she does not know Greek! Duncan, the physician, observed aloud that it was surprising that the demon, who knew everything, should commit barbarisms and solecisms in Latin, and not be able to answer in Greek. The young Superior, who was then upon her bed, turned toward the wall to weep, and said in an undertone to Father Barré, 'I can not go on with this, father.' I repeated her words aloud, and infuriated all the exorcists; they cried out that I ought to know that there are demons more ignorant than peasants, and said that as to their power and physical strength, it could not be doubted, since the spirits named Grésil des Trones, Aman des Puissance, and Asmodeus, had promised to carry off the *calotte* of Monsieur de Laubardemont. They were preparing for this, when the physician Duncan, a learned and upright man, but somewhat of a scoffer, took it into his head to pull a cord he discovered fastened to a column like a bell-rope, and which hung down just close to the referendary's head; whereupon they called him a Huguenot, and I am satisfied that if Maréchal de Brézé were not his protector, it would have gone ill with him. The Comte du Lude then came forward with his customary *sang-froid*, and begged the exorcists to perform before him. Father Lactantius, the Capuchin with the dark visage and hard look, proceeded with Sister Agnes and Sister Claire; he raised both his hands, looking at them as a serpent would look at two dogs, and cried in a terrible voice, '*Quis te misit, Diabole?*' and the two sisters answered, as with one voice, 'Urbanus.' He was about to continue, when Monsieur du Lude, taking out of his pocket, with an air of veneration, a small gold box, said that he had in it a relic left by his ancestors, and that though not doubting the fact of the possession, he wished to test it. Father Lactantius seized the box with delight, and hardly had he touched the foreheads of the two sisters with it when they made great leaps and twisted about their hands and feet. Lactantius shouted forth his exorcisms; Barré threw himself upon his knees with all the old women; and Mignon and the judges applauded. The impassible Laubardemont made the sign of the cross, without being struck dead for it! When Monsieur du Lude took back his box the nuns became still. 'I think,' said Lactantius, insolently, 'that you will not question your relics now.' 'No more than I do the possession,' answered Monsieur du Lude, opening his box and showing that it was empty. 'Monsieur, you mock us,' said Lactantius. I was indignant at these mummeries, and said to him, 'Yes, Monsieur, as you mock God and men.' And this,

my dear friend, is the reason why you see me in my
seven-league boots, so heavy that they hurt my legs,
and with pistols; for our friend Laubardemont has ordered my person to be seized, and I don't choose it to
be seized, old as it is."

"What, is he so powerful, then?" cried Cinq-Mars.

"More so than is supposed — more so than could be
believed. I know that the possessed Abbess is his
niece, and that he is provided with an order in council
directing him to judge, without being deterred by any
appeals lodged in Parliament, the Cardinal having prohibited the latter from taking cognizance of the matter
of Urbain Grandier."

"And what are his offences?" asked the young man,
already deeply interested.

"Those of a strong mind and of a great genius, an
inflexible will which has irritated power against him,
and a profound passion which has driven his heart and
him to commit the only mortal sin with which I believe
he can be reproached; and it was only by violating the
sanctity of his private papers, which they tore from
Jeanne d'Estièvre, his mother, an old woman of eighty,
that they discovered his love for the beautiful Madeleine de Brou. This girl had refused to marry, and
wished to take the veil. May that veil have concealed
from her the spectacle of this day! The eloquence of
Grandier and his angelic beauty drove the women half
mad; they came miles and miles to hear him. I have
seen them swoon during his sermons; they declared
him an angel, and touched his garment and kissed his
hands when he descended from the pulpit. It is cer-

tain that, unless it be his beauty, nothing could equal the sublimity of his discourses, ever full of inspiration. The pure honey of the gospel combined on his lips with the flashing flame of the prophecies; and one recognized in the sound of his voice a heart overflowing with holy pity for the evils to which mankind are subject, and filled with tears, ready to flow for us."

The good priest paused, for his own voice and eyes were filled with tears; his round and naturally joyous face was more touching than a graver one under the same circumstances, for it seemed as if it bade defiance to sadness. Cinq-Mars, even more moved, pressed his hand without speaking, fearful of interrupting him. The Abbé took out a red handkerchief, wiped his eyes, and continued:

"This is the second attack upon Urbain by his combined enemies. He had already been accused of bewitching the nuns; but, examined by holy prelates, by enlightened magistrates, and learned physicians, he was immediately acquitted, and the judges indignantly imposed silence upon these devils in human form. The good and pious Archbishop of Bordeaux, who had himself chosen the examiners of these pretended exorcists, drove the prophets away and shut up their hell. But, humiliated by the publicity of the result, annoyed at seeing Grandier kindly received by our good King when he threw himself at his feet at Paris, they saw that if he triumphed they were lost, and would be universally regarded as impostors. Already the convent of the Ursulines was looked upon only as a theatre for disgraceful comedies, and the nuns themselves as shameless actresses. More than a hundred persons, furious against the Curé, had compromised themselves in the hope of destroying him. Their plot, instead of being abandoned, has gained strength by its first check; and here are the means that have been set to work by his implacable enemies.

"Do you know a man called *L'Eminence Grise*, that formidable Capuchin whom the Cardinal employs in all things, consults upon some, and always despises? It was to him that the Capuchins of Loudun addressed themselves. A woman of this place, of low birth, named Hamon, having been so fortunate as to please the Queen when she passed through Loudun, was taken into her service. You know the hatred that separates her court from that of the Cardinal; you know that Anne of Austria and Monsieur de Richelieu have for some time disputed for the King's favor, and that, of her two suns, France never knew in the evening which would rise next morning. During a temporary eclipse of the Cardinal, a satire appeared, issuing from the planetary system of the Queen; it was called, *La cordonnière de la reine-mère.* Its tone and language were vulgar; but it contained things so insulting about the birth and person of the Cardinal that the enemies of the minister took it up and gave it a publicity which irritated him. It revealed, it is said, many intrigues and mysteries which he had deemed impenetrable. He read this anonymous work, and desired to know its author. It was just at this time that the Capuchins of this town wrote to Father Joseph that a constant correspondence between Grandier and La Hamon left no doubt in their

minds as to his being the author of this diatribe. It
was in vain that he had previously published religious
books, prayers, and meditations, the style of which
alone ought to have absolved him from having put his
hand to a libel written in the language of the market-
place; the Cardinal, long since prejudiced against Urbain, was determined to fix upon him as the culprit.
He remembered that when he was only prior of Cous-
say, Grandier disputed precedence with him and gained
it; I fear this achievement of precedence in life will
make poor Grandier precede the Cardinal in death
also."

A melancholy smile played upon the lips of the good
Abbé as he uttered this involuntary pun.

"What! do you think this matter will go so far as
death?"

"Ay, my son, even to death; they have already taken
away all the documents connected with his former ab-
solution that might have served for his defence, despite
the opposition of his poor mother, who preserved them
as her son's license to live. Even now they affect to
regard a work against the celibacy of priests, found
among his papers, as destined to propagate schism. It
is a culpable production, doubtless, and the love which
dictated it, however pure it may be, is an enormous sin
in a man consecrated to God alone; but this poor
priest was far from wishing to encourage heresy, and it
was simply, they say, to appease the remorse of Mademoiselle de Brou that he composed the work. It was
so evident that his real faults would not suffice to con-
demn him to death that they have revived the accusa-

tion of sorcery, long since disposed of; but, feigning to believe this, the Cardinal has established a new tribunal in this town, and has placed Laubardemont at its head, —a sure sign of death. Heaven grant that you never become acquainted with what the corruption of governments call *coups-d'état!*"

At this moment a terrible shriek sounded from beyond the wall of the courtyard; the Abbé arose in terror, as did Cinq-Mars.

"It is the cry of a woman," said the old man.

"'Tis heartrending!" exclaimed Cinq-Mars. "What is it?" he asked his people, who had all rushed out into the courtyard.

They answered that they heard nothing further.

"Well, well," said the Abbé, "make no noise." He then shut the window, and put his hands before his eyes.

"Ah, what a cry was that, my son!" he said, with his face of an ashy paleness—"what a cry! It pierced my very soul; some calamity has happened. Ah, holy Virgin! it has so agitated me that I can talk with you no more. Why did I hear it, just as I was speaking to you of your future career? My dear child, may God bless you! Kneel!"

Cinq-Mars did as he was desired, and knew by a kiss upon his head that he had been blessed by the old man, who then raised him, saying:

"Go, my son, the time is advancing; they might find you with me. Go, leave your people and horses here; wrap yourself in a cloak, and go; I have much to write ere the hour when darkness shall allow me to depart for Italy."

They embraced once more, promising to write to each other, and Henri quitted the house. The Abbé, still following him with his eyes from the window, cried:

"Be prudent, whatever may happen," and sent him with his hands one more paternal blessing, saying, "Poor child! poor child!"

CHAPTER IV

THE TRIAL

Oh, vendetta di Dio, quanto tu dei
Esser temuta da ciascun che legge
Cio, che fu manifesto agli occhi miei.—DANTE.

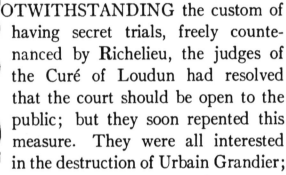

NOTWITHSTANDING the custom of having secret trials, freely countenanced by Richelieu, the judges of the Curé of Loudun had resolved that the court should be open to the public; but they soon repented this measure. They were all interested in the destruction of Urbain Grandier; but they desired that the indignation of the country should in some degree sanction the sentence of death they had received orders to pass and to carry into effect.

Laubardemont was a kind of bird of prey, whom the Cardinal always let loose when he required a prompt and sure agent for his vengeance; and on this occasion he fully justified the choice that had been made of him. He committed but one error— that of allowing a public trial, contrary to the usual custom; his object had been to intimidate and to dismay. He dismayed, indeed, but he created also a feeling of indignant horror.

[60]

The throng without the gates had waited there two hours, during which time the sound of hammers indicated that within the great hall they were hastily completing their mysterious preparations. At length the archers laboriously turned upon their hinges the heavy gates opening into the street, and the crowd eagerly rushed in. The young Cinq-Mars was carried along with the second enormous wave, and, placed behind a thick column, stood there, so as to be able to see without being seen. He observed with vexation that the group of dark-clad citizens was near him; but the great gates, closing, left the part of the court where the people stood in such darkness that there was no likelihood of his being recognized. Although it was only midday, the hall was lighted with torches; but they were nearly all placed at the farther end, where rose the judges' bench behind a long table. The chairs, tables, and steps were all covered with black cloth, and cast a livid hue over the faces of those near them. A seat reserved for the prisoner was placed upon the left, and on the crape robe which covered him flames were represented in gold embroidery to indicate the nature of the offence. Here sat the accused, surrounded by archers, with his hands still bound in chains, held by two monks, who, with simulated terror, affected to start from him at his slightest motion, as if they held a tiger or enraged wolf, or as if the flames depicted on his robe could communicate themselves to their clothing. They also carefully kept his face from being seen in the least degree by the people.

ALFRED DE VIGNY

The impassible countenance of M. de Laubardemont was there to dominate the judges of his choice; almost a head taller than any of them, he sat upon a seat higher than theirs, and each of his glassy and uneasy glances seemed to convey a command. He wore a long, full scarlet robe, and a black cap covered his head; he seemed occupied in arranging papers, which he then passed to the judges. The accusers, all ecclesiastics, sat upon the right hand of the judges; they wore their albs and stoles. Father Lactantius was distinguishable among them by his simple Capuchin habit, his tonsure, and the extreme hardness of his features. In a side gallery sat the Bishop of Poitiers, hidden from view; other galleries were filled with veiled women. Below the bench of judges a group of men and women, the dregs of the populace, stood behind six young Ursuline nuns, who seemed full of disgust at their proximity; these were the witnesses.

The rest of the hall was filled with an enormous crowd, gloomy and silent, clinging to the arches, the gates, and the beams, and full of a terror which communicated itself to the judges, for it arose from an interest in the accused. Numerous archers, armed with long pikes, formed an appropriate frame for this lugubrious picture.

At a sign from the President, the witnesses withdrew through a narrow door opened for them by an usher. As the Superior of the Ursulines passed M. de Laubardemont she was heard to say to him, "You have deceived me, Monsieur." He remained immovable, and she went on. A profound silence reigned throughout the whole assembly.

Rising with all the gravity he could assume, but still with visible agitation, one of the judges, named Houmain, Judge-Advocate of Orléans, read a sort of indictment in a voice so low and hoarse that it was impossible to follow it. He made himself heard only when what he had to say was intended to impose upon the minds of the people. He divided the evidence into two classes: one, the depositions of seventy-two witnesses; the other, more convincing, that resulting from "the exorcisms of the reverend fathers here present," said he, crossing himself.

Fathers Lactantius, Barré, and Mignon bowed low, repeating the sacred sign.

"Yes, my lords," said Houmain, addressing the judges, "this bouquet of white roses and this manuscript, signed with the blood of the magician, a counterpart of the contract he has made with Lucifer, and which he was obliged to carry about him in order to preserve his power, have been recognized and brought before you. We read with horror these words written at the bottom of the parchment: '*The original is in hell, in Lucifer's private cabinet.*'"

A roar of laughter, which seemed to come from stentorian lungs, was heard in the throng. The president reddened, and made a sign to the archers, who in vain endeavored to discover the disturber. The Judge-Advocate continued:

"The demons have been forced to declare their names by the mouths of their victims. Their names and deeds are deposited upon this table. They are called Astaroth, of the order of Seraphim; Eazas, Celsus, Acaos, Cedron, Asmodeus, of the order of Thrones; Alex, Zebulon, Cham, Uriel, and Achas, of the order of Principalities, and so on, for their number is infinite. For their actions, who among us has not been a witness of them?"

A prolonged murmur arose from the gathering, but, upon some halberdiers advancing, all became silent.

"We have seen, with grief, the young and respectable Superior of the Ursulines tear her bosom with her own hands and grovel in the dust; we have seen the sisters, Agnes, Claire, and others, deviate from the modesty of their sex by impassioned gestures and unseemly laughter. When impious men have inclined to doubt the presence of the demons, and we ourselves felt our convictions shaken, because they refused to answer to unknown questions in Greek or Arabic, the reverend fathers have, to establish our belief, deigned to explain to us that the malignity of evil spirits being extreme, it was not surprising that they should feign this ignorance in order that they might be less pressed with questions; and that in their answers they had committed various solecisms and other grammatical faults in order to bring contempt upon themselves, so that out of this disdain the holy doctors might leave them in quiet. Their hatred is so inveterate that just before performing one of their miraculous feats, they suspended a rope from a beam in order to involve the reverend personages in a suspicion of fraud, whereas it has been deposed on oath by credible people that there never had been a cord in that place.

"But, my lords, while Heaven was thus miraculously explaining itself by the mouths of its holy interpreters, another light has just been thrown upon us. At the very time the judges were absorbed in profound meditation, a loud cry was heard near the hall of council; and upon going to the spot, we found the body of a young lady of high birth. She had just exhaled her last breath in the public street, in the arms of the reverend Father Mignon, Canon; and we learned from the said father here present, and from several other grave personages, that, suspecting the young lady to be possessed, by reason of the current rumor for some time past of the admiration Urbain Grandier had for her, an idea of testing it happily occurred to the Canon, who suddenly said, approaching her, 'Grandier has just been put to death,' whereat she uttered one loud scream and fell dead, deprived by the demon of the time necessary for giving her the assistance of our holy Mother, the Catholic Church." ·

A murmur of indignation arose from the crowd, among whom the word "Assassin" was loudly re-echoed; the halberdiers commanded silence with a loud voice, but it was obtained rather by the judge resuming his address, the general curiosity triumphing.

"Oh, infamy!" he continued, seeking to fortify himself by exclamations; "upon her person was found this work, written by the hand of Urbain Grandier," and he took from among his papers a book bound in parchment.

5 [65]

ALFRED DE VIGNY

"Heavens!" cried Urbain from his seat.

"Look to your prisoner!" cried the judge to the archers who surrounded him.

"No doubt the demon is about to manifest himself," said Father Lactantius, in a sombre voice; "tighten his bonds." He was obeyed.

The Judge-Advocate continued, "Her name was Madeleine de Brou, aged nineteen."

"O God! this is too much!" cried the accused, as he fell fainting on the ground.

The assembly was deeply agitated; for a moment there was an absolute tumult.

"Poor fellow! he loved her," said some.

"So good a lady!" cried the women.

Pity began to predominate. Cold water was thrown upon Grandier, without his being taken from the court, and he was tied to his seat. The Judge-Advocate went on:

"We are directed to read the beginning of this book to the court," and he read as follows:

"'It is for thee, dear and gentle Madeleine, in order to set at rest thy troubled conscience, that I have described in this book one thought of my soul. All those thoughts tend to thee, celestial creature, because in thee they return to the aim and object of my whole existence; but the thought I send thee, as 'twere a flower, comes from thee, exists only in thee, and returns to thee alone.

"'Be not sad because thou lovest me; be not afflicted because I adore thee. The angels of heaven, what is it that they do? The souls of the blessed, what is it that is promised them? Are we less pure than the angels? Are our souls less separated from the earth than they will be after death? Oh, Madeleine, what

[66]

is there in us wherewith the Lord can be displeased? Can it be that we pray together, that with faces prostrate in the dust before His altars, we ask for early death to take us while yet youth and love are ours? Or that, musing together beneath the funereal trees of the churchyard, we yearned for one grave, smiling at the idea of death, and weeping at life? Or that, when thou kneelest before me at the tribunal of penitence, and, speaking in the presence of God, canst find naught of evil to reveal to me, so wholly have I kept thy soul in the pure regions of heaven? What, then, could offend our Creator? Perhaps—yes! perhaps some spirit of heaven may have envied me my happiness when on Easter morn I saw thee kneeling before me, purified by long austerities from the slight stain which original sin had left in thee! Beautiful, indeed, wert thou! Thy glance sought thy God in heaven, and my trembling hand held His image to thy pure lips, which human lip had never dared to breathe upon. Angelic being! I alone participated in the secret of the Lord, in the one secret of the entire purity of thy soul; I it was that united thee to thy Creator, who at that moment descended also into my bosom. Ineffable espousals, of which the Eternal himself was the priest, you alone were permitted between the virgin and her pastor! the sole joy of each was to see eternal happiness beginning for the other, to inhale together the perfumes of heaven, to drink in already the harmony of the spheres, and to feel assured that our souls, unveiled to God and to ourselves alone, were worthy together to adore Him.

"'What scruple still weighs upon thy soul, O my sister? Dost thou think I have offered too high a worship to thy virtue? Fearest thou so pure an admiration should deter me from that of the Lord?'"

Houmain had reached this point when the door through which the witnesses had withdrawn suddenly opened. The judges anxiously whispered together. Laubardemont, uncertain as to the meaning of this, signed to the fathers to let him know whether this was some scene executed by their orders; but, seated at some distance from him, and themselves taken by surprise, they could not make him understand that they had not prepared this interruption. Besides, ere they could exchange looks, to the amazement of the assembly, three women, *en chemise*, with naked feet, each with a cord round her neck and a wax taper in her hand, came through the door and advanced to the middle of the platform. It was the Superior of the Ursulines, followed by Sisters Agnes and Claire. Both the latter were weeping; the Superior was very pale, but her bearing was firm, and her eyes were fixed and tearless. She knelt; her companions followed her example. Everything was in such confusion that no one thought of checking them; and in a clear, firm voice she pronounced these words, which resounded in every corner of the hall:

"In the name of the Holy Trinity, I, Jeanne de Belfiel, daughter of the Baron de Cose, I, the unworthy Superior of the Convent of the Ursulines of Loudun, ask pardon of God and man for the crime I have committed in accusing the innocent Urbain Grandier. My possession was feigned, my words were dictated; remorse overwhelms me."

"Bravo!" cried the spectators, clapping their hands. The judges arose; the archers, in doubt, looked at the president; he shook in every limb, but did not change countenance.

"Let all be silent," he said, in a sharp voice; "archers, do your duty."

This man felt himself supported by so strong a hand
that nothing could affright him—for no thought of
Heaven ever visited him.

"What think you, my fathers?" said he, making a
sign to the monks.

"That the demon seeks to save his friend. *Ob-
mutesce, Satanas!*" cried Father Lactantius, in a terrible voice, affecting to exorcise the Superior.

Never did fire applied to gunpowder produce an
effect more instantaneous than did these two words.
Jeanne de Belfiel started up in all the beauty of twenty,
which her awful nudity served to augment; she seemed
a soul escaped from hell appearing to her seducer.
With her dark eyes she cast fierce glances upon the
monks; Lactantius lowered his beneath that look.
She took two steps toward him with her bare feet,
beneath which the scaffolding rung, so energetic was
her movement; the taper seemed, in her hand, the
sword of the avenging angel.

"Silence, impostor!" she cried, with warmth; "the
demon who possessed me was yourself. You deceived
me; you said he was not to be tried. To-day, for the
first time, I know that he is to be tried; to-day, for the
first time, I know that he is to be murdered. And I
will speak!"

"Woman, the demon bewilders thee."

"Say, rather, that repentence enlightens me. Daugh-
ters, miserable as myself, arise; is he not innocent?"

"We swear he is," said the two young lay sisters,
still kneeling and weeping, for they were not animated
with so strong a resolution as that of the Superior.

Agnes, indeed, had hardly uttered these words when turning toward the people, she cried, "Help me! they will punish me; they will kill me!" And hurrying away her companion, she drew her into the crowd, who affectionately received them. A thousand voices swore to protect them. Imprecations arose; the men struck their staves against the floor; the officials dared not prevent the people from passing the sisters on from one to another into the street.

During this strange scene the amazed and panic-struck judges whispered; M. Laubardemont looked at the archers, indicating to them the points they were especially to watch, among which, more particularly, was that occupied by the group in black. The accusers looked toward the gallery of the Bishop of Poitiers, but discovered no expression in his dull countenance. He was one of those old men of whom death appears to take possession ten years before all motion entirely ceases in them. His eyes seemed veiled by a half sleep; his gaping mouth mumbled a few vague and habitual words of prayer without meaning or application; the entire amount of intelligence he retained was the ability to distinguish the man who had most power, and him he obeyed, regardless at what price. He had accordingly signed the sentence of the doctors of the Sorbonne which declared the nuns possessed, without even deducing thence the consequence of the death of Urbain; the rest seemed to him one of those more or less lengthy ceremonies, to which he paid not the slightest attention — accustomed as he was to see and live among them, himself an indispensable part and parcel of them. He therefore gave no sign of life on this occasion, merely preserving an air at once perfectly noble and expressionless.

Meanwhile, Father Lactantius, having had a moment to recover from the sudden attack made upon him, turned toward the president and said:

"Here is a clear proof, sent us by Heaven, of the possession, for the Superior never before has forgotten the modesty and severity of her order."

"Would that all the world were here to see me!" said Jeanne de Belfiel, firm as ever. "I can not be sufficiently humiliated upon earth, and Heaven will reject me, for I have been your accomplice."

Perspiration appeared upon the forehead of Laubardemont, but he tried to recover his composure. "What absurd tale is this, Sister; what has influenced you herein?"

The voice of the girl became sepulchral; she collected all her strength, pressed her hand upon her heart as if she desired to stay its throbbing, and, looking at Urbain Grandier, answered, "Love."

A shudder ran through the assembly. Urbain, who since he had fainted had remained with his head hanging down as if dead, slowly raised his eyes toward her, and returned entirely to life only to undergo a fresh sorrow. The young penitent continued

"Yes, the love which he rejected, which he never fully knew, which I have breathed in his discourses, which my eyes drew in from his celestial countenance, which his very counsels against it have increased.

ALFRED DE VIGNY
Yes, Urbain is pure as an angel, but good as a man
who has loved. I knew not that he had loved! It
was a crime; but, by my mother, I am an Italian! I
see Urbain, to have him as a friend, to see him daily."
She was silent for a moment, then exclaimed, "People,

She prostrated herself before Urbain and burst into
a torrent of tears.

Urbain raised his closely bound hands, and giving
her his benediction, said, gently:

"Go, Sister; I pardon thee in the name of Him
whom I shall soon see. I have before said to you,

The blood rose a second time to Laubardemont's

"I have not quitted her bosom," said Urbain.

"Remove the girl," said the President.

When the archers went to obey, they found that she
force that she was of a livid hue and almost lifeless.
Fear had driven all the women from the assembly;

[72]

many had been carried out fainting, but the hall was no less crowded. The ranks thickened, for the men out of the streets poured in.

The judges arose in terror, and the president attempted to have the hall cleared; but the people, putting on their hats, stood in alarming immobility. The archers were not numerous enough to repel them. It became necessary to yield; and accordingly Laubardemont in an agitated voice announced that the council would retire for half an hour. He broke up the sitting; the people remained gloomily, each man fixed firmly to his place.

CHAPTER V

THE MARTYRDOM

La torture interroge, et la douleur répond.
RAYNOUARD, *Les Templiers.*

HE continuous interest of this half-trial, its preparations, its interruptions, all had held the minds of the people in such attention that no private conversations had taken place. Some irrepressible cries had been uttered, but simultaneously, so that no man could accuse his neighbor. But when the people were left to themselves, there was an explosion of clamorous sentences.

There was at this period enough of primitive simplicity among the lower classes for them to be persuaded by the mysterious tales of the political agents who were deluding them; so that a large portion of the throng in the hall of trial, not venturing to change their judgment, though upon the manifest evidence just given them, awaited in painful suspense the return of the judges, interchanging with an air of mystery and inane importance the usual remarks prompted by imbecility on such occasions.

"One does not know what to think, Monsieur?"

"Truly, Madame, most extraordinary things have happened."

"We live in strange times!"

"I suspected this; but, i' faith, it is not wise to say what one thinks."

"We shall see what we shall see," and so on— the unmeaning chatter of the crowd, which merely serves to show that it is at the command of the first who chooses to sway it. Stronger words were heard from the group in black.

"What! shall we let them do as they please, in this manner? What! dare to burn our letter to the King!"

"If the King knew it!"

"The barbarian impostors! how skilfully is their plot contrived! What! shall murder be committed under our very eyes? Shall we be afraid of these archers?"

"No, no, no!" rang out in trumpet-like tones.

Attention was turned toward the young advocate, who, standing on a branch, began tearing to pieces a roll of paper; then he cried:

"Yes, I tear and scatter to the winds the defence I had prepared for the accused. They have suppressed discussion; I am not allowed to speak for him. I can only speak to you, people; I rejoice that I can do so. You heard these infamous judges. Which of them can hear the truth? Which of them is worthy to listen to an honest man? Which of them will dare to meet his gaze? But what do I say? They all know the truth. They carry it in their guilty breasts; it stings their hearts like a serpent. They tremble in their lair, where doubtless they are devouring their victim; they tremble because they have heard the cries of three deluded women. What was I about to do? I was about to speak in behalf of Urbain Grandier! But what eloquence could equal that of those unfortunates? What words could better have shown you his innocence? Heaven has taken up arms for him in bringing them to repentance and to devotion; Heaven will finish its work——"

"*Vade retro, Satanas*," was heard through a high window in the hall.

Fournier stopped for a moment, then said:

"You hear these voices parodying the divine language? If I mistake not, these instruments of an infernal power are, by this song, preparing some new spell."

"But," cried those who surrounded him, "what shall we do? What have they done with him?"

"Remain here; be immovable, be silent," replied the young advocate. "The inertia of a people is all-powerful; that is its 'rue wisdom, that its strength. Observe them closely, and in silence; and you will make them tremble."

"They surely will not dare to appear here again," said the Comte du Lude.

"I should like to look once more at the tall scoundrel in red," said Grand-Ferré, who had lost nothing of what had occurred.

"And that good gentleman, the Curé," murmured old Father Guillaume Leroux, looking at all his indignant parishioners, who were talking together in a low tone, measuring and counting the archers, ridiculing their dress, and beginning to point them out to the observation of the other spectators.

Cinq-Mars, still leaning against the pillar behind which he had first placed himself, still wrapped in his black cloak, eagerly watched all that passed, lost not a word of what was said, and filled his heart with hate and bitterness. Violent desires for slaughter and revenge, a vague desire to strike, took possession of him, despite himself; this is the first impression which evil produces on the soul of a young man. Later, sadness takes the place of fury, then indifference and scorn, later still, a calculating admiration for great villains who have been successful; but this is only when, of the two elements which constitute man, earth triumphs over spirit.

Meanwhile, on the right of the hall near the judges' platform, a group of women were watching attentively a child about eight years old, who had taken it into his head to climb up to a cornice by the aid of his sister Martine, whom we have seen the subject of jest with the young soldier, Grand-Ferré. The child, having nothing to look at after the court had left the hall, had climbed to a small window which admitted a faint light, and which he imagined to contain a swallow's nest or some other treasure for a boy; but after he was well established on the cornice, his hands grasping the bars of an old shrine of Jerome, he wished himself anywhere else, and cried out:

"Oh, sister, sister, lend me your hand to get down!"

"What do you see there?" asked Martine.

"Oh, I dare not tell; but I want to get down," and he began to cry.

"Stay there, my child; stay there!" said all the women. "Don't be afraid; tell us all that you see."

"Well, then, they've put the Curé between two great boards that squeeze his legs, and there are cords round the boards."

"Ah! that is the rack," said one of the townsmen. "Look again, my little friend, what do you see now?"

The child, more confident, looked again through the window, and then, withdrawing his head, said:

"I can not see the Curé now, because all the judges stand round him, and are looking at him, and their great robes prevent me from seeing. There are also some Capuchins, stooping down to whisper to him."

Curiosity attracted more people to the boy's perch; every one was silent, waiting anxiously to catch his words, as if their lives depended on them.

"I see," he went on, "the executioner driving four little pieces of wood between the cords, after the Capuchins have blessed the hammer and nails. Ah, heavens! Sister, how enraged they seem with him, because he will not speak. Mother! mother! give me your hand, I want to come down!"

Instead of his mother, the child, upon turning round, saw only men's faces, looking up at him with a mournful eagerness, and signing him to go on. He dared not descend, and looked again through the window, trembling.

"Oh! I see Father Lactantius and Father Barré themselves forcing in more pieces of wood, which squeeze his legs. Oh, how pale he is! he seems praying. There, his head falls back, as if he were dying! Oh, take me away!"

And he fell into the arms of the young Advocate, of M. du Lude, and of Cinq-Mars, who had come to support him.

"*Deus stetit in synagoga deorum: in medio autem Deus dijudicat*—" chanted strong, nasal voices, issuing from the small window, which continued in full chorus one of the psalms, interrupted by blows of the hammer—an infernal deed beating time to celestial songs. One might have supposed himself near a smithy, except that the blows were dull, and manifested to the ear that the anvil was a man's body.

"Silence!" said Fournier, "He speaks. The chanting and the blows stop."

A weak voice within said, with difficulty, "Oh, my fathers, mitigate the rigor of your torments, for you will reduce my soul to despair, and I might seek to destroy myself!"

At this the fury of the people burst forth like an explosion, echoing along the vaulted roofs; the men sprang fiercely upon the platform, thrust aside the surprised and hesitating archers; the unarmed crowd drove them back, pressed them, almost suffocated them against the walls, and held them fast, then dashed against the doors which led to the torture chamber, and, making them shake beneath their blows, threatened to drive them in; imprecations resounded from a thousand menacing voices and terrified the judges within.

ALFRED DE VIGNY

"They are gone; they have taken him away!" cried a man who had climbed to the little window.

The multitude at once stopped short, and changing the direction of their steps, fled from this detestable place and spread rapidly through the streets, where an extraordinary confusion prevailed.

Night had come on during the long sitting, and the rain was pouring in torrents. The darkness was terrifying. The cries of women slipping on the pavement or driven back by the horses of the guards; the shouts of the furious men; the ceaseless tolling of the bells which had been keeping time with the strokes of the question; the roll of distant thunder—all combined to increase the disorder. If the ear was astonished, the eyes were no less so. A few dismal torches lighted up the corners of the streets; their flickering gleams showed soldiers, armed and mounted, dashing along, regardless of the crowd, to assemble in the Place de St.-Pierre; tiles were sometimes thrown at them on their way, but, missing the distant culprit, fell upon some unoffending neighbor. The confusion was bewildering, and became still more so, when, hurrying through all the streets toward the Place de St.-Pierre, the people found it barricaded on all sides, and filled with mounted guards and archers. Carts, fastened to the posts at each corner, closed each entrance, and sentinels, armed with arquebuses, were stationed close to the carts. In the centre of the Place rose a pile composed of enormous beams placed crosswise upon one another, so as to form a perfect square; these were covered with a whiter and lighter wood;

an enormous stake arose from the centre of the scaffold. A man clothed in red and holding a lowered torch stood near this sort of mast, which was visible from a long distance. A huge chafing-dish, covered on account of the rain, was at his feet.

At this spectacle, terror inspired everywhere a profound silence; for an instant nothing was heard but the sound of the rain, which fell in floods, and of the thunder, which came nearer and nearer.

Meanwhile, Cinq-Mars, accompanied by MM. du Lude and Fournier and all the more important personages of the town, had sought refuge from the storm under the peristyle of the church of Ste.-Croix, raised upon twenty stone steps. The pile was in front, and from this height they could see the whole of the square. The centre was entirely clear, large streams of water alone traversed it; but all the windows of the houses were gradually lighted up, and showed the heads of the men and women who thronged them.

The young D'Effiat sorrowfully contemplated this menacing preparation. Brought up in sentiments of honor, and far removed from the black thoughts which hatred and ambition arouse in the heart of man, he could not conceive that such wrong could be done without some powerful and secret motive. The audacity of such a condemnation seemed to him so enormous that its very cruelty began to justify it in his eyes; a secret horror crept into his soul, the same that silenced the people. He almost forgot the interest with which the unhappy Urbain had inspired him, in thinking whether it were not possible that some

6 [81]

secret correspondence with the infernal powers had justly provoked such excessive severity; and the public revelations of the nuns, and the statement of his respected tutor, faded from his memory, so powerful is success, even in the eyes of superior men! so strongly does force impose upon men, despite the voice of conscience!

The young traveller was asking himself whether it were not probable that the torture had forced some monstrous confession from the accused, when the obscurity which surrounded the church suddenly ceased. Its two great doors were thrown open; and by the light of an infinite number of flambeaux, appeared all the judges and ecclesiastics, surrounded by guards. Among them was Urbain, supported, or rather carried, by six men clothed as Black Penitents—for his limbs, bound with bandages saturated with blood, seemed broken and incapable of supporting him. It was at most two hours since Cinq-Mars had seen him, and yet he could hardly recognize the face he had so closely observed at the trial. All color, all roundness of form had disappeared from it; a livid pallor covered a skin yellow and shining like ivory; the blood seemed to have left his veins; all the life that remained within him shone from his dark eyes, which appeared to have grown twice as large as before, as he looked languidly around him; his long, chestnut hair hung loosely down his neck and over a white shirt, which entirely covered him—or rather a sort of robe with large sleeves, and of a yellowish tint, with an odor of sulphur about it; a long, thick cord encircled his neck and fell upon his breast. He looked like an apparition; but it was the apparition of a martyr.

Urbain stopped, or, rather, was set down upon the peristyle of the church; the Capuchin Lactantius placed a lighted torch in his right hand, and held it there, as he said to him, with his hard inflexibility:

"Do penance, and ask pardon of God for thy crime of magic."

The unhappy man raised his voice with great difficulty, and with his eyes to heaven said:

"In the name of the living God, I cite thee, Laubardemont, false judge, to appear before Him in three years. They have taken away my confessor, and I have been fain to pour out my sins into the bosom of God Himself, for my enemies surround me. I call that God of mercy to witness I never have dealt in magic. I have known no mysteries but those of the Catholic religion, apostolic and Roman, in which I die; I have sinned much against myself, but never against God and our Lord——"

"Cease!" cried the Capuchin, affecting to close his mouth ere he could pronounce the name of the Saviour. "Obdurate wretch, return to the demon who sent thee!"

He signed to four priests, who, approaching with sprinklers in their hands, exorcised with holy water the air the magician breathed, the earth he touched, the wood that was to burn him. During this ceremony, the Judge-Advocate hastily read the decree, dated the 18th of August, 1639, *declaring Urbain Grandier duly attainted and convicted of the crime of sor-*

[83]

cery, witchcraft, and possession, in the persons of sundry Ursuline nuns of Loudun, and others, laymen, etc.

The reader, dazzled by a flash of lightning, stopped for an instant, and, turning to M. de Laubardemont, asked whether, considering the awful weather, the execution could not be deferred till the next day.

"The decree," coldly answered Laubardemont, "commands execution within twenty-four hours. Fear not the incredulous people; they will soon be convinced."

All the most important persons of the town and many strangers were under the peristyle, and now advanced, Cinq-Mars among them.

"The magician never has been able to pronounce the name of the Saviour, and repels his image."

Lactantius at this moment issued from the midst of the Penitents, with an enormous iron crucifix in his hand, which he seemed to hold with precaution and respect; he extended it to the lips of the sufferer, who indeed threw back his head, and collecting all his strength, made a gesture with his arm, which threw the cross from the hands of the Capuchin.

"You see," cried the latter, "he has thrown down the cross!"

A murmur arose, the meaning of which was doubtful.

"Profanation!" cried the priests.

The procession moved toward the pile.

Meanwhile, Cinq-Mars, gliding behind a pillar, had eagerly watched all that passed; he saw with astonishment that the cross, in falling upon the steps, which were more exposed to the rain than the platform, smoked and made a noise like molten lead when thrown into water. While the public attention was elsewhere engaged, he advanced and touched it lightly with his bare hand, which was immediately scorched. Seized with indignation, with all the fury of a true heart, he took up the cross with the folds of his cloak, stepped up to Laubardemont, and, striking him with it on the forehead, cried:

"Villain, I brand thee with the mark of this red-hot iron!"

The crowd heard these words and rushed forward.

"Arrest this madman!" cried the unworthy magistrate.

He was himself seized by the hands of men who cried:

"Justice! justice, in the name of the King!"

"We are lost!" said Lactantius; "to the pile, to the pile!"

The Penitents dragged Urbain toward the Place, while the judges and archers reëntered the church, struggling with the furious citizens; the executioner, having no time to tie up the victim, hastened to lay him on the wood, and to set fire to it. But the rain still fell in torrents, and each piece of wood had no sooner caught the flame than it became extinguished. In vain did Lactantius and the other canons themselves seek to stir up the fire; nothing could overcome the water which fell from heaven.

Meanwhile, the tumult which had begun in the peristyle of the church extended throughout the square. The cry of "Justice!" was repeated and circulated, with the information of what had been discovered; two barricades were forced, and despite three volleys of musketry, the archers were gradually driven back toward the centre of the square. In vain they spurred their horses against the crowd; it overwhelmed them with its swelling waves. Half an hour passed in this struggle, the guards still receding toward the pile, which they concealed as they pressed closer upon it.

"On! on!" cried a man; "we will deliver him; do not strike the soldiers, but let them fall back. See, Heaven will not permit him to die! The fire is out; now, friend, one effort more! That is well! Throw down that horse! Forward! On!"

The guard was broken and dispersed on all sides. The crowd rushed to the pile, but no more light was there: all had disappeared, even the executioner. They tore up and threw aside the beams; one of them was still burning, and its light showed under a mass of ashes and ensanguined mire a blackened hand, preserved from the fire by a large iron bracelet and chain. A woman had the courage to open it; the fingers clasped a small ivory cross and an image of St. Magdalen.

"These are his remains," she said, weeping.

"Say, the relics of a martyr!" exclaimed a citizen, baring his head.

CHAPTER VI

Les vergers languissants altérés de chaleurs,
Balancent des rameaux dépourvus de feuillages;
Il semble que l'hiver ne quitte pas les cieux.

Maria, JULES LEFEVRE.

EANWHILE, Cinq-Mars, amid the excitement which his outbreak had provoked, felt his left arm seized by a hand as hard as iron, which, drawing him from the crowd to the foot of the steps, pushed him behind the wall of the church, and he then saw the dark face of old Grandchamp, who said to him in a sharp voice:

"Sir, your attack upon thirty musketeers in a wood at Chaumont was nothing, because we were near you, though you knew it not, and, moreover, you had to do with men of honor; but here 'tis different. Your horses and people are at the end of the street; I request you to mount and leave the town, or to send me back to Madame la Maréchale, for I am responsible for your limbs, which you expose so freely."

Cinq-Mars was somewhat astonished at this rough mode of having a service done him, was not sorry to extricate himself thus from the affair, having had time to reflect how very awkward it might be for him to be recognized, after striking the head of the judicial authority, the agent of the very Cardinal who was to present him to the King. He observed also that around him was assembled a crowd of the lowest class of people, among whom he blushed to find himself. He therefore followed his old domestic without argument, and found the other three servants waiting for him. Despite the rain and wind he mounted, and was soon upon the highroad with his escort, having put his horse to a gallop to avoid pursuit.

He had, however, hardly left Loudun when the sandy road, furrowed by deep ruts completely filled with water, obliged him to slacken his pace. The rain continued to fall heavily, and his cloak was almost saturated. He felt a thicker one thrown over his shoulders; it was his old valet, who had approached him, and thus exhibited toward him a maternal solicitude.

"Well, Grandchamp," said Cinq-Mars, "now that we are clear of the riot, tell me how you came to be there when I had ordered you to remain at the Abbé's."

"*Parbleu*, Monsieur!" answered the old servant, in a grumbling tone, "do you suppose that I should obey you any more than I did Monsieur le Maréchal? When my late master, after telling me to remain in his tent, found me behind him in the cannon's smoke, he made no complaint, because he had a fresh horse ready when his own was killed, and he only scolded me for a moment in his thoughts; but, truly, during the forty years I served him, I never saw him act as

you have in the fortnight I have been with you. Ah!"
he added with a sigh, "things are going strangely;
and if we continue thus, there's no knowing what will
be the end of it."

"But knowest thou, Grandchamp, that these scoun-
drels had made the crucifix red hot?—a thing at which
no honest man would have been less enraged than I."

"Except Monsieur le Maréchal, your father, who
would not have done at all what you have done,
Monsieur."

"What, then, would he have done?"

"He would very quietly have let this curé be burned
by the other curés, and would have said to me, 'Grandchamp, see that my horses have oats, and let no one
steal them'; or, 'Grandchamp, take care that the
rain does not rust my sword or wet the priming of
my pistols'; for Monsieur le Maréchal thought of
everything, and never interfered in what did not con-
cern him. That was his great principle; and as he
was, thank Heaven, alike good soldier and good general, he was always as careful of his arms as a recruit,
and would not have stood up against thirty young
gallants with a dress rapier."

Cinq-Mars felt the force of the worthy servitor's
epigrammatic scolding, and feared that he had followed him beyond the wood of Chaumont; but he
would not ask, lest he should have to give explanations
or to tell a falsehood or to command silence, which
would at once have been taking him into confidence
on the subject. As the only alternative, he spurred
his horse and rode ahead of his old domestic; but the

latter had not yet had his say, and instead of keeping behind his master, he rode up to his left and continued the conversation.

"Do you suppose, Monsieur, that I should allow you to go where you please? No, Monsieur, I am too deeply impressed with the respect I owe to Madame la Marquise, to give her an opportunity of saying to me: 'Grandchamp, my son has been killed with a shot or with a sword; why were you not before him?' Or, 'He has received a stab from the stiletto of an Italian, because he went at night beneath the window of a great princess; why did you not seize the assassin?' This would be very disagreeable to me, Monsieur, for I never have been reproached with anything of the kind. Once Monsieur le Maréchal lent me to his nephew, Monsieur le Comte, to make a campaign in the Netherlands, because I know Spanish. I fulfilled the duty with honor, as I always do. When Monsieur le Comte received a bullet in his heart, I myself brought back his horses, his mules, his tent, and all his equipment, without so much as a pocket-handkerchief being missed; and I can assure you that the horses were as well dressed and harnessed when we reëntered Chaumont as if Monsieur le Comte had been about to go a-hunting. And, accordingly, I received nothing but compliments and agreeable things from the whole family, just in the way I like."

"Well, well, my friend," said Henri d'Effiat, "I may some day, perhaps, have these horses to take back; but in the mean time take this great purse of gold, which I have well-nigh lost two or three times, and thou shalt pay for me everywhere. The money wearies me."

"Monsieur le Maréchal did not so, Monsieur. He had been superintendent of finances, and he counted every farthing he paid out of his own hand. I do not think your estates would have been in such good condition, or that you would have had so much money to count yourself, had he done otherwise; have the goodness, therefore, to keep your purse, whose contents, I dare swear, you do not know."

"Faith, not I."

Grandchamp sent forth a profound sigh at his master's disdainful exclamation.

"Ah, Monsieur le Marquis! Monsieur le Marquis! When I think that the great King Henri, before my eyes, put his chamois gloves into his pocket to keep the rain from spoiling them; when I think that Monsieur de Rosni refused him money when he had spent too much; when I think——"

"When thou dost think, thou art egregiously tedious, my old friend," interrupted his master; "and thou wilt do better in telling me what that black figure is that I think I see walking in the mire behind us."

"It looks like some poor peasant woman who, perhaps, wants alms of us. She can easily follow us, for we do not go at much of a pace in this sand, wherein our horses sink up to the hams. We shall go to the Landes perhaps some day, Monsieur, and you will see a country all the same as this sandy road, and great, black firs all the way along. It looks like a churchyard; this is an exact specimen of it. Look,

the rain has ceased, and we can see a little ahead;
there is nothing but furze-bushes on this great plain,
without a village or a house. I don't know where
we can pass the night; but if you will take my advice,
you will let us cut some boughs and bivouac where we
are. You shall see how, with a little earth, I can
make a hut as warm as a bed."

"I would rather go on to the light I see in the
horizon," said Cinq-Mars; "for I fancy I feel rather
feverish, and I am thirsty. But fall back, I would
ride alone; rejoin the others and follow."

Grandchamp obeyed; he consoled himself by giving Germain, Louis, and Etienne lessons in the art
of reconnoitring a country by night.

Meanwhile, his young master was overcome with
fatigue. The violent emotions of the day had profoundly affected his mind; and the long journey on
horseback, the last two days passed almost without
nourishment, owing to the hurried pressure of events,
the heat of the sun by day, the icy coldness of the
night, all contributed to increase his indisposition and
to weary his delicate frame. For three hours he rode
in silence before his people, yet the light he had seen
in the horizon seemed no nearer; at last he ceased
to follow it with his eyes, and his head, feeling heavier
and heavier, sank upon his breast. He gave the reins
to his tired horse, which of its own accord followed
the high-road, and, crossing his arms, allowed himself
to be rocked by the monotonous motion of his fellow-
traveller, which frequently stumbled against the large
stones that strewed the road. The rain had ceased,

as had the voices of his domestics, whose horses followed in the track of their master's. The young man abandoned himself to the bitterness of his thoughts; he asked himself whether the bright object of his hopes would not flee from him day by day, as that phosphoric light fled from him in the horizon, step by step. Was it probable that the young Princess, almost forcibly recalled to the gallant court of Anne of Austria, would always refuse the hands, perhaps royal ones, that would be offered to her? What chance that she would resign herself to renounce a present throne, in order to wait till some caprice of fortune should realize romantic hopes, or take a youth almost in the lowest rank of the army and lift him to the elevation she spoke of, till the age of love should be passed? How could he be certain that even the vows of Marie de Gonzaga were sincere?

"Alas!" he said, "perhaps she has blinded herself as to her own sentiments; the solitude of the country had prepared her soul to receive deep impressions. I came; she thought I was he of whom she had dreamed. Our age and my love did the rest. But when at court, she, the companion of the Queen, has learned to contemplate from an exalted position the greatness to which I aspire, and which I as yet see only from a very humble distance; when she shall suddenly find herself in actual possession of the future she aims at, and measures with a more correct eye the long road I have to travel; when she shall hear around her vows like mine, pronounced by lips which could undo me with a word, with a word destroy him whom she awaits as her husband, her lord—oh, madman that I have been!—she will see all her folly, and will be incensed at mine."

Thus did doubt, the greatest misery of love, begin to torture his unhappy heart; he felt his hot blood rush to his head and oppress it. Ever and anon he fell forward upon the neck of his horse, and a half sleep weighed down his eyes; the dark firs that bordered the road seemed to him gigantic corpses travelling beside him. He saw, or thought he saw, the same woman clothed in black, whom he had pointed out to Grandchamp, approach so near as to touch his horse's mane, pull his cloak, and then run off with a jeering laugh; the sand of the road seemed to him a river running beneath him, with opposing current, back toward its source. This strange sight dazzled his worn eyes; he closed them and fell asleep on his horse.

Presently, he felt himself stopped, but he was numbed with cold and could not move. He saw peasants, lights, a house, a great room into which they carried him, a wide bed, whose heavy curtains were closed by Grandchamp; and he fell asleep again, stunned by the fever that whirred in his ears.

Dreams that followed one another more rapidly than grains of sand before the wind rushed through his brain; he could not catch them, and moved restlessly on his bed. Urbain Grandier on the rack, his mother in tears, his tutor armed, Bassompierre loaded with chains, passed before him, making signs of farewell; at last, as he slept, he instinctively put his hand to his head to stay the passing dream, which then seemed to unfold itself before his eyes like pictures in shifting sands.

He saw a public square crowded with a foreign people, a northern people, who uttered cries of joy, but they were savage cries; there was a line of guards, ferocious soldiers—these were Frenchmen. "Come with me," said the soft voice of Marie de Gonzaga, who took his hand. "See, I wear a diadem; here is thy throne, come with me." And she hurried him on, the people still shouting. He went on, a long way. "Why are you sad, if you are a queen?" he said, trembling. But she was pale, and smiled and spoke not. She ascended, step after step, up to a throne, and seated herself. "Mount!" said she, forcibly pulling his hand. But, at every movement, the massive stairs crumbled beneath his feet, so that he could not ascend. "Give thanks to love," she continued; and her hand, now more powerful, raised him to the throne. The people still shouted. He bowed low to kiss that helping hand, that adored hand; it was the hand of the executioner!

"Oh, heavens!" exclaimed Cinq-Mars, as, heaving a deep sigh, he opened his eyes. A flickering lamp lighted the ruinous chamber of the inn; he again closed his eyes, for he had seen, seated on his bed, a woman, a nun, young and beautiful! He thought he was still dreaming, but she grasped his hand firmly. He opened his burning eyes, and fixed them upon her.

"Is it you, Jeanne de Belfiel? The rain has

drenched your veil and your black hair! Why are you here, unhappy woman?"

"Hark! awake not my Urbain; he sleeps there in the next room. Ay, my hair is indeed wet, and my feet—see, my feet that were once so white, see how the mud has soiled them. But I have made a vow —I will not wash them till I have seen the King, and until he has granted me Urbain's pardon. I am going to the army to find him; I will speak to him as Grandier taught me to speak, and he will pardon him. And listen, I will also ask thy pardon, for I read it in thy face that thou, too, art condemned to death. Poor youth! thou art too young to die, thy curling hair is beautiful; but yet thou art condemned, for thou hast on thy brow a line that never deceives. The man thou hast struck will kill thee. Thou hast made too much use of the cross; it is that which will bring evil upon thee. Thou hast struck with it, and thou wearest it round thy neck by a hair chain. Nay, hide not thy face; have I said aught to afflict thee, or is it that thou lovest, young man? Ah, reassure thyself, I will not tell all this to thy love. I am mad, but I am gentle, very gentle; and three days ago I was beautiful. Is she also beautiful? Ah! she will weep some day! Yet, if she can weep, she will be happy!"

And then suddenly Jeanne began to recite the service for the dead in a monotonous voice, but with incredible rapidity, still seated on the bed, and turning the beads of a long rosary.

Suddenly the door opened; she looked up, and fled through another door in the partition.

"What the devil's that—an imp or an angel, saying the funeral service over you, and you under the clothes, as if you were in a shroud?"

This abrupt exclamation came from the rough voice of Grandchamp, who was so astonished at what he had seen that he dropped the glass of lemonade he was bringing in. Finding that his master did not answer, he became still more alarmed, and raised the bedclothes. Cinq-Mars's face was crimson, and he seemed asleep, but his old domestic saw that the blood rushing to his head had almost suffocated him; and, seizing a jug full of cold water, he dashed the whole of it in his face. This military remedy rarely fails to effect its purpose, and Cinq-Mars returned to himself with a start.

"Ah! it is thou, Grandchamp; what frightful dreams I have had!"

"*Peste!* Monsieur le Marquis, your dreams, on the contrary, are very pretty ones. I saw the tail of the last as I came in; your choice is not bad."

"What dost mean, blockhead?"

"Nay, not a blockhead, Monsieur; I have good eyes, and I have seen what I have seen. But, really ill as you are, Monsieur le Maréchal would never——"

"Thou art utterly doting, my friend; give me some drink, I am parched with thirst. Oh, heavens! what a night! I still see all those women."

"All those women, Monsieur? Why, how many are here?"

"I am speaking to thee of a dream, blockhead.

7 [97]

Why standest there like a post, instead of giving me some drink?"

"Enough, Monsieur; I will get more lemonade." And going to the door, he called over the staircase, "Germain! Etienne! Louis!"

The innkeeper answered from below: "Coming, Monsieur, coming; they have been helping me to catch the mad-woman."

"What mad-woman?" said Cinq-Mars, rising in bed.

The host entered, and, taking off his cotton cap, said, respectfully: "Oh, nothing, Monsieur le Marquis, only a mad-woman that came here last night on foot, and whom we put in the next room; but she has escaped, and we have not been able to catch her."

"Ah!" exclaimed Cinq-Mars, returning to himself and putting his hand to his eyes, "it was not a dream, then. And my mother, where is she? and the Maréchal, and—Ah! and yet it is but a fearful dream! Leave me."

As he said this, he turned toward the wall, and again pulled the clothes over his head.

The innkeeper, in amazement, touched his forehead three times with his finger, looking at Grandchamp as if to ask him whether his master were also mad.

Grandchamp motioned him away in silence, and in order to watch the rest of the night by the side of Cinq-Mars, who was in a deep sleep, he seated himself in a large armchair, covered with tapestry, and began to squeeze lemons into a glass of water with an air as grave and severe as Archimedes calculating the condensing power of his mirrors.

CHAPTER VII

Men have rarely the courage to be wholly good or wholly bad.
                                                    MACHIAVELLI.

ET us leave our young traveller sleeping; he will soon pursue a long and beautiful route. Since we are at liberty to turn to all points of the map, we will fix our eyes upon the city of Narbonne.

Behold the Mediterranean, not far distant, washing with its blue waters the sandy shores. Penetrate into that city resembling Athens; and to find him who reigns there, follow that dark and irregular street, mount the steps of the old archiepiscopal palace, and enter the first and largest of its apartments.

This was a very long salon, lighted by a series of high lancet windows, of which the upper part only retained the blue, yellow, and red panes that shed a mysterious light through the apartment. A large round table occupied its entire breadth, near the great fireplace; around this table, covered with a colored cloth and scattered with papers and portfolios, were seated, bending over their pens, eight secretaries copying letters which were handed to them from a smaller table. Other men quietly arranged the completed papers in the shelves of a bookcase, partly filled with books bound in black.

Notwithstanding the number of persons assembled in the room, one might have heard the movements of the wings of a fly. The only interruption to the silence was the sound of pens rapidly gliding over paper, and a shrill voice dictating, stopping every now and then to cough. This voice proceeded from a great armchair placed beside the fire, which was blazing, notwithstanding the heat of the season and of the country. It was one of those armchairs that you still see in old castles, and which seem made to read one's self to sleep in, so easy is every part of it. The sitter sinks into a circular cushion of down; if the head leans back, the cheeks rest upon pillows covered with silk, and the seat juts out so far beyond the elbows that one may believe the provident upholsterers of our forefathers sought to provide that the book should make no noise in falling so as to awaken the sleeper.

But we will quit this digression, and speak of the man who occupied the chair, and who was very far from sleeping. He had a broad forehead, bordered with thin white hair, large, mild eyes, a wan face, to which a small, pointed, white beard gave that air of subtlety and finesse noticeable in all the portraits of the period of Louis XIII. His mouth was almost without lips, which Lavater deems an indubitable sign of an evil mind, and it was framed in a pair of slight gray moustaches and a *royale* — an ornament then in fashion, which somewhat resembled a comma in form. The old man wore a close red cap, a large *robe-de-chambre*, and purple silk stockings; he was no less a personage than Armand Duplessis, Cardinal de Richelieu.

Near him, around the small table, sat four youths from fifteen to twenty years of age; these were pages, or domestics, according to the term then in use, which signified *familiars*, friends of the house. This custom was a relic of feudal patronage, which still existed in our manners. The younger members of high families received wages from the great lords, and were devoted to their service in all things, challenging the first comer at the wish of their patron. The pages wrote letters from the outline previously given them by the Cardinal, and after their master had glanced at them, passed them to the secretaries, who made fair copies. The Duke, for his part, wrote on his knee private notes upon small slips of paper, inserting them in almost all the packets before sealing them, which he did with his own hand.

He had been writing a short time, when, in a mirror before him, he saw the youngest of his pages writing something on a sheet of paper much smaller than the official sheet. He hastily wrote a few words, and then slipped the paper under the large sheet which, much against his inclination, he had to fill; but, seated behind the Cardinal, he hoped that the difficulty with which the latter turned would prevent him from seeing the little manœuvre he had tried to exercise with much dexterity. Suddenly Richelieu said to him, dryly, "Come here, Monsieur Olivier."

These words came like a thunder-clap on the poor boy, who seemed about sixteen. He rose at once, however, and stood before the minister, his arms hanging at his side and his head lowered.

The other pages and the secretaries stirred no more than soldiers when a comrade is struck down by a ball, so accustomed were they to this kind of summons. The present one, however, was more energetic than usual.

"What were you writing?"

"My lord, what your Eminence dictated."

"What!"

"My lord, the letter to Don Juan de Braganza."

"No evasions, Monsieur; you were writing something else."

"My lord," said the page, with tears in his eyes, "it was a letter to one of my cousins."

"Let me see it."

The page trembled in every limb and was obliged to lean against the chimney-piece, as he said, in a hardly audible tone, "It is impossible."

"Monsieur le Vicomte Olivier d'Entraigues," said the minister, without showing the least emotion, "you are no longer in my service." The page withdrew. He knew that there was no reply; so, slipping his letter into his pocket, and opening the folding-doors just wide enough to allow his exit, he glided out like a bird escaped from the cage.

The minister went on writing the note upon his knee.

The secretaries redoubled their silent zeal, when

suddenly the two wings of the door were thrown back and showed, standing in the opening, a Capuchin, who, bowing, with his arms crossed over his breast, seemed waiting for alms or for an order to retire. He had a dark complexion, and was deeply pitted with smallpox; his eyes, mild, but somewhat squinting, were almost hidden by his thick eyebrows, which met in the middle of his forehead; on his mouth played a crafty, mischievous, and sinister smile; his beard was straight and red, and his costume was that of the order of St. Francis in all its repulsiveness, with sandals on his bare feet, that looked altogether unfit to tread upon carpet.

Such as he was, however, this personage appeared to create a great sensation throughout the room; for, without finishing the phrase, the line, or even the word begun, every person rose and went out by the door where he was still standing—some saluting him as they passed, others turning away their heads, and the young pages holding their fingers to their noses, but not till they were behind him, for they seemed to have a secret fear of him. When they had all passed out, he entered, making a profound reverence, because the door was still open; but, as soon as it was shut, unceremoniously advancing, he seated himself near the Cardinal, who, having recognized him by the general movement he created, saluted him with a dry and silent inclination of the head, regarding him fixedly, as if awaiting some news and unable to avoid knitting his brows, as at the aspect of a spider or some other disagreeable creature.

ALFRED DE VIGNY

The Cardinal could not resist this movement of displeasure, because he felt himself obliged, by the presence of his agent, to resume those profound and painful conversations from which he had for some days been free, in a country whose pure air, favorable to him, had somewhat soothed the pain of his malady; that malady had changed to a slow fever, but its intervals were long enough to enable him to forget during its absence that it must return. Giving, therefore, a little rest to his hitherto indefatigable mind, he had been awaiting, for the first time in his life perhaps, without impatience, the return of the couriers he had sent in all directions, like the rays of a sun which alone gave life and movement to France. He had not expected the visit he now received, and the sight of one of those men, whom, to use his own expression, he "steeped in crime," rendered all the habitual disquietudes of his life more present to him, without entirely dissipating the cloud of melancholy which at that time obscured his thoughts.

The beginning of his conversation was tinged with the gloomy hue of his late reveries; but he soon became more animated and vigorous than ever, when his powerful mind had reëntered the real world.

His confidant, seeing that he was expected to break the silence, did so in this abrupt fashion:

"Well, my lord, of what are you thinking?"

"Alas, Joseph, of what should we all think, but of our future happiness in a better life? For many days I have been reflecting that human interests have too much diverted me from this great thought; and I repent me of having spent some moments of my leisure in profane works, such as my tragedies, *Europe* and *Mirame*, despite the glory they have already gained me among our brightest minds—a glory which will extend unto futurity."

Father Joseph, full of what he had to say, was at first surprised at this opening; but he knew his master too well to betray his feelings, and, well skilled in changing the course of his ideas, replied:

"Yes, their merit is very great, and France will regret that these immortal works are not followed by similar productions."

"Yes, my dear Joseph; but it is in vain that such men as Boisrobert, Claveret, Colletet, Corneille, and, above all, the celebrated Mairet, have proclaimed these tragedies the finest that the present or any past age has produced. I reproach myself for them, I swear to you, as for a mortal sin, and I now, in my hours of repose, occupy myself only with my *Méthode des Controverses*, and my book on the *Perfection du Chrétien*. I remember that I am fifty-six years old, and that I have an incurable malady."

"These are calculations which your enemies make as precisely as your Eminence," said the priest, who began to be annoyed with this conversation, and was eager to talk of other matters.

The blood mounted to the Cardinal's face.

"I know it! I know it well!" he said; "I know all their black villainy, and I am prepared for it. But what news is there?"

"According to our arrangement, my lord, we have

removed Mademoiselle d'Hautefort, as we removed Mademoiselle de la Fayette before her. So far it is well; but her place is not filled, and the King——"

"Well!"

"The King has ideas which he never had before."

"Ha! and which come not from me? 'Tis well, truly," said the minister, with an ironic sneer.

"What, my lord, leave the place of the favorite vacant for six whole days? It is not prudent; pardon me for saying so."

"He has ideas—ideas!" repeated Richelieu, with a kind of terror; "and what are they?"

"He talks of recalling the Queen-mother," said the Capuchin, in a low voice; "of recalling her from Cologne."

"Marie de Médicis!" cried the Cardinal, striking the arms of his chair with his hands. "No, by Heaven, she shall not again set her foot upon the soil of France, whence I drove her, step by step! England has not dared to receive her, exiled by me; Holland fears to be crushed by her; and *my* kingdom to receive her! No, no, such an idea could not have originated with himself! To recall my enemy! to recall his mother! What perfidy! He would not have dared to think of it."

Then, having mused for a moment, he added, fixing a penetrating look still full of burning anger upon Father Joseph:

"But in what terms did he express this desire? Tell me his precise words."

"He said publicly, and in the presence of Monsieur:

'I feel that one of the first duties of a Christian is to be a good son, and I will resist no longer the murmurs of my conscience.'"

"Christian! conscience! these are not his expressions. It is Father Caussin—it is his confessor who is betraying me," cried the Cardinal. "Perfidious Jesuit! I pardoned thee thy intrigue with La Fayette; but I will not pass over thy secret counsels. I will have this confessor dismissed, Joseph; he is an enemy to the State, I see it clearly. But I myself have acted with negligence for some days past; I have not sufficiently hastened the arrival of the young d'Effiat, who will doubtless succeed. He is handsome and intellectual, they say. What a blunder! I myself merit disgrace. To leave that fox of a Jesuit with the King, without having given him my secret instructions, without a hostage, a pledge, or his fidelity to my orders! What neglect! Joseph, take a pen, and write what I shall dictate for the other confessor, whom we will choose better. I think of Father Sirmond."

Father Joseph sat down at the large table, ready to write, and the Cardinal dictated to him those duties, of a new kind, which shortly afterward he dared to have given to the King, who received them, respected them, and learned them by heart as the commandments of the Church. They have come down to us, —a terrible monument of the empire that a man may seize upon by means of circumstances, intrigues, and audacity:

"I. A prince should have a prime minister, and that minister three qualities: (1) He should have no passion but for his prince;

(2) He should be able and faithful; (3) He should be an ecclesiastic.

"II. A prince ought perfectly to love his prime minister.

"III. Ought never to change his prime minister.

"IV. Ought to tell him all things.

"V. To give him free access to his person.

"VI. To give him sovereign authority over his people.

"VII. Great honors and large possessions.

"VIII. A prince has no treasure more precious than his prime minister.

"IX. A prince should not put faith in what people say against his prime minister, nor listen to any such slanders.

"X. A prince should reveal to his prime minister all that is said against him, *even though he has been bound to keep it secret.*

"XI. A prince should prefer not only the well-being of the State, but also his prime minister, to all his relations."

Such were the commandments of the god of France, less astonishing in themselves than the terrible naïveté which made him bequeath them to posterity, as if posterity also must believe in him.

While he dictated his instructions, reading them from a small piece of paper, written with his own hand, a deep melancholy seemed to possess him more and more at each word; and when he had ended, he fell back in his chair, his arms crossed, and his head sunk on his breast.

Father Joseph, dropping his pen, arose and was inquiring whether he were ill, when he heard issue from the depths of his chest these mournful and memorable words:

"What utter weariness! what endless trouble! If the ambitious man could see me, he would flee to a desert. What is my power? A miserable reflection of the royal power; and what labors to fix upon my star that incessantly wavering ray! For twenty years I have been in vain attempting it. I can not comprehend that man. He dare not flee me; but they take him from me—he glides through my fingers. What things could I not have done with his hereditary rights, had I possessed them? But, employing such infinite calculation in merely keeping one's balance, what of genius remains for high enterprises? I hold Europe in my hand, yet I myself am suspended by a trembling hair. What is it to me that I can cast my eyes confidently over the map of Europe, when all my interests are concentrated in his narrow cabinet, and its few feet of space give me more trouble to govern than the whole country besides? See, then, what it is to be a prime minister! Envy me, my guards, if you can."

His features were so distorted as to give reason to fear some accident; and at the same moment he was seized with a long and violent fit of coughing, which ended in a slight hemorrhage. He saw that Father Joseph, alarmed, was about to seize a gold bell that stood on the table, and, suddenly rising with all the vivacity of a young man, he stopped him, saying:

"'Tis nothing, Joseph; I sometimes yield to these fits of depression; but they do not last long, and I leave them stronger than before. As for my health, I know my condition perfectly; but that is not the business in hand. What have you done at Paris? I am glad to know the King has arrived in Béarn, as

I wished; we shall be able to keep a closer watch upon him. How did you induce him to come away?"

"A battle at Perpignan."

"That is not bad. Well, we can arrange it for him; that occupation will do as well as another just now. But the young Queen, what says she?"

"She is still furious against you; her correspondence discovered, the questioning to which you had subjected her——"

"Bah! a madrigal and a momentary submission on my part will make her forget that I have separated her from her house of Austria and from the country of her Buckingham. But how does she occupy herself?"

"In machinations with Monsieur. But as we have his entire confidence, here are the daily accounts of their interviews."

"I shall not trouble myself to read them; while the Duc de Bouillon remains in Italy I have nothing to fear in that quarter. She may have as many petty plots with Gaston in the chimney-corner as she pleases; he never got beyond his excellent intentions, forsooth! He carries nothing into effect but his withdrawal from the kingdom. He has had his third dismissal; I will manage a fourth for him whenever he pleases; he is not worth the pistol-shot you had the Comte de Soissons settled with, and yet the poor Comte had scarce more energy than he."

And the Cardinal, reseating himself in his chair, began to laugh gayly enough for a statesman.

"I always laugh when I think of their expedition to Amiens. They had me between them. Each had fully five hundred gentlemen with him, armed to the teeth, and all going to despatch me, like Concini; but the great Vitry was not there. They very quietly let me talk for an hour with them about the hunt and the *Fête Dieu*, and neither of them dared make a sign to their cut-throats. I have since learned from Chavigny that for two long months they had been waiting that happy moment. For myself, indeed, I observed nothing, except that little villain, the Abbé de Gondi,* who prowled near me, and seemed to have something hidden under his sleeve; it was he that made me get into the coach."

"*Apropos* of the Abbé, my lord, the Queen insists upon making him coadjutor."

"She is mad! he will ruin her if she connects herself with him; he's a musketeer in canonicals, the devil in a cassock. Read his *Histoire de Fiesque;* you may see himself in it. He will be nothing while I live."

"How is it that with a judgment like yours you bring another ambitious man of his age to court?"

"That is an entirely different matter. This young Cinq-Mars, my friend, will be a mere puppet. He will think of nothing but his ruff and his shoulder-knots; his handsome figure assures me of this. I know that he is gentle and weak; it was for this reason I preferred him to his elder brother. He will do whatever we wish."

"Ah, my lord," said the monk, with an expression of doubt, "I never place much reliance on people

* Afterward Cardinal de Retz.

whose exterior is so calm; the hidden flame is often all the more dangerous. Recollect the Maréchal d'Effiat, his father."

"But I tell you he is a boy, and I shall bring him up; while Gondi is already an accomplished conspirator, an ambitious knave who sticks at nothing. He has dared to dispute Madame de la Meilleraie with me. Can you conceive it? He dispute with me! A petty priestling, who has no other merit than a little lively small-talk and a cavalier air. Fortunately, the husband himself took care to get rid of him."

Father Joseph, who listened with equal impatience to his master when he spoke of his *bonnes fortunes* or of his verses, made, however, a grimace which he meant to be very sly and insinuating, but which was simply ugly and awkward; he fancied that the expression of his mouth, twisted about like a monkey's, conveyed, "Ah! who can resist your Eminence?" But his Eminence only read there, "I am a clown who knows nothing of the great world"; and, without changing his voice, he suddenly said, taking up a despatch from the table:

"The Duc de Rohan is dead, that is good news; the Huguenots are ruined. He is a lucky man. I had him condemned by the Parliament of Toulouse to be torn in pieces by four horses, and here he dies quietly on the battlefield of Rheinfeld. But what matters? The result is the same. Another great head is laid low! How they have fallen since that of Montmorency! I now see hardly any that do not bow before me. We have already punished almost

" Ah, who can resist your eminence ? "

[From the Original Drawing by A. Duvivier.]

whose exterior is so calm; the hidden flame is often all the more danger———. Recollect the Maréchal d'Effiat, his father."

"But I tell you he is a boy, and I shall bring him ... an accomplished con... ambitious knave who sticks at nothing. de la Meilleraie ... the ... Can you conceive it? He dispute with me! A poor priestling who has no other merit than a little lively small-talk and a cavalier air. Fortunately, the husband himself took care to get rid of him."

Father Joseph, who listened with equal impatience to his master when he spoke of his *bonnes fortunes* or of his verses, made, however, a grimace which he meant to be very sly and insinuating, but which was simply ugly and awkward; he fancied that the expression of his mouth, twisted about like a monkey's, conveyed, "Ah! who can resist your Eminence?" But his Eminence only read there, "I am a clown who knows nothing of the great world"; and, without changing his voice, he suddenly said, taking up a despatch from the table:

"The Duc de Rohan is dead, that is good news, the Huguenots are ruined. He is a lucky man. I had him condemned by the Parliament of Toulouse to be torn in pieces by four horses, and here he dies quietly on the battlefield of Rheinfeld. But what matters? The result is the same. Another great head is laid low! How they have fallen since that of Montmorency! I now see hardly any that do not bow before me. We have already punished almost

[From the Original Drawing by A. Dunoier.]

Ah, who can resist your eminence.

all our dupes of Versailles; assuredly they have nothing with which to reproach me. I simply exercise against them the law of retaliation, treating them as they would have treated me in the council of the Queen-mother. The old dotard Bassompierre shall be doomed for perpetual imprisonment, and so shall the assassin Maréchal de Vitry, for that was the punishment they voted me. As for Marillac, who counselled death, I reserve death for him at the first false step he makes, and I beg thee, Joseph, to remind me of him; we must be just to all. The Duc de Bouillon still keeps up his head proudly on account of his Sedan, but I shall make him yield. Their blindness is truly marvellous! They think themselves all free to conspire, not perceiving that they are merely fluttering at the ends of the threads that I hold in my hand, and which I lengthen now and then to give them air and space. Did the Huguenots cry out as one man at the death of their dear duke?"

"Less so than at the affair of Loudun, which is happily concluded."

"What! Happily? I hope that Grandier is dead?"

"Yes; that is what I meant. Your Eminence may be fully satisfied. All was settled in twenty-four hours. He is no longer thought of. Only Laubardemont committed a slight blunder in making the trial public. This caused a little tumult; but we have a description of the rioters, and measures have been taken to seek them out."

"This is well, very well. Urbain was too superior

a man to be left there; he was turning Protestant. I
would wager that he would have ended by abjuring.
His work against the celibacy of priests made me conjecture this; and in cases of doubt, remember, Joseph,
it is always best to cut the tree before the fruit is
gathered. These Huguenots, you see, form a regular
republic in the State. If once they had a majority in
France, the monarchy would be lost, and they would
establish some popular government which might be
durable."

"And what deep pain do they daily cause our holy
Father the Pope!" said Joseph.

"Ah," interrupted the Cardinal, "I see; thou
wouldst remind me of his obstinacy in not giving
thee the hat. Be tranquil; I will speak to-day on the
subject to the new ambassador we are sending, the
Maréchal d'Estrées, and he will, on his arrival, doubtless obtain that which has been in train these two
years—thy nomination to the cardinalate. I myself
begin to think that the purple would become thee
well, for it does not show blood-stains."

And both burst into laughter—the one as a master,
overwhelming the assassin whom he pays with his
utter scorn; the other as a slave, resigned to all the
humiliation by which he rises.

The laughter which the ferocious pleasantry of the
old minister had excited had hardly subsided, when
the door opened, and a page announced several couriers who had arrived simultaneously from different
points. Father Joseph arose, and, leaning against the
wall like an Egyptian mummy, allowed nothing to

appear upon his face but an expression of stolid contemplation. Twelve messengers entered successively, attired in various disguises; one appeared to be a Swiss soldier, another a sutler, a third a master-mason. They had been introduced into the palace by a secret stairway and corridor, and left the cabinet by a door opposite that at which they had entered, without any opportunity of meeting one another or communicating the contents of their despatches. Each laid a rolled or folded packet of papers on the large table, spoke for a moment with the Cardinal in the embrasure of a window and withdrew. Richelieu had risen on the entrance of the first messenger, and, careful to do all himself, had received them all, listened to all, and with his own hand had closed the door upon all. When the last was gone, he signed to Father Joseph, and, without speaking, both proceeded to unfold, or, rather, to tear open, the packets of despatches, and in a few words communicated to each other the substance of the letters.

"The Duc de Weimar pursues his advantage; the Duc Charles is defeated. Our General is in good spirits; here are some of his lively remarks at table. Good!"

"Monseigneur le Vicomte de Turenne has retaken the towns of Lorraine; and here are his private conversations——"

"Oh! pass over them; they can not be dangerous. He is ever a good and honest man, in no way mixing himself up with politics; so that some one gives him a little army to play at chess with, no matter against whom, he is content. We shall always be good friends."

"The Long Parliament still endures in England. The Commons pursue their project; there are massacres in Ireland. The Earl of Strafford is condemned to death."

"To death! Horrible!"

"I will read: 'His Majesty Charles I has not had the courage to sign the sentence, but he has appointed four commissioners.'"

"Weak king, I abandon thee! Thou shalt have no more of our money. Fall, since thou art ungrateful! Unhappy Wentworth!"

A tear rose in the eyes of Richelieu as he said this; the man who had but now played with the lives of so many others wept for a minister abandoned by his prince. The similarity between that position and his own affected him, and it was his own case he deplored in the person of the foreign minister. He ceased to read aloud the despatches that he opened, and his confidant followed his example. He examined with scrupulous attention the detailed accounts of the most minute and secret actions of each person of any importance—accounts which he always required to be added to the official despatches made by his able spies. All the despatches to the King passed through his hands, and were carefully revised so as to reach the King amended to the state in which he wished him to read them. The private notes were all carefully burned by the monk after the Cardinal had ascertained their contents. The latter, however, seemed by no means satisfied, and he was walking quickly to and fro with gestures expressive of anxiety, when the door opened, and a thirteenth courier entered. This one seemed a boy hardly fourteen years old; he held under his arm a packet sealed with black for the King, and gave to the Cardinal only a small letter, of which a stolen glance from Joseph could collect but four words. The Cardinal started, tore the billet into a thousand pieces, and, bending down to the ear of the boy, spoke to him for a long time; all that Joseph heard was, as the messenger went out:

"Take good heed to this; not until twelve hours from this time.'"

During this aside of the Cardinal, Joseph was occupied in concealing an infinite number of libels from Flanders and Germany, which the minister always insisted upon seeing, however bitter they might be to him. In this respect, be affected a philosophy which he was far from possessing, and to deceive those around him he would sometimes pretend that his enemies were not wholly wrong, and would outwardly laugh at their pleasantries; but those who knew his character better detected bitter rage lurking under this apparent moderation, and knew that he was never satisfied until he had got the hostile book condemned by the parliament to be burned in the Place de Grève, as "injurious to the King, in the person of his minister, the most illustrious Cardinal," as we read in the decrees of the time, and that his only regret was that the author was not in the place of his book—a satisfaction he gave himself whenever he could, as in the case of Urbain Grandier.

ALFRED DE VIGNY

It was his colossal pride which he thus avenged, without avowing it even to himself—nay, laboring for a length of time, sometimes for a whole twelvemonth together, to persuade himself that the interest of the State was concerned in the matter. Ingenious in connecting his private affairs with the affairs of France, he had convinced himself that she bled from the wounds which he received. Joseph, careful not to irritate his ill-temper at this moment, put aside and concealed a book entitled *Mystères Politiques du Cardinal de la Rochelle;* also another, attributed to a monk of Munich, entitled *Questions quolibétiques, ajustées au temps présent, et Impiété Sanglante du dieu Mars.* The worthy advocate Aubery, who has given us one of the most faithful histories of the most eminent Cardinal, is transported with rage at the mere title of the first of these books, and exclaims that "the great minister had good reason to glorify himself that his enemies, inspired against their will with the same enthusiasm which conferred the gift of rendering oracles upon the ass of Balaam, upon Caiaphas and others, who seemed most unworthy of the gift of prophecy, called him with good reason Cardinal de la Rochelle, since three years after their writing he reduced that town; thus Scipio was called Africanus for having subjugated that PROVINCE!" Very little was wanting to make Father Joseph, who had necessarily the same feelings, express his indignation in the same terms; for he remembered with bitterness the ridiculous part he had played in the siege of Rochelle, which, though not a *province* like Africa, had ventured to resist the

[118]

most eminent Cardinal, and into which Father Joseph, piquing himself on his military skill, had proposed to introduce the troops through a sewer. However, he restrained himself, and had time to conceal the libel in the pocket of his brown robe ere the minister had dismissed his young courier and returned to the table.

"And now to depart, Joseph," he said. "Open the doors to all that court which besieges me, and let us go to the King, who awaits me at Perpignan; this time I have him for good."

The Capuchin drew back, and immediately the pages, throwing open the gilded doors, announced in succession the greatest lords of the period, who had obtained permission from the King to come and salute the minister. Some, even, under the pretext of illness or business, had departed secretly, in order not to be among the last at Richelieu's reception; and the unhappy monarch found himself almost as alone as other kings find themselves on their deathbeds. But with him, the throne seemed, in the eyes of the court, his dying couch, his reign a continual last agony, and his minister a threatening successor.

Two pages, of the first families of France, stood at the door, where the ushers announced each of the persons whom Father Joseph had found in the anteroom. The Cardinal, still seated in his great armchair, remained motionless as the common couriers entered, inclined his head to the more distinguished, and to princes alone put his hands on the elbows of his chair and slightly rose; each person, having pro-

foundly saluted him, stood before him near the fireplace, waited till he had spoken to him, and then, at a
wave of his hand, completed the circuit of the room,
and went out by the same door at which he had entered, paused for a moment to salute Father Joseph,
who aped his master, and who for that reason had
been named "his Gray Eminence," and at last quitted
the palace, unless, indeed, he remained standing behind the chair, if the minister had signified that he
should, which was considered a token of very great
favor.

He allowed to pass several insignificant persons, and
many whose merits were useless to him; the first
whom he stopped in the procession was the Maréchal d'Estrées, who, about to set out on an embassy
to Rome, came to make his adieux; those behind him
stopped short. This circumstance warned the courtiers in the anteroom that a longer conversation than
usual was on foot, and Father Joseph, advancing to
the threshold, exchanged with the Cardinal a glance
which seemed to say, on the one side, "Remember the
promise you have just made me," on the other, "Set
your mind at rest." At the same time, the expert
Capuchin let his master see that he held upon his
arm one of his victims, whom he was forming into a
docile instrument; this was a young gentleman who
wore a very short green cloak, a *pourpoint* of the same
color, close-fitting red breeches, with glittering gold
garters below the knee—the costume of the pages of
Monsieur. Father Joseph, indeed, spoke to him secretly, but not in the way the Cardinal imagined; for

he contemplated being his equal, and was preparing other connections, in case of defection on the part of the prime minister.

"Tell Monsieur not to trust in appearances, and that he has no servant more faithful than I. The Cardinal is on the decline, and my conscience tells me to warn against his faults him who may inherit the royal power during the minority. To give your great Prince a proof of my faith, tell him that it is intended to arrest his friend, Puy-Laurens, and that he had better be kept out of the way, or the Cardinal will put him in the Bastille."

While the servant was thus betraying his master, the master, not to be behindhand with him, betrayed his servant. His self-love, and some remnant of respect to the Church, made him shudder at the idea of seeing a contemptible agent invested with the same hat which he himself wore as a crown, and seated as high as himself, except as to the precarious position of minister. Speaking, therefore, in an undertone to the Maréchal d'Estrées, he said:

"It is not necessary to importune Urbain VIII any further in favor of the Capuchin you see yonder; it is enough that his Majesty has deigned to name him for the cardinalate. One can readily conceive the repugnance of his Holiness to clothe this mendicant in the Roman purple."

Then, passing on to general matters, he continued:

"Truly, I know not what can have cooled the Holy Father toward us; what have we done that was not for the glory of our Holy Mother, the Catholic Church?

ALFRED DE VIGNY

I myself said the first mass at Rochelle, and you see for yourself, Monsieur le Maréchal, that our habit is everywhere; and even in your armies, the Cardinal de la Vallette has commanded gloriously in the palatinate."

"And has just made a very fine *retreat*," said the Maréchal, laying a slight emphasis upon the word.

The minister continued, without noticing this little outburst of professional jealousy, and raising his voice, said:

"God has shown that He did not scorn to send the spirit of victory upon his Levites, for the Duc de Weimar did not more powerfully aid in the conquest of Lorraine than did this pious Cardinal, and never was a naval army better commanded than by our Archbishop of Bordeaux at Rochelle."

It was well known that at this very time the minister was incensed against this prelate, whose haughtiness was so overbearing, and whose impertinent ebullitions were so frequent as to have involved him in two very disagreeable affairs at Bordeaux. Four years before, the Duc d'Epernon, then governor of Guyenne, followed by all his train and by his troops, meeting him among his clergy in a procession, had called him an insolent fellow, and given him two smart blows with his cane; whereupon the Archbishop had excommunicated him. And again, recently, despite this lesson, he had quarrelled with the Maréchal de Vitry, from whom he had received "twenty blows with a cane or stick, which you please," wrote the Cardinal-

Duke to the Cardinal de la Vallette, "and I think he would like to excommunicate all France." In fact, he did excommunicate the Maréchal's baton, remembering that in the former case the Pope had obliged the Duc d'Epernon to ask his pardon; but M. Vitry, who had caused the Maréchal d'Ancre to be assassinated, stood too high at court for that, and the Archbishop, in addition to his beating, got well scolded by the minister.

M. d'Estrées thought, therefore, sagely that there might be some irony in the Cardinal's manner of referring to the warlike talents of the Archbishop, and he answered, with perfect *sang-froid:*

"It is true, my lord, no one can say that it was upon the sea he was beaten."

His Eminence could not restrain a smile at this; but seeing that the electrical effect of that smile had created others in the hall, as well as whisperings and conjectures, he immediately resumed his gravity, and familiarly taking the Maréchal's arm, said:

"Come, Monsieur l'Ambassadeur, you are ready at repartee. With you I should not fear Cardinal Albornos, or all the Borgias in the world—no, nor all the efforts of their Spain with the Holy Father."

Then, raising his voice, and looking around, as if addressing himself to the silent, and, so to speak, captive assembly, he continued:

"I hope that we shall no more be reproached, as formerly, for having formed an alliance with one of the greatest men of our day; but as Gustavus Adolphus is dead, the Catholic King will no longer have any pretext for soliciting the excommunication of the most Christian King. How say you, my dear lord?" addressing himself to the Cardinal de la Vallette, who now approached, fortunately without having heard the late allusion to himself. "Monsieur d'Estrées, remain near our chair; we have still many things to say to you, and you are not one too many in our conversations, for we have no secrets. Our policy is frank and open to all men; the interest of his Majesty and of the State—nothing more."

The Maréchal made a profound bow, fell back behind the chair of the minister, and gave place to the Cardinal de la Vallette, who, incessantly bowing and flattering and swearing devotion and entire obedience to the Cardinal, as if to expiate the obduracy of his father, the Duc d'Epernon, received in return a few vague words, to no meaning or purpose, the Cardinal all the while looking toward the door, to see who should follow. He had even the mortification to find himself abruptly interrupted by the minister, who cried at the most flattering period of his honeyed discourse:

"Ah! is that you at last, my dear Fabert? How I have longed to see you, to talk of the siege!"

The General, with a brusque and awkward manner, saluted the Cardinal-Generalissimo, and presented to him the officers who had come from the camp with him. He talked some time of the operations of the siege, and the Cardinal seemed to be paying him court now, in order to prepare him afterward for receiving his orders even on the field of battle; he spoke to the officers who accompanied him, calling them by their names, and questioning them about the camp.

They all stood aside to make way for the Duc d'Angoulême—that Valois, who, having struggled against Henri IV, now prostrated himself before Richelieu. He solicited a command, having been only third in rank at the siege of Rochelle. After him came young Mazarin, ever supple and insinuating, but already confident in his fortune.

The Duc d'Halluin came after them; the Cardinal broke off the compliments he was addressing to the others, to utter, in a loud voice:

"Monsieur le Duc, I inform you with pleasure that the King has made you a marshal of France; you will sign yourself Schomberg, will you not, at Leucate, delivered, as we hope, by you? But pardon me, here is Monsieur de Montauron, who has doubtless something important to communicate."

"Oh, no, my lord, I would only say that the poor young man whom you deigned to consider in your service is dying of hunger."

"Pshaw! at such a moment to speak of things like this! Your little Corneille will not write anything good; we have only seen *Le Cid* and *Les Horaces* as yet. Let him work, let him work! it is known that he is in my service, and that is disagreeable. However, since you interest yourself in the matter, I give him a pension of five hundred crowns on my privy purse."

The Chancellor of the Exchequer retired, charmed with the liberality of the minister, and went home to receive with great affability the dedication of *Cinna,* wherein the great Corneille compares his soul to that of Augustus, and thanks him for having given alms *à quelques Muses.*

The Cardinal, annoyed by this importunity, rose, observing that the day was advancing, and that it was time to set out to visit the King.

At this moment, and as the greatest noblemen present were offering their arms to aid him in walking, a man in the robe of a referendary advanced toward him, saluting him with a complacent and confident smile which astonished all the people there, accustomed to the great world, seeming to say: "We have secret affairs together; you shall see how agreeable he makes himself to me. I am at home in his cabinet." His heavy and awkward manner, however, betrayed a very inferior being; it was Laubardemont.

Richelieu knit his brows when he saw him, and cast a glance at Joseph; then, turning toward those who surrounded him, he said, with bitter scorn:

"Is there some criminal about us to be apprehended?"

Then, turning his back upon the discomfited Laubardemont, the Cardinal left him redder than his robe, and, preceded by the crowd of personages who were to escort him in carriages or on horseback, he descended the great staircase of the palace.

All the people and the authorities of Narbonne viewed this royal departure with amazement.

The Cardinal entered alone a spacious square litter, in which he was to travel to Perpignan, his infirmities not permitting him to go in a coach, or to perform the journey on horseback. This kind of moving chamber contained a bed, a table, and a small chair for the page who wrote or read for him. This machine, covered with purple damask, was carried by eighteen men, who were relieved at intervals of a league; they were selected among his guards, and always performed this service of honor with uncovered heads, however hot or wet the weather might be. The Duc d'Angoulême, the Maréchals de Schomberg and d'Estrées, Fabert, and other dignitaries were on horseback beside the litter; after them, among the most prominent were the Cardinal de la Vallette and Mazarin, with Chavigny, and the Maréchal de Vitry, anxious to avoid the Bastille, with which it was said he was threatened.

Two coaches followed for the Cardinal's secretaries, physicians, and confessor; then eight others, each with four horses, for his gentlemen, and twenty-four mules for his luggage. Two hundred musketeers on foot marched close behind him, and his company of men-at-arms of the guard and his light-horse, all gentlemen, rode before and behind him on splendid horses.

Such was the equipage in which the prime minister proceeded to Perpignan; the size of the litter often made it necessary to enlarge the roads, and knock down the walls of some of the towns and villages on the way, into which it could not otherwise enter, "so that," say the authors and manuscripts of the time, full of a sincere admiration for all this luxury—"so

that he seemed a conqueror entering by the breach."
We have sought in vain with great care in these documents, for any account of proprietors or inhabitants of these dwellings so making room for his passage who shared in this admiration; but we have been unable to find any mention of such.

CHAPTER VIII

THE INTERVIEW

Mon génie étonné tremble devant le sien.

HE pompous *cortège* of the Cardinal halted at the beginning of the camp. All the armed troops were drawn up in the finest order; and amid the sound of cannon and the music of each regiment the litter traversed a long line of cavalry and infantry, formed from the outermost tent to that of the minister, pitched at some distance from the royal quarters, and which its purple covering distinguished at a distance. Each general of division obtained a nod or a word from the Cardinal, who at length reaching his tent and, dismissing his train, shut himself in, waiting for the time to present himself to the King. But, before him, every person of his escort had repaired thither individually, and, without entering the royal abode, had remained in the long galleries covered with striped stuff, and arranged as became avenues leading to the Prince. The courtiers walking in groups, saluted one another and shook hands, regarding each other haughtily, according to their connections or the lords to whom they belonged. Others whispered together, and showed signs of astonishment, pleasure, or anger, which showed that something extraordinary had taken place. Among a thousand others, one singular dialogue occurred in a corner of the principal gallery.

"May I ask, Monsieur l'Abbé, why you look at me so fixedly?"

"*Parbleu!* Monsieur de Launay, it is because I'm curious to see what you will do. All the world abandons your Cardinal-Duke since your journey into Touraine; if you do not believe it, go and ask the people of Monsieur or of the Queen. You are behindhand ten minutes by the watch with the Cardinal de la Vallette, who has just shaken hands with Rochefort and the gentlemen of the late Comte de Soissons, whom I shall regret as long as I live."

"Monsieur de Gondi, I understand you; is it a challenge with which you honor me?"

"Yes, Monsieur le Comte," answered the young Abbé, saluting him with all the gravity of the time; "I sought an occasion to challenge you in the name of Monsieur d'Attichi, my friend, with whom you had something to do at Paris."

"Monsieur l'Abbé, I am at your command. I will seek my seconds; do you the same."

"On horseback, with sword and pistol, I suppose?" added Gondi, with the air of a man arranging a party of pleasure, lightly brushing the sleeve of his cassock.

"If you please," replied the other. And they separated for a time, saluting one another with the greatest politeness, and with profound bows.

A brilliant crowd of gentlemen circulated around

them in the gallery. They mingled with it to procure friends for the occasion. All the elegance of the costumes of the day was displayed by the court that morning—small cloaks of every color, in velvet or in satin, embroidered with gold or silver; crosses of St. Michael and of the Holy Ghost; the ruffs, the sweeping hat-plumes, the gold shoulder-knots, the chains by which the long swords hung: all glittered and sparkled, yet not so brilliantly as did the fiery glances of those warlike youths, or their sprightly conversation, or their intellectual laughter. Amid the assembly grave personages and great lords passed on, followed by their numerous gentlemen.

The little Abbé de Gondi, who was very short-sighted, made his way through the crowd, knitting his brows and half shutting his eyes, that he might see the better, and twisting his moustache, for ecclesiastics wore them in those days. He looked closely at every one in order to recognize his friends, and at last stopped before a young man, very tall and dressed in black from head to foot; his sword, even, was of quite dark, bronzed steel. He was talking with a captain of the guards, when the Abbé de Gondi took him aside.

"Monsieur de Thou," said he, "I need you as my second in an hour, on horseback, with sword and pistol, if you will do me that honor."

"Monsieur, you know I am entirely at your service on all occasions. Where shall we meet?"

"In front of the Spanish bastion, if you please."

"Pardon me for returning to a conversation that

greatly interests me. I will be punctual at the rendezvous."

And De Thou quitted him to rejoin the Captain.
He had said all this in the gentlest of voices with
unalterable coolness, and even with somewhat of an
abstracted manner.

The little Abbé squeezed his hand with warm satisfaction, and continued his search.

He did not so easily effect an agreement with the
young lords to whom he addressed himself; for they
knew him better than did De Thou, and when they
saw him coming they tried to avoid him, or laughed
at him openly, and would not promise to serve him.

"Ah, Abbé! there you are hunting again; I'll swear
it's a second you want," said the Duc de Beaufort.

"And I wager," added M. de la Rochefoucauld,
"that it's against one of the Cardinal-Duke's people."

"You are both right, gentlemen; but since when
have you laughed at affairs of honor?"

"The saints forbid I should," said M. de Beaufort.
"Men of the sword like us ever reverence tierce,
quarte, and octave; but as for the folds of the cassock, I know nothing of them."

"*Pardieu!* Monsieur, you know well enough that
it does not embarrass my wrist, as I will prove to him
who chooses; as to the gown itself, I should like to
throw it into the gutter."

"Is it to tear it that you fight so often?" asked
La Rochefoucauld. "But remember, my dear Abbé,
that you yourself are within it."

Gondi turned to look at the clock, wishing to lose

no more time in such sorry jests; but he had no better success elsewhere. Having stopped two gentlemen in the service of the young Queen, whom he thought ill-affected toward the Cardinal, and consequently glad to measure weapons with his creatures, one of them said to him very gravely:

"Monsieur de Gondi, you know what has just happened; the King has said aloud, 'Whether our imperious Cardinal wishes it or not, the widow of Henri le Grand shall no longer remain in exile.' *Imperious!* the King never before said anything so strong as that, Monsieur l'Abbé, mark that. *Imperious!* it is open disgrace. Certainly no one will dare to speak to him; no doubt he will quit the court this very day."

"I have heard this, Monsieur, but I have an affair——"

"It is lucky for you he stopped short in the middle of *your* career."

"An affair of honor——"

"Whereas Mazarin is quite a friend of yours."

"But will you, or will you not, listen to me?"

"Yes, a friend indeed! your adventures are always uppermost in his thoughts. Your fine duel with Monsieur de Coutenan about the pretty little pin-maker, —he even spoke of it to the King. Adieu, my dear Abbé, we are in great haste; adieu, adieu!" And, taking his friend's arm, the young mocker, without listening to another word, walked rapidly down the gallery and disappeared in the throng.

The poor Abbé was much mortified at being able to get only one second, and was watching sadly the

passing of the hour and of the crowd, when he perceived a young gentleman whom he did not know,
seated at a table, leaning on his elbow with a pensive
air; he wore mourning which indicated no connection
with any great house or party, and appeared to await,
without any impatience, the time for attending the
King, looking with a heedless air at those who surrounded him, and seeming not to notice or to know
any of them.

Gondi looked at him a moment, and accosted him
without hesitation:

"Monsieur, I have not the honor of your acquaint-
ance, but a fencing-party can never be unpleasant to
a man of honor; and if you will be my second, in a
quarter of an hour we shall be on the ground. I am
Paul de Gondi; and I have challenged Monsieur de
Launay, one of the Cardinal's clique, but in other
respects a very gallant fellow."

The unknown, apparently not at all surprised at
this address, replied, without changing his attitude:
"And who are his seconds?"

"Faith, I don't know; but what matters it who
serves him? We stand no worse with our friends for
having exchanged a thrust with them."

The stranger smiled nonchalantly, paused for an instant to pass his hand through his long chestnut hair,
and then said, looking idly at a large, round watch
which hung at his waist:

"Well, Monsieur, as I have nothing better to do,
and as I have no friends here, I am with you; it will
pass the time as well as anything else."

And, taking his large, black-plumed hat from the table, he followed the warlike Abbé, who went quickly before him, often running back to hasten him on, like a child running before his father, or a puppy that goes backward and forward twenty times before it gets to the end of a street.

Meanwhile, two ushers, attired in the royal livery, opened the great curtains which separated the gallery from the King's tent, and silence reigned. The courtiers began to enter slowly, and in succession, the temporary dwelling of the Prince. He received them all gracefully, and was the first to meet the view of each person introduced.

Before a very small table surrounded with gilt arm-chairs stood Louis XIII, encircled by the great officers of the crown. His dress was very elegant: a kind of fawn-colored vest, with open sleeves, ornamented with shoulder-knots and blue ribbons, covered him down to the waist. Wide breeches reached to the knee, and the yellow-and-red striped stuff of which they were made was ornamented below with blue ribbons. His riding-boots, reaching hardly more than three inches above the ankle, were turned over, showing so lavish a lining of lace that they seemed to hold it as a vase holds flowers. A small mantle of blue velvet, on which was embroidered the cross of the Holy Ghost, covered the King's left arm, which rested on the hilt of his sword.

His head was uncovered, and his pale and noble face was distinctly visible, lighted by the sun, which penetrated through the top of the tent. The small, pointed beard then worn augmented the appearance of thinness in his face, while it added to its melancholy expression. By his lofty brow, his classic profile, his aquiline nose, he was at once recognized as a prince of the great race of Bourbon. He had all the characteristic traits of his ancestors except their penetrating glance; his eyes seemed red from weeping, and veiled with a perpetual drowsiness; and the weakness of his vision gave him a somewhat vacant look.

He called around him, and was attentive to, the greatest enemies of the Cardinal, whom he expected every moment; and, balancing himself with one foot over the other, an hereditary habit of his family, he spoke quickly, but pausing from time to time to make a gracious inclination of the head, or a gesture of the hand, to those who passed before him with low reverences.

The court had been thus paying its respects to the King for two hours before the Cardinal appeared; the whole court stood in close ranks behind the Prince, and in the long galleries which extended from his tent. Already longer intervals elapsed between the names of the courtiers who were announced.

"Shall we not see our cousin the Cardinal?" said the King, turning, and looking at Montrésor, one of Monsieur's gentlemen, as if to encourage him to answer.

"He is said to be very ill just now, Sire," was the answer.

"And yet I do not see how any but your Majesty can cure him," said the Duc de Beaufort.

"We cure nothing but the king's evil," replied Louis; "and the complaints of the Cardinal are always so mysterious that we own we can not understand them."

The Prince thus essayed to brave his minister, gaining strength in jests, the better to break his yoke, insupportable, but so difficult to remove. He almost thought he had succeeded in this, and, sustained by the joyous air surrounding him, he already privately congratulated himself on having been able to assume the supreme empire, and for the moment enjoyed all the power of which he fancied himself possessed. An involuntary agitation in the depth of his heart had warned him indeed that, the hour passed, all the burden of the State would fall upon himself alone; but he talked in order to divert the troublesome thought, and, concealing from himself the doubt he had of his own inability to reign, he set his imagination to work upon the result of his enterprises, thus forcing himself to forget the tedious roads which had led to them. Rapid phrases succeeded one another on his lips.

"We shall soon take Perpignan," he said to Fabert, who stood at some distance.

"Well, Cardinal, Lorraine is ours," he added to La Vallette. Then, touching Mazarin's arm:

"It is not so difficult to manage a State as is supposed, eh?"

The Italian, who was not so sure of the Cardinal's disgrace as most of the courtiers, answered, without compromising himself:

"Ah, Sire, the late successes of your Majesty at

home and abroad prove your sagacity in choosing your instruments and in directing them, and——"

But the Duc de Beaufort, interrupting him with that self-confidence, that loud voice and overbearing air, which subsequently procured him the surname of Important, cried out, vehemently:

"*Pardieu!* Sire, it needs only to will. A nation is driven like a horse, with spur and bridle; and as we are all good horsemen, your Majesty has only to choose among us."

This fine sally had not time to take effect, for two ushers cried, simultaneously, "His Eminence!"

The King's face flushed involuntarily, as if he had been surprised *en flagrant délit*. But immediately gaining confidence, he assumed an air of resolute haughtiness, which was not lost upon the minister.

The latter, attired in all the pomp of a cardinal, leaning upon two young pages, and followed by his captain of the guards and more than five hundred gentlemen attached to his house, advanced toward the King slowly and pausing at each step, as if forced to it by his sufferings, but in reality to observe the faces before him. A glance sufficed.

His suite remained at the entrance of the royal tent; of all those within it, not one was bold enough to salute him, or to look toward him. Even La Vallette feigned to be occupied in a conversation with Montrésor; and the King, who desired to give him an unfavorable reception, greeted him lightly and continued a private conversation in a low voice with the Duc de Beaufort.

The Cardinal was therefore forced, after the first salute, to stop and pass to the side of the crowd of courtiers, as if he wished to mingle with them, but in reality to test them more closely; they all recoiled as at the sight of a leper. Fabert alone advanced toward him with the frank, brusque air habitual with him, and, making use of the terms belonging to his profession, said:

"Well, my lord, you make a breach in the midst of them like a cannon-ball; I ask pardon in their name."

"And you stand firm before me as before the enemy," said the Cardinal; "you will have no cause to regret it in the end, my dear Fabert."

Mazarin also approached the Cardinal, but with caution, and, giving to his mobile features an expression of profound sadness, made him five or six very low bows, turning his back to the group gathered around the King, so that in the latter quarter they might be taken for those cold and hasty salutations which are made to a person one desires to be rid of, and, on the part of the Duke, for tokens of respect, blended with a discreet and silent sorrow.

The minister, ever calm, smiled disdainfully; and, assuming that firm look and that air of grandeur which he always wore in the hour of danger, he again leaned upon his pages, and, without waiting for a word or a glance from his sovereign, he suddenly resolved upon his line of conduct, and walked directly toward him, traversing the whole length of the tent. No one had lost sight of him, although all affected not to observe him. Every one now became silent, even those who were conversing with the King. All the courtiers bent forward to see and to hear.

Louis XIII turned toward him in astonishment, and, all presence of mind totally failing him, remained motionless and waited with an icy glance—his sole force, but a force very effectual in a prince.'

The Cardinal, on coming close to the monarch, did not bow; and, without changing his attitude, with his eyes lowered and his hands placed on the shoulders of the two boys half bending, he said:

"Sire, I come to implore your Majesty at length to grant me the retirement for which I have long sighed. My health is failing; I feel that my life will soon be ended. Eternity approaches me, and before rendering an account to the eternal King, I would render one to my earthly sovereign. It is eighteen years, Sire, since you placed in my hands a weak and divided kingdom; I return it to you united and powerful. Your enemies are overthrown and humiliated. My work is accomplished. I ask your Majesty's permission to retire to Citeaux, of which I am abbot, and where I may end my days in prayer and meditation."

The King, irritated by some haughty expressions in this address, showed none of the signs of weakness which the Cardinal had expected, and which he had always seen in him when he had threatened to resign the management of affairs. On the contrary, feeling that he had the eyes of the whole court upon him, Louis looked upon him with the air of a king, and coldly replied:

"We thank you, then, for your services, Monsieur le Cardinal, and wish you the repose you desire."

Richelieu was deeply moved, but no indication of his anger appeared upon his countenance. "Such was the coldness with which you left Montmorency to die," he said to himself; "but you shall not escape me thus." He then continued aloud, bowing at the same time:

"The only recompense I ask for my services is that your Majesty will deign to accept from me, as a gift, the Palais-Cardinal I have erected at my own expense in Paris."

The King, astonished, bowed his assent. A murmur of surprise for a moment agitated the attentive court.

"I also throw myself at your Majesty's feet, to beg that you will grant me the revocation of an act of rigor, which I solicited (I publicly confess it), and which I perhaps regarded too hastily beneficial to the repose of the State. Yes, when I was of this world, I was too forgetful of my early sentiments of personal respect and attachment, in my eagerness for the public welfare; but now that I already enjoy the enlightenment of solitude, I see that I have done wrong, and I repent."

The attention of the spectators was redoubled, and the uneasiness of the King became visible.

"Yes, there is one person, Sire, whom I have always loved, despite her wrong toward you, and the banishment which the affairs of the kingdom forced me to bring about for her; a person to whom I have owed much, and who should be very dear to you, nowithstanding her armed attempts against you; a person, in a word, whom I implore you to recall from exile—the Queen Marie de Médicis, your mother!"

The King uttered an involuntary exclamation, so little did he expect to hear that name. A repressed agitation suddenly appeared upon every face. All waited in silence the King's reply. Louis XIII looked for a long time at his old minister without speaking, and this look decided the fate of France; in that instant he called to mind all the indefatigable services of Richelieu, his unbounded devotion, his wonderful capacity, and was surprised at himself for having wished to part with him. He felt deeply affected at this request, which had probed for the exact cause of his anger at the bottom of his heart, and uprooted it, thus taking from his hands the only weapon he had against his old servant. Filial love brought words of pardon to his lips and tears into his eyes. Rejoicing to grant what he desired most of all things in the world, he extended his hands to the Duke with all the nobleness and kindliness of a Bourbon. The Cardinal bowed and respectfully kissed it; and his heart, which should have burst with remorse, only swelled in the joy of a haughty triumph.

The King, deeply touched, abandoning his hand to him, turned gracefully toward his court and said, with a trembling voice:

"We often deceive ourselves, gentlemen, and especially in our knowledge of so great a politician as this.

I hope he will never leave us, since his heart is as good as his head."

Cardinal de la Vallette instantly seized the sleeve of the King's mantle, and kissed it with all the ardor of a lover, and the young Mazarin did much the same with Richelieu himself, assuming, with admirable Italian suppleness, an expression radiant with joy and tenderness. Two streams of flatterers hastened, one toward the King, the other toward the minister; the former group, not less adroit than the second, although less direct, addressed to the Prince thanks which could be heard by the minister, and burned at the feet of the one incense which was intended for the other. As for Richelieu, bowing and smiling to right and left, he stepped forward and stood at the right hand of the King as his natural place. A stranger entering would rather have thought, indeed, that it was the King who was on the Cardinal's left hand. The Maréchal d'Estrées, all the ambassadors, the Duc d'Angoulême, the Duc d'Halluin (Schomberg), the Maréchal de Châtillon, and all the great officers of the crown surrounded him, each waiting impatiently for the compliments of the others to be finished, in order to pay his own, fearing lest some one else should anticipate him with the flattering epigram he had just improvised, or the phrase of adulation he was inventing.

As for Fabert, he had retired to a corner of the tent, and seemed to have paid no particular attention to the scene. He was chatting with Montrésor and the gentlemen of Monsieur, all sworn enemies of the Cardinal, because, out of the throng he avoided, he had found none but these to speak to. This conduct would have seemed extremely tactless in one less known; but although he lived in the midst of the court, he was ever ignorant of its intrigues. It was said of him that he returned from a battle he had gained, like the King's hunting-horse, leaving the dogs to caress their master and divide the quarry, without seeking even to remember the part he had had in the triumph.

The storm, then, seemed entirely appeased, and to the violent agitations of the morning succeeded a gentle calm. A respectful murmur, varied with pleasant laughter and protestations of attachment, was all that was heard in the tent. The voice of the Cardinal arose from time to time: "The poor Queen! We shall, then, soon again see her! I never had dared to hope for such happiness while I lived!" The King listened to him with full confidence, and made no attempt to conceal his satisfaction. "It was assuredly an idea sent to him from on high," he said; "this good Cardinal, against whom they had so incensed me, was thinking only of the union of my family. Since the birth of the Dauphin I have not tasted greater joy than at this moment. The protection of the Holy Virgin is manifested over our kingdom."

At this moment, a captain of the guards came up and whispered in the King's ear.

"A courier from Cologne?" said the King; "let him wait in my cabinet."

Then, unable to restrain his impatience, "I will go! I will go!" he said, and entered alone a small, square tent attached to the larger one. In it he saw a young courier holding a black portfolio, and the curtains closed upon the King.

The Cardinal, left sole master of the court, concentrated all its homage; but it was observed that he no longer received it with his former presence of mind. He inquired frequently what time it was, and exhibited an anxiety which was not assumed; his hard, unquiet glances turned toward the smaller tent. It suddenly opened; the King appeared alone, and stopped on the threshold. He was paler than usual, and trembled in every limb; he held in his hand a large letter with five black seals.

"Gentlemen," said he, in a loud but broken voice, "the Queen has just died at Cologne; and I perhaps am not the first to hear of it," he added, casting a severe look toward the impassible Cardinal, "but God knows all! To horse in an hour, and attack the lines! Maréchals, follow me." And he turned his back abruptly, and reëntered his cabinet with them.

The court retired after the minister, who, without giving any sign of sorrow or annoyance, went forth as gravely as he had entered, but now a victor.

CHAPTER IX

Il papa, alzato le mani e fattomi un patente crocione supra la mia figura, mi disse, che mi benediva e che mi perdonava tutti gli omicidii che io avevo mai fatti, et tutti quelli che mai io farei in servizio della Chiesa apostolica.—BENVENUTO CELLINI.

THERE are moments in our life when we long ardently for strong excitement to drown our petty griefs—times when the soul, like the lion in the fable, wearied with the continual attacks of the gnat, earnestly desires a mightier enemy and real danger. Cinq-Mars found himself in this condition of mind, which always results from a morbid sensibility in the organic constitution and a perpetual agitation of the heart. Weary of continually turning over in his mind a combination of the events which he desired, and of those which he dreaded; weary of calculating his chances to the best of his power; of summoning to his assistance all that his education had taught him concerning the lives of illustrious men, in order to compare it with his present situation; oppressed by his regrets, his dreams, predictions, fancies, and all that imaginary world in which he had lived during his solitary journey—he breathed freely upon find-

[146]

ing himself thrown into a real world almost as full of
agitation; and the realizing of two actual dangers
restored circulation to his blood, and youth to his
whole being.

Since the nocturnal scene at the inn near Loudun,
he had not been able to resume sufficient empire over
his mind to occupy himself with anything save his
cherished though sad reflections; and consumption
was already threatening him, when happily he arrived
at the camp of Perpignan, and happily also had the
opportunity of accepting the proposition of the Abbé
de Gondi—for the reader has no doubt recognized
Cinq-Mars in the person of that young stranger in
mourning, so careless and so melancholy, whom the
duellist in the cassock invited to be his second.

He had ordered his tent to be pitched as a volunteer
in the street of the camp assigned to the young noblemen who were to be presented to the King and were
to serve as aides-de-camp to the Generals; he soon
repaired thither, and was quickly armed, horsed, and
cuirassed, according to the custom of the time, and
set out alone for the Spanish bastion, the place of
rendezvous. He was the first arrival, and found that
a small plot of turf, hidden among the works of the
besieged place, had been well chosen by the little
Abbé for his homicidal purposes; for besides the
probability that no one would have suspected officers
of engaging in a duel immediately beneath the town
which they were attacking, the body of the bastion
separated them from the French camp, and would
conceal them like an immense screen. It was wise

to take these precautions, for at that time it cost a man his head to give himself the satisfaction of risking his body.

While waiting for his friends and his adversaries, Cinq-Mars had time to examine the southern side of Perpignan, before which he stood. He had heard that these works were not those which were to be attacked, and he tried in vain to account for the besieger's projects. Between this southern face of the town, the mountains of Albère, and the Col du Perthus, there might have been advantageous lines of attack, and redoubts against the accessible point; but not a single soldier was stationed there. All the forces seemed directed upon the north of Perpignan, upon the most difficult side, against a brick fort called the Castillet, which surmounted the gate of Nôtre-Dame. He discovered that a piece of ground, apparently marshy, but in reality very solid, led up to the very foot of the Spanish bastion; that this post was guarded with true Castilian negligence, although its sole strength lay entirely in its defenders; for its battlements, almost in ruin, were furnished with four pieces of cannon of enormous calibre, embedded in the turf, and thus rendered immovable, and impossible to be directed against a troop advancing rapidly to the foot of the wall.

It was easy to see that these enormous pieces had discouraged the besiegers from attacking this point, and had kept the besieged from any idea of addition to its means of defence. Thus, on the one side, the vedettes and advanced posts were at a distance, and on the other, the sentinels were few and ill supported. A young Spaniard, carrying a long gun, with its rest suspended at his side and the burning match in his right hand, who was walking with nonchalance upon the rampart, stopped to look at Cinq-Mars, who was riding about the ditches and moats.

"*Señor caballero*," he cried, "are you going to take the bastion by yourself on horseback, like Don Quixote—Quixada de la Mancha?"

At the same time he detached from his side the iron rest, planted it in the ground, and supported upon it the barrel of his gun in order to take aim, when a grave and older Spaniard, enveloped in a dirty brown cloak, said to him in his own tongue:

"*Ambrosio de demonio*, do you not know that it is forbidden to throw away powder uselessly, before sallies or attacks are made, merely to have the pleasure of killing a boy not worth your match? It was in this very place that Charles the Fifth threw the sleeping sentinel into the ditch and drowned him. Do your duty, or I shall follow his example."

Ambrosio replaced the gun upon his shoulder, the rest at his side, and continued his walk upon the rampart.

Cinq-Mars had been little alarmed at this menacing gesture, contenting himself with tightening the reins of his horse and bringing the spurs close to his sides, knowing that with a single leap of the nimble animal he should be carried behind the wall of a hut which stood near by, and should thus be sheltered from the Spanish fusil before the operation of the fork and match could be completed. He knew, too, that a tacit convention between the two armies prohibited marksmen from firing upon the sentinels; each party would have regarded it as assassination. The soldier who had thus prepared to attack Cinq-Mars must have been ignorant of this understanding. Young D'Effiat, therefore, made no visible movement; and when the sentinel had resumed his walk upon the rampart, he again betook himself to his ride upon the turf, and presently saw five cavaliers directing their course toward him. The first two, who came on at full gallop, did not salute him, but, stopping close to him, leaped to the ground, and he found himself in the arms of the Counsellor de Thou, who embraced him tenderly, while the little Abbé de Gondi, laughing heartily, cried:

"Behold another Orestes recovering his Pylades, and at the moment of immolating a rascal who is not of the family of the King of kings, I assure you."

"What! is it you, my dear Cinq-Mars?" cried De Thou; "and I knew not of your arrival in the camp! Yes, it is indeed you; I recognize you, although you are very pale. Have you been ill, my dear friend? I have often written to you; for my boyish friendship has always remained in my heart."

"And I," answered Henri d'Effiat, "I have been very culpable toward you; but I will relate to you all the causes of my neglect. I can speak of them, but I was ashamed to write them. But how good you are! Your friendship has never relaxed."

"I knew you too well," replied De Thou; "I knew

that there could be no real coldness between us, and that my soul had its echo in yours."

With these words they embraced once more, their eyes moist with those sweet tears which so seldom flow in one's life, but with which it seems, nevertheless, the heart is always charged, so much relief do they give in flowing.

This moment was short; and during these few words, Gondi had been pulling them by their cloaks, saying:

"To horse! to horse, gentlemen! *Pardieu!* you will have time enough to embrace, if you are so affectionate; but do not delay. Let our first thought be to have done with our good friends who will soon arrive. We are in a fine position, with those three villains there before us, the archers close by, and the Spaniards up yonder! We shall be under three fires."

He was still speaking, when De Launay, finding himself at about sixty paces from his opponents, with his seconds, who were chosen from his own friends rather than from among the partisans of the Cardinal, put his horse to a canter, advanced gracefully toward his young adversaries, and gravely saluted them.

"Gentlemen, I think that we shall do well to select our men, and to take the field; for there is talk of attacking the lines, and I must be at my post."

"We are ready, Monsieur," said Cinq-Mars; "and as for selecting opponents, I shall be very glad to become yours, for I have not forgotten the Maréchal de Bassompierre and the wood of Chaumont. You know my opinion concerning your insolent visit to my mother."

ALFRED DE VIGNY

"You are very young, Monsieur. In regard to Madame, your mother, I fulfilled the duties of a man of the world; toward the Maréchal, those of a captain of the guard; here, those of a gentleman toward Monsieur l'Abbé, who has challenged me; afterward I shall have that honor with you."

"If I permit you," said the Abbé, who was already on horseback.

They took sixty paces of ground—all that was afforded them by the extent of the meadow that enclosed them. The Abbé de Gondi was stationed between De Thou and his friend, who sat nearest the ramparts, upon which two Spanish officers and a score of soldiers stood, as in a balcony, to witness this duel of six persons—a spectacle common enough to them. They showed the same signs of joy as at their bull-fights, and laughed with that savage and bitter laugh which their temperament derives from their admixture of Arab blood.

At a sign from Gondi, the six horses set off at full gallop, and met, without coming in contact, in the middle of the arena; at that instant, six pistol-shots were heard almost together, and the smoke covered the combatants.

When it dispersed, of the six cavaliers and six horses but three men and three animals were on their legs. Cinq-Mars was on horseback, giving his hand to his adversary, as calm as himself; at the other end of the field, De Thou stood by his opponent, whose horse he had killed, and whom he was helping to rise. As for Gondi and De Launay, neither was to be seen.

Cinq-Mars, looking about for them anxiously, perceived the Abbé's horse, which, caracoling and cur-
vetting, was dragging after him the future cardinal,
whose foot was caught in the stirrup, and who was
swearing as if he had never studied anything but the
language of the camp. His nose and hands were
stained and bloody with his fall and with his efforts
to seize the grass; and he was regarding with con-
siderable dissatisfaction his horse, which in spite of
himself he irritated with his spurs, making its way to
the trench, filled with water, which surrounded the
bastion, when, happily, Cinq-Mars, passing between
the edge of the swamp and the animal, seized its bridle
and stopped its career.

"Well, my dear Abbé, I see that no great harm
has come to you, for you speak with decided energy."

"*Corbleu!*" cried Gondi, wiping the dust out of his
eyes, "to fire a pistol in the face of that giant I had
to lean forward and rise in my stirrups, and thus I
lost my balance; but I fancy that he is down, too."

"You are right, sir," said De Thou, coming up;
"there is his horse swimming in the ditch with its
master, whose brains are blown out. We must think
now of escaping."

"Escaping! That, gentlemen, will be rather difficult,"
said the adversary of Cinq-Mars, approaching. "Hark!
there is the cannon-shot, the signal for the attack.
I did not expect it would have been given so soon.
If we return we shall meet the Swiss and the foot-
soldiers, who are marching in this direction."

"Monsieur de Fontrailles says well," said De Thou;

"but if we do not return, here are these Spaniards, who are running to arms, and whose balls we shall presently have whistling about our heads."

"Well, let us hold a council," said Gondi; "summon Monsieur de Montrésor, who is uselessly occupied in searching for the body of poor De Launay. You have not wounded him, Monsieur De Thou?"

"No, Monsieur l'Abbé; not every one has so good an aim as you," said Montrésor, bitterly, limping from his fall. "We shall not have time to continue with the sword."

"As to continuing, I will not consent to it, gentlemen," said Fontrailles; "Monsieur de Cinq-Mars has behaved too nobly toward me. My pistol went off too soon, and his was at my very cheek—I feel the coldness of it now—but he had the generosity to withdraw it and fire in the air. I shall not forget it; and I am his in life and in death."

"We must think of other things now," interrupted Cinq-Mars; "a ball has just whistled past my ear. The attack has begun on all sides; and we are surrounded by friends and by enemies."

In fact, the cannonading was general; the citadel, the town, and the army were covered with smoke. The bastion before them as yet was unassailed, and its guards seemed less eager to defend it than to observe the fate of the other fortifications.

"I believe that the enemy has made a sally," said Montrésor, "for the smoke has cleared from the plain, and I see masses of cavalry charging under the protection of the battery."

"Gentlemen," said Cinq-Mars, who had not ceased to observe the walls, "there is a very decided part which we could take, an important share in this— we might enter this ill-guarded bastion."

"An excellent idea, Monsieur," said Fontrailles; "but we are but five against at least thirty, and are in plain sight and easily counted."

"Faith, the idea is not bad," said Gondi; "it is better to be shot up there than hanged down here, as we shall be if we are found, for De Launay must be already missed by his company, and all the court knows of our quarrel."

"*Parbleu!* gentlemen," said Montrésor, "help is coming to us."

A numerous troop of horse, in great disorder, advanced toward them at full gallop; their red uniform made them visible from afar. It seemed to be their intention to halt on the very ground on which were our embarrassed duellists, for hardly had the first cavalier reached it when cries of "Halt!" were repeated and prolonged by the voices of the chiefs who were mingled with their cavaliers.

"Let us go to them; these are the men-at-arms of the King's guard," said Fontrailles. "I recognize them by their black cockades. I see also many of the light-horse with them; let us mingle in the disorder, for I fancy they are *ramenés.*"

This is a polite phrase signifying in military language "put to rout." All five advanced toward the noisy and animated troops, and found that this conjecture was right. But instead of the consternation which one might expect in such a case, they found nothing but a youthful and rattling gayety, and heard only bursts of laughter from the two companies.

"Ah, *pardieu!* Cahuzac," said one, "your horse runs better than mine; I suppose you have exercised it in the King's hunts!"

"Ah, I see, 'twas that we might be the sooner *rallied* that you arrived here first," answered the other.

"I think the Marquis de Coislin must be mad, to make four hundred of us charge eight Spanish regiments."

"Ha! ha! Locmaria, your plume is a fine ornament; it looks like a weeping willow. If we follow that, it will be to our burial."

"Gentlemen, I said to you before," angrily replied the young officer, "that I was sure that Capuchin Joseph, who meddles in everything, was mistaken in telling us to charge, upon the part of the Cardinal. But would you have been satisfied if those who have the honor of commanding you had refused to charge?"

"No, no, no!" answered all the young men, at the same time forming themselves quickly into ranks.

"I said," interposed the old Marquis de Coislin, who, despite his white head, had all the fire of youth in his eyes, "that if you were commanded to mount to the assault on horseback, you would do it."

"Bravo! bravo!" cried all the men-at-arms, clapping their hands.

"Well, Monsieur le Marquis," said Cinq-Mars, approaching, "here is an opportunity to execute what you have promised. I am only a volunteer; but an

instant ago these gentlemen and I examined this bastion, and I believe that it is possible to take it."

"Monsieur, we must first examine the ditch to
see——"

At this moment a ball from the rampart of which
they were speaking struck in the head the horse of
the old captain, laying it low.

"Locmaria, De Mouy, take the command, and to
the assault!" cried the two noble companies, believing
their leader dead.

"Stop a moment, gentlemen," said old Coislin,
rising, "I will lead you, if you please. Guide us,
Monsieur volunteer, for the Spaniards invite us to
this ball, and we must reply politely."

Hardly had the old man mounted another horse,
which one of his men brought him, and drawn his
sword, when, without awaiting his order, all these
ardent youths, preceded by Cinq-Mars and his friends,
whose horses were urged on by the squadrons behind,
had thrown themselves into the morass, wherein, to
their great astonishment and to that of the Spaniards,
who had counted too much upon its depth, the horses
were in the water only up to their hams; and in spite
of a discharge of grape-shot from the two largest
pieces, all reached pell-mell a strip of land at the foot
of the half-ruined ramparts. In the ardor of the rush,
Cinq-Mars and Fontrailles, with the young Locmaria,
forced their horses upon the rampart itself; but a
brisk fusillade killed the three animals, which rolled
over their masters.

"Dismount all, gentlemen!" cried old Coislin;

"forward with pistol and sword! Abandon your horses!"

All obeyed instantly, and threw themselves in a mass upon the breach.

Meantime, De Thou, whose coolness never quitted him any more than his friendship, had not lost sight of the young Henri, and had received him in his arms when his horse fell. He helped him to rise, restored to him his sword, which he had dropped, and said to him, with the greatest calmness, notwithstanding the balls which rained on all sides:

"My friend, do I not appear very ridiculous amid all this skirmish, in my costume of Counsellor in Parliament?"

"*Parbleu!*" said Montrésor, advancing, "here's the Abbé, who quite justifies you."

And, in fact, little Gondi, pushing on among the light horsemen, was shouting, at the top of his voice: "Three duels and an assault. I hope to get rid of my cassock at last!"

Saying this, he cut and thrust at a tall Spaniard.

The defence was not long. The Castilian soldiers were no match for the French officers, and not one of them had time or courage to recharge his carbine.

"Gentlemen, we will relate this to our mistresses in Paris," said Locmaria, throwing his hat into the air; and Cinq-Mars, De Thou, Coislin, De Mouy, Londigny, officers of the red companies, and all the young noblemen, with swords in their right hands and pistols in their left, dashing, pushing, and doing each other by their eagerness as much harm as they did the enemy, finally rushed upon the platform of the bastion, as water poured from a vase, of which the opening is too small, leaps out in interrupted gushes.

Disdaining to occupy themselves with the vanquished soldiers, who cast themselves at their feet, they left them to look about the fort, without even disarming them, and began to examine their conquest, like schoolboys in vacation, laughing with all their hearts, as if they were at a pleasure-party.

A Spanish officer, enveloped in his brown cloak, watched them with a sombre air.

"What demons are these, Ambrosio?" said he to a soldier. "I never have met with any such before in France. If Louis XIII has an entire army thus composed, it is very good of him not to conquer all Europe."

"Oh, I do not believe they are very numerous; they must be some poor adventurers, who have nothing to lose and all to gain by pillage."

"You are right," said the officer; "I will try to persuade one of them to let me escape."

And slowly approaching, he accosted a young lighthorseman, of about eighteen, who was sitting apart from his comrades upon the parapet. He had the pink-and-white complexion of a young girl; his delicate hand held an embroidered handkerchief, with which he wiped his forehead and his golden locks He was consulting a large, round watch set with rubies, suspended from his girdle by a knot of ribbons.

The astonished Spaniard paused. Had he not seen this youth overthrow his soldiers, he would not have believed him capable of anything beyond singing a romance, reclined upon a couch. But, filled with the suggestion of Ambrosio, he thought that he might have stolen these objects of luxury in the pillage of the apartments of a woman; so, going abruptly up to him, he said:

"*Hombre!* I am an officer; will you restore me to liberty, that I may once more see my country?"

The young Frenchman looked at him with the gentle expression of his age, and, thinking of his own family, he said:

"Monsieur, I will present you to the Marquis de Coislin, who will, I doubt not, grant your request; is your family of Castile or of Aragon?"

"Your Coislin will ask the permission of somebody else, and will make me wait a year. I will give you four thousand ducats if you will let me escape."

That gentle face, those girlish features, became infused with the purple of fury; those blue eyes shot forth lightning; and, exclaiming, "Money to me! away, fool!" the young man gave the Spaniard a ringing box on the ear. The latter, without hesitating, drew a long poniard from his breast, and, seizing the arm of the Frenchman, thought to plunge it easily into his heart; but, nimble and vigorous, the youth caught him by the right arm, and, lifting it with force above his head, sent it back with the weapon it held upon the head of the Spaniard, who was furious with rage.

"Eh! eh! Softly, Olivier!" cried his comrades, running from all directions; "there are Spaniards enough on the ground already."

And they disarmed the hostile officer.

"What shall we do with this lunatic?" said one.

"I should not like to have him for my *valet-de-chambre*," returned another.

"He deserves to be hanged," said a third; "but, faith, gentlemen, we don't know how to hang. Let us send him to that battalion of Swiss which is now passing across the plain."

And the calm and sombre Spaniard, enveloping himself anew in his cloak, began the march of his own accord, followed by Ambrosio, to join the battalion, pushed by the shoulders and urged on by five or six of these young madcaps.

Meantime, the first troop of the besiegers, astonished at their success, had followed it out to the end; Cinq-Mars, so advised by the aged Coislin, had made with him the circuit of the bastion, and found to their vexation that it was completely separated from the city, and that they could not follow up their advantage. They, therefore, returned slowly to the platform, talking by the way, to rejoin De Thou and the Abbé de Gondi, whom they found laughing with the young light-horsemen.

"We have Religion and Justice with us, gentlemen; we could not fail to triumph."

"No doubt, for they fought as hard as we."

There was silence at the approach of Cinq-Mars, and they remained for an instant whispering and asking his name; then all surrounded him, and took his hand with delight.

"Gentlemen, you are right," said their old captain;

"he is, as our fathers used to say, *the best doer of the day*. He is a volunteer, who is to be presented to-day to the King by the Cardinal."

"By the Cardinal! We will present him ourselves. Ah, do not let him be a *Cardinalist;* he is too good a fellow for that!" exclaimed all the young men, with vivacity.

"Monsieur, I will undertake to disgust you with him," said Olivier d'Entraigues, approaching Cinq-Mars, "for I have been his page. Rather serve in the red companies; come, you will have good comrades there."

The old Marquis saved Cinq-Mars the embarrassment of replying, by ordering the trumpets to sound and rally his brilliant companies. The cannon was no longer heard, and a soldier announced that the King and the Cardinal were traversing the lines to examine the results of the day. He made all the horses pass through the breach, which was tolerably wide, and ranged the two companies of cavalry in battle array, upon a spot where it seemed impossible that any but infantry could penetrate.

CHAPTER X

THE RECOMPENSE

Ah! comme du butin ces guerriers trop jaloux
Courent bride abattue au-devant des mes coups,
Agitez tous leurs sens d'une rage insensée,
Tambour, fifre, trompette, ôtez-leur la pensée.
N. Lemercier, Panhypocrisiade.

CARDINAL RICHELIEU had said to himself, "To soften the first paroxysm of the royal grief, to open a source of emotions which shall turn from its sorrow this wavering soul, let this city be besieged; I consent. Let Louis go; I will allow him to strike a few poor soldiers with the blows which he wishes, but dares not, to inflict upon me. Let his anger drown itself in this obscure blood; I agree. But this caprice of glory shall not derange my fixed designs; this city shall not fall yet. It shall not become French forever until two years have past; it shall come into my nets only on the day upon which I have fixed in my own mind. Thunder, bombs, and cannons; meditate upon your operations, skilful captains; hasten, young warriors. I shall silence your noise, I shall dissipate your projects, and make your efforts abortive; all shall end in vain smoke, for I shall conduct in order to mislead you."

ALFRED DE VIGNY

This is the substance of what passed in the bald head of the Cardinal before the attack of which we have witnessed a part. He was stationed on horseback, upon one of the mountains of Salces, north of the city; from this point he could see the plain of Roussillon before him, sloping to the Mediterranean. Perpignan, with its ramparts of brick, its bastions, its citadel, and its spire, formed upon this plain an oval and sombre mass on its broad and verdant meadows; the vast mountains surrounded it, and the valley, like an enormous bow curved from north to south, while, stretching its white line in the east, the sea looked like its silver cord. On his right rose that immense mountain called the Canigou, whose sides send forth two rivers into the plain below. The French line extended to the foot of this western barrier. A crowd of generals and of great lords were on horseback behind the minister, but at twenty paces' distance and profoundly silent.

Cardinal Richelieu had at first followed slowly the line of operations, but had later returned and stationed himself upon this height, whence his eye and his thought hovered over the destinies of besiegers and besieged. The whole army had its eyes upon him, and could see him from every point. All looked upon him as their immediate chief, and awaited his gesture before they acted. France had bent beneath his yoke a long time; and admiration of him shielded all his actions to which another would have been often subjected. At this moment, for instance, no one thought of smiling, or even of feeling surprised, that the cuirass should clothe the priest; and the severity of his character and aspect suppressed every thought of ironical comparisons or injurious conjectures. This day the Cardinal appeared in a costume entirely martial: he wore a reddish-brown coat, embroidered with gold, a water-colored cuirass, a sword at his side, pistols at his saddle-bow, and he had a plumed hat; but this he seldom put on his head, which was still covered with the red cap. Two pages were behind him; one carried his gauntlets, the other his casque, and the captain of his guards was at his side.

As the King had recently named him generalissimo of his troops, it was to him that the generals sent for their orders; but he, knowing only too well the secret motives of his master's present anger, affected to refer to that Prince all who sought a decision from his own mouth. It happened as he had foreseen; for he regulated and calculated the movements of that heart as those of a watch, and could have told with precision through what sensations it had passed. Louis XIII came and placed himself at his side; but he came as a pupil, forced to acknowledge that his master is in the right. His air was haughty and dissatisfied, his language brusque and dry. The Cardinal remained impassible. It was remarked that the King, in consulting him, employed the words of command, thus reconciling his weakness and his power of place, his irresolution and his pride, his ignorance and his pretensions, while his minister dictated laws to him in a tone of the most profound obedience.

"I will have them attack immediately, Cardinal,"

said the Prince on coming up; "that is to say," he added, with a careless air, "when all your preparations are made, and you have fixed upon the hour with our generals."

. "Sire, if I might venture to express my judgment, I should be glad did your Majesty think proper to begin the attack in a quarter of an hour, for that will give time enough to advance the third line."

"Yes, yes; you are right, Monsieur le Cardinal! I think so, too. I will go and give my orders myself; I wish to do everything myself. Schomberg, Schomberg! in a quarter of an hour I wish to hear the signal-gun; I command it."

And Schomberg, taking the command of the right wing, gave the order, and the signal was made.

The batteries, arranged long since by the Maréchal de la Meilleraie, began to batter a breach, but slowly, because the artillerymen felt that they had been directed to attack two impregnable points; and because, with their experience, and above all with the common sense and quick perception of French soldiers, any one of them could at once have indicated the point against which the attack should have been directed. The King was surprised at the slowness of the firing.

"La Meilleraie," said he, impatiently, "these batteries do not play well; your cannoneers are asleep."

The principal artillery officers were present as well as the Maréchal; but no one answered a syllable. They had looked toward the Cardinal, who remained as immovable as an equestrian statue, and they imitated his example. The answer must have been that the fault was not with the soldiers, but with him who had ordered this false disposition of the batteries; and this was Richelieu himself, who, pretending to believe them more useful in that position, had stopped the remarks of the chiefs.

The King, astonished at this silence, and, fearing that he had committed some gross military blunder by his question, blushed slightly, and, approaching the group of princes who had accompanied him, said, in order to reassure himself:

"D'Angoulême, Beaufort, this is very tiresome, is it not? We stand here like mummies."

Charles de Valois drew near and said:

"It seems to me, Sire, that they are not employing here the machines of the engineer Pompée-Targon."

"*Parbleu!*" said the Duc de Beaufort, regarding Richelieu fixedly, "that is because we were more eager to take Rochelle than Perpignan at the time that Italian came. Here we have not an engine ready, not a mine, not a petard beneath these walls; and the Maréchal de la Meilleraie told me this morning that he had proposed to bring some with which to open the breach. It was neither the Castillet, nor the six great bastions which surround it, nor the half-moon, we should have attacked. If we go on in this way, the great stone arm of the citadel will show us its fist a long time yet."

The Cardinal, still motionless, said not a single word; he only made a sign to Fabert, who left the group in attendance, and ranged his horse behind that of Richelieu, close to the captain of his guards.

ALFRED DE VIGNY

The Duc de la Rochefoucauld, drawing near the King, said:

"I believe, Sire, that our inactivity makes the enemy insolent, for look! here is a numerous sally, directing itself straight toward your Majesty; and the regiments of Biron and De Ponts fall back after firing."

"Well!" said the King, drawing his sword, "let us charge and force those villains back again. Bring on the cavalry with me, D'Angoulême. Where is it, Cardinal?"

"Behind that hill, Sire, there are in column six regiments of dragoons, and the carabineers of La Roque; below you are my men-at-arms and my light horse, whom I pray your Majesty to employ, for those of your Majesty's guard are ill guided by the Marquis de Coislin, who is ever too zealous. Joseph, go tell him to return."

He whispered to the Capuchin, who had accompanied him, huddled up in military attire, which he wore awkwardly, and who immediately advanced into the plain.

In the mean time, the compact columns of the old Spanish infantry issued from the gate of Nôtre-Dame like a dark and moving forest, while from another gate proceeded the heavy cavalry, which drew up on the plain. The French army, in battle array at the foot of the hill where the King stood, behind fortifications of earth, behind redoubts and fascines of turf, perceived with alarm the men-at-arms and the light horse pressed between these two forces, ten times their superior in numbers.

"Sound the charge!" cried Louis XIII; "or my old Coislin is lost."

And he descended the hill, with all his suite as ardent as himself; but before he reached the plain and was at the head of his musketeers, the two companies had taken their course, dashing off with the rapidity of lightning, and to the cry of *"Vive le Roi!"* They fell upon the long column of the enemy's cavalry like two vultures upon a serpent; and, making a large and bloody gap, they passed beyond, and rallied behind the Spanish bastion, leaving the enemy's cavalry so astonished that they thought only of re-forming their own ranks, and not of pursuing.

The French army uttered a burst of applause; the King paused in amazement. He looked around him, and saw a burning desire for attack in all eyes; the valor of his race shone in his own. He paused yet another instant in suspense, listening, intoxicated, to the roar of the cannon, inhaling the odor of the powder; he seemed to receive another life, and to become once more a Bourbon. All who looked on him felt as if they were commanded by another man, when, raising his sword and his eyes toward the sun, he cried:

"Follow me, brave friends! here I am King of France!"

His cavalry, deploying, dashed off with an ardor which devoured space, and, raising billows of dust from the ground, which trembled beneath them, they were in an instant mingled with the Spanish cavalry, and both were swallowed up in an immense and fluctuating cloud.

ALFRED DE VIGNY

"Now! now!" cried the Cardinal, in a voice of thunder, from his elevation, "now remove the guns from their useless position! Fabert, give your orders; let them be all directed upon the infantry which slowly approaches to surround the King. Haste! save the King!"

Immediately the Cardinal's suite, until then sitting erect as so many statues, were in motion. The generals gave their orders; the aides-de-camp galloped off into the plain, where, leaping over the ditches, barriers, and palisades, they arrived at their destination as soon as the thought that directed them and the glance that followed them.

Suddenly the few and interrupted flashes which had shone from the discouraged batteries became a continual and immense flame, leaving no room for the smoke, which rose to the sky in an infinite number of light and floating wreaths; the volleys of cannon, which had seemed like far and feeble echoes, changed into a formidable thunder whose roll was as rapid as that of drums beating the charge; while from three opposite points large red flashes from fiery mouths fell upon the dark columns which issued from the besieged city.

Meantime, without changing his position, but with ardent eyes and imperative gestures, Richelieu ceased not to multiply his orders, casting upon those who received them a look which implied a sentence of death if he was not instantly obeyed.

"The King has overthrown the cavalry; but the foot still resist. Our batteries have only killed, they have not conquered. Forward with three regiments of infantry instantly, Gassion, La Meilleraie, and Lesdiguières! Take the enemy's columns in flank. Order the rest of the army to cease from the attack, and to remain motionless throughout the whole line. Bring paper! I will write myself to Schomberg."

A page alighted and advanced, holding a pencil and paper. The minister, supported by four men of his suite, also alighted, but with difficulty, uttering a cry, wrested from him by pain; but he conquered it by an effort, and seated himself upon the carriage of a cannon. The page presented his shoulder as a desk; and the Cardinal hastily penned that order which contemporary manuscripts have transmitted to us, and which might well be imitated by the diplomatists of our day, who are, it seems, more desirous to maintain themselves in perfect balance between two ideas than to seek those combinations which decide the destinies of the world, regarding the clear and obvious dictates of true genius as beneath their profound subtlety.

"M. le Maréchal, do not risk anything, and reflect before you attack. When you are thus told that the King desires you not to risk anything, you are not to understand that his Majesty forbids you to fight at all; but his intention is that you do not engage in a general battle unless it be with a notable hope of gain from the advantage which a favorable situation may present, the responsibility of the battle naturally falling upon you."

These orders given, the old minister, still seated upon the gun-carriage, his arms resting upon the touch-hole, and his chin upon his arms, in the attitude of one who adjusts and points a cannon, continued in silence to watch the battle, like an old wolf, which, sated with victims and torpid with age, contemplates in the plain the ravages of a lion among a herd of cattle, which he himself dares not attack. From time to time his eye brightens; the smell of blood rejoices him, and he laps his burning tongue over his toothless jaw.

On that day, it was remarked by his servants—or, in other words, by all surrounding him—that from the time of his rising until night he took no nourishment, and so fixed all the application of his soul on the events which he had to conduct that he triumphed over his physical pains, seeming, by forgetting, to have destroyed them. It was this power of attention, this continual presence of mind, that raised him almost to genius. He would have attained it quite, had he not lacked native elevation of soul and generous sensibility of heart.

Everything happened upon the field of battle as he had wished, fortune attending him there as well as in the cabinet. Louis XIII claimed with eager hand the victory which his minister had procured for him; he had contributed himself, however, only that grandeur which consists in personal valor.

The cannon had ceased to roar when the broken columns of infantry fell back into Perpignan; the remainder had met the same fate, was already within the walls, and on the plain no living man was to be seen, save the glittering squadrons of the King, who followed him, forming ranks as they went.

He returned at a slow walk, and contemplated with

satisfaction the battlefield swept clear of enemies; he passed haughtily under the very fire of the Spanish guns, which, whether from lack of skill, or by a secret agreement with the Prime Minister, or from very shame to kill a king of France, only sent after him a few balls, which, passing two feet above his head, fell in front of the lines, and merely served to increase the royal reputation for courage.

At every step, however, that he took toward the spot where Richelieu awaited him, the King's countenance changed and visibly fell; he lost all the flush of combat; the noble sweat of triumph dried upon his brow. As he approached, his usual pallor returned to his face, as if having the right to sit alone on a royal head; his look lost its fleeting fire, and at last, when he joined the Cardinal, a profound melancholy entirely possessed him. He found the minister as he had left him, on horseback; the latter, still coldly respectful, bowed, and after a few words of compliment, placed himself near Louis to traverse the lines and examine the results of the day, while the princes and great lords, riding at some distance before and behind, formed a crowd around them.

The wily minister was careful not to say a word or to make a gesture that could suggest the idea that he had had the slightest share in the events of the day; and it was remarkable that of all those who came to hand in their reports, there was not one who did not seem to divine his thoughts, and exercise care not to compromise his occult power by open obedience. All reports were made to the King. The Cardinal then traversed, by the side of the Prince, the right of the camp, which had not been under his view from the height where he had remained; and he saw with satisfaction that Schomberg, who knew him well, had acted precisely as his master had directed, bringing into action only a few of the light troops, and fighting just enough not to incur reproach for inaction, and not enough to obtain any distinct result. This line of conduct charmed the minister, and did not displease the King, whose vanity cherished the idea of having been the sole conqueror that day. He even wished to persuade himself, and to have it supposed, that all the efforts of Schomberg had been fruitless, saying to him that he was not angry with him, that he had himself just had proof that the enemy before him was less despicable than had been supposed.

"To show you that you have lost nothing in our estimation," he added, "we name you a knight of our order, and we give you public and private access to our person."

The Cardinal affectionately pressed his hand as he passed him, and the Maréchal, astonished at this deluge of favors, followed the Prince with his bent head, like a culprit, recalling, to console himself, all the brilliant actions of his career which had remained unnoticed, and mentally attributing to them these unmerited rewards to reconcile them to his conscience.

The King was about to retrace his steps, when the Duc de Beaufort, with an astonished air, exclaimed:

"But, Sire, have I still the powder in my eyes, or have I been sun-struck? It appears to me that I see upon yonder bastion several cavaliers in red uniforms who greatly resemble your light horse whom we thought to be killed."

The Cardinal knitted his brows.

"Impossible, Monsieur," he said; "the imprudence of Monsieur de Coislin has destroyed his Majesty's men-at-arms and those cavaliers. It is for that reason I ventured just now to say to the King that if the useless corps were suppressed, it might be very advantageous from a military point of view."

"*Pardieu!* your Eminence will pardon me," answered the Duc de Beaufort; "but I do not deceive myself, and there are seven or eight of them driving prisoners before them."

"Well! let us go to the point," said the King; "if I find my old Coislin there I shall be very glad."

With great caution, the horses of the King and his suite passed across the marsh, and with infinite astonishment their riders saw on the ramparts the two red companies in battle array as on parade.

"*Vive Dieu!*" cried Louis; "I think that not one of them is missing! Well, Marquis, you keep your word—you take walls on horseback."

"In my opinion, this point was ill chosen," said Richelieu, with disdain; "it in no way advances the taking of Perpignan, and must have cost many lives."

"Faith, you are right," said the King, for the first time since the intelligence of the Queen's death addressing the Cardinal without dryness; "I regret the blood which must have been spilled here."

"Only two of own young men have been wounded

in the attack, Sire," said old Coislin; "and we have gained new companions-in-arms, in the volunteers who guided us."

"Who are they?" said the Prince.

"Three of them have modestly retired, Sire; but the youngest, whom you see, was the first who proposed the assault, and the first to venture his person in making it. The two companies claim the honor of presenting him to your Majesty."

Cinq-Mars, who was on horseback behind the old captain, took off his hat and showed his pale face, his large, dark eyes, and his long, chestnut hair.

"Those features remind me of some one," said the King; "what say you, Cardinal?"

The latter, who had already cast a penetrating glance at the newcomer, replied:

"Unless I am mistaken, this young man is——"

"Henri d'Effiat," said the volunteer, bowing.

"Sire, it is the same whom I had announced to your Majesty, and who was to have been presented to you by me; the second son of the Maréchal."

"Ah!" said Louis, warmly, "I am glad to see the son of my old friend presented by this bastion. It is a suitable introduction, my boy, for one bearing your name. You will follow us to the camp, where we have much to say to you. But what! you here, Monsieur de Thou? Whom have you come to judge?"

"Sire," answered Coislin, "he has condemned to death, without judging, sundry Spaniards, for he was the second to enter the place."

"I struck no one, Monsieur," interrupted De Thou,

reddening; "it is not my business. Herein I have no merit; I merely accompanied my friend, Monsieur de Cinq-Mars."

"We approve your modesty as well as your bravery, and we shall not forget this. Cardinal, is there not some presidency vacant?"

Richelieu did not like De Thou. And as the sources of his dislike were always mysterious, it was difficult to guess the cause of this animosity; it revealed itself in a cruel word that escaped him. The motive was a passage in the history of the President De Thou— the father of the young man now in question—wherein he stigmatized, in the eyes of posterity, a granduncle of the Cardinal, an apostate monk, sullied with every human vice.

Richelieu, bending to Joseph's ear, whispered:

"You see that man; his father put my name into his history. Well, I will put his into mine." And, truly enough, he subsequently wrote it in blood. At this moment, to avoid answering the King, he feigned not to have heard his question, and to be wholly intent upon the merit of Cinq-Mars and the desire to see him well placed at court.

"I promised you beforehand to make him a captain in my guards," said the Prince; "let him be nominated to-morrow. I would know more of him, and raise him to a higher fortune, if he pleases me. Let us now retire; the sun has set, and we are far from our army. Tell my two good companies to follow us."

The minister, after repeating the order, omitting the

implied praise, placed himself on the King's right hand, and the whole court quitted the bastion, now confided to the care of the Swiss, and returned to the camp.

The two red companies defiled slowly through the breach which they had effected with such promptitude; their countenances were grave and silent.

Cinq-Mars went up to his friend.

"These are heroes but ill recompensed," said he; "not a favor, not a compliment."

"I, on the other hand," said the simple De Thou —"I, who came here against my will—receive one. Such are courts, such is life; but above us is the true Judge, whom men can not blind."

"This will not prevent us from meeting death to-morrow, if necessary," said the young Olivier, laughing.

CHAPTER XI

THE BLUNDERS

Quand vint le tour de saint Guilin,
Il jeta trois dés sur la table.
Ensuite il regarda le diable,
Et lui dit d'un air très-malin:
Jouons donc cette vieille femme!
Qui de nous deux aura son âme!

Ancienne Légende.

IN order to appear before the King, Cinq-Mars had been compelled to mount the charger of one of the light horse, wounded in the affair, having lost his own at the foot of the rampart. As the two companies were marching out, he felt some one touch his shoulder, and, turning round, saw old Grandchamp leading a very beautiful gray horse.

"Will Monsieur le Marquis mount a horse of his own?" said he. "I have put on the saddle and bousings of velvet embroidered in gold that remained in the trench. Alas, when I think that a Spaniard might have taken it, or even a Frenchman! For just now there are so many people who take all they find, as if it were their own; and then, as the proverb says, 'What falls in the ditch is for the soldier.' They might

[179]

also have taken the four hundred gold crowns that
Monsieur le Marquis, be it said without reproach,
forgot to take out of the holsters. And the pistols!
Oh, what pistols! I bought them in Germany; and
here they are as good as ever, and with their locks
perfect. It was quite enough to kill the poor little
black horse, that was born in England as sure as I
was at Tours in Touraine, without also exposing these
valuables to pass into the hands of the enemy."

While making this lamentation, the worthy man
finished saddling the gray horse. The column was
long enough filing out to give him time to pay scrupulous attention to the length of the stirrups and of
the bands, all the while continuing his harangue.

"I beg your pardon, Monsieur, for being somewhat
slow about this; but I sprained my arm slightly in
lifting Monsieur de Thou, who himself raised Monsieur le Marquis during the grand scuffle."

"How camest thou there at all, stupid?" said Cinq-
Mars. "That is not thy business. I told thee to
remain in the camp."

"Oh, as to remaining in the camp, that is out of
the question. I can't stay there; when I hear a mus-
ket-shot, I should be ill did I not see the flash. As
for my business, that is to take care of your horses,
and you are on them. Monsieur, think you I should
not have saved, had I been able, the life of the poor
black horse down there in the trench? Ah, how I
loved him!—a horse that gained three races in his
time—a time too short for those who loved him as I
loved him! He never would take his corn but from

his dear Grandchamp; and then he would caress me with his head. The end of my left ear that he carried away one day—poor fellow!—proves it, for it was not out of ill-will he bit it off; quite the contrary. You should have heard how he neighed with rage when any one else came near him; that was the reason why he broke Jean's leg. Good creature, I loved him so!

"When he fell I held him on one side with one hand and M. de Locmaria with the other. I thought at first that both he and that gentleman would recover; but unhappily only one of them returned to life, and that was he whom I least knew. You seem to be laughing at what I say about your horse, Monsieur; you forget that in times of war the horse is the soul of the cavalier. Yes, Monsieur, his soul; for what is it that intimidates the infantry? It is the horse! It certainly is not the man, who, once seated, is little more than a bundle of hay. Who is it that performs the fine deeds that men admire? The horse. There are times when his master, who a moment before would rather have been far away, finds himself victorious and rewarded for his horse's valor, while the poor beast gets nothing but blows. Who is it gains the prize in the race? The horse, that sups hardly better than usual, while the master pockets the gold, and is envied by his friends and admired by all the lords as if he had run himself. Who is it that hunts the roebuck, yet puts but a morsel in his own mouth? Again, the horse; sometimes the horse is even eaten himself, poor animal! I remember in a campaign

with Monsieur le Maréchal, it happened that——
But what is the matter, Monsieur, you grow pale?"

"Bind up my leg with something—a handkerchief,
a strap, or what you will. I feel a burning pain there;
I know not what."

"Your boot is cut, Monsieur. It may be some ball;
however, lead is the friend of man."

"It is no friend of mine, at all events."

"Ah, who loves, chastens! Lead must not be ill
spoken of! What is that——"

While occupied in binding his master's leg below
the knee, the worthy Grandchamp was about to hold
forth in praise of lead as absurdly as he had in praise
of the horse, when he was forced, as well as Cinq-
Mars, to hear a warm and clamorous dispute among
some Swiss soldiers who had remained behind the
other troops. They were talking with much ges-
ticulation, and seemed busied with two men among
a group of about thirty soldiers.

D'Effiat, still holding out his leg to his servant, and
leaning on the saddle of his horse, tried, by listening
attentively, to understand the subject of the colloquy;
but he knew nothing of German, and could not comprehend the dispute. Grandchamp, who, still holding the boot, had also been listening very seriously,
suddenly burst into loud laughter, holding his sides
in a manner not usual with him.

"Ha, ha, ha! Monsieur, here are two sergeants disputing which they ought to hang of the two Spaniards
there; for your red comrades did not take the trouble
to tell them. One of the Swiss says that it's the

officer, the other that it's the soldier; a third has just made a proposition for meeting the difficulty."

"And what does he say?"

"He suggests that they hang them both."

"Stop! stop!" cried Cinq-Mars to the soldiers, attempting to walk; but his leg would not support him.

"Put me on my horse, Grandchamp."

"Monsieur, you forget your wound."

"Do as I command, and then mount thyself."

The old servant grumblingly obeyed, and then galloped off, in fulfilment of another imperative order, to stop the Swiss, who were just about to hang their two prisoners to a tree, or to let them hang themselves; for the officer, with the *sang-froid* of his nation, had himself passed the running noose of a rope around his own neck, and, without being told, had ascended a small ladder placed against the tree, in order to tie the other end of the rope to one of its branches. The soldier, with the same calm indifference, was looking on at the Swiss disputing around him, while holding the ladder.

Cinq-Mars arrived in time to save them, gave his name to the Swiss sergeant, and, employing Grandchamp as interpreter, said that the two prisoners were his, and that he would take them to his tent; that he was a captain in the guards, and would be responsible for them. The German, ever exact in discipline, made no reply; the only resistance was on the part of the prisoner. The officer, still on the top of the ladder, turned round, and speaking thence as from a pulpit, said, with a sardonic laugh:

"I should much like to know what you do here? Who told you I wished to live?"

"I do not ask to know anything about that," said Cinq-Mars; "it matters not to me what becomes of you afterward. All I propose now is to prevent an act which seems to me unjust and cruel. You may kill yourself afterward, if you like."

"Well said," returned the ferocious Spaniard; "you please me. I thought at first you meant to affect the generous in order to oblige me to be grateful, which is a thing I detest. Well, I consent to come down; but I shall hate you as much as ever, for you are a Frenchman. Nor do I thank you, for you only discharge a debt you owe me, since it was I who this morning kept you from being shot by this young soldier while he was taking aim at you; and he is a man who never missed a chamois in the mountains of Léon."

"Be it as you will," said Cinq-Mars; "come down."

It was his character ever to assume with others the mien they wore toward him; and the rudeness of the Spaniard made him as hard as iron toward him.

"A proud rascal that, Monsieur," said Grandchamp; "in your place Monsieur le Maréchal would certainly have left him on his ladder. Come, Louis, Etienne, Germain, escort Monsieur's prisoners—a fine acquisition, truly! If they bring you any luck, I shall be very much surprised."

Cinq-Mars, suffering from the motion of his horse, rode only at the pace of his prisoners on foot, and was accordingly at a distance behind the red companies, who followed close upon the King. He meditated on his way what it could be that the Prince desired to say to him. A ray of hope presented to his mind the figure of Marie de Mantua in the distance; and for a moment his thoughts were calmed. But all his future lay in that brief sentence—"to please the King"; and he began to reflect upon all the bitterness in which his task might involve him.

At that moment he saw approaching his friend, De Thou, who, anxious at his remaining behind, had sought him in the plain, eager to aid him if necessary.

"It is late, my friend; night approaches. You have delayed long; I feared for you. Whom have you here? What has detained you? The King will soon be asking for you."

Such were the rapid inquiries of the young counsellor, whose anxiety, more than the battle itself, had made him lose his accustomed serenity.

"I was slightly wounded; I bring a prisoner, and I was thinking of the King. What can he want me for, my friend? What must I do if he proposes to place me about his person? I must please him; and at this thought—shall I own it?—I am tempted to fly. But I trust that I shall not have that fatal honor. 'To please,' how humiliating the word! 'to obey' quite the opposite! A soldier runs the chance of death, and there's an end. But in what base compliances, what sacrifices of himself, what compositions with his conscience, what degradation of his own thought, may not a courtier be involved! Ah, De Thou, my dear De Thou! I am not made for the court; I feel it, though I have seen it but for a moment. There is in my temperament a certain savageness, which education has polished only on the surface. At a distance, I thought myself adapted to live in this all-powerful world; I even desired it, led by a cherished hope of my heart. But I shuddered at the first step; I shuddered at the mere sight of the Cardinal. The recollection of the last of his crimes, at which I was present, kept me from addressing him. He horrifies me; I never can endure to be near him. The King's favor, too, has that about it which dismays me, as if I knew it would be fatal to me."

"I am glad to perceive this apprehension in you; it may be most salutary," said De Thou, as they rode on. "You are about to enter into contact with power. Before, you did not even conceive it; now you will touch it with your very hand. You will see what it is, and what hand hurls the lightning. Heaven grant that that lightning may never strike you! You will probably be present in those councils which regulate the destiny of nations; you will see, you will perchance originate, those caprices whence are born sanguinary wars, conquests, and treaties; you will hold in your hand the drop of water which swells into mighty torrents. It is only from high places that men can judge of human affairs; you must look from the mountain-top ere you can appreciate the littleness of those things which from below appear to us great."

"Ah, were I on those heights, I should at least learn the lesson you speak of; but this Cardinal, this man to whom I must be under obligation, this man whom I know too well by his works—what will he be to me?"

"A friend, a protector, no doubt," answered De Thou.

"Death were a thousand times preferable to his friendship! I hate his whole being, even his very name; he spills the blood of men with the cross of the Redeemer!"

"What horrors are you saying, my friend? You will ruin yourself if you reveal your sentiments respecting the Cardinal to the King."

"Never mind; in the midst of these tortuous ways, I desire to take a new one, the right line. My whole opinion, the opinion of a just man, shall be unveiled to the King himself, if he interrogate me, even should it cost me my head. I have at last seen this King, who has been described to me as so weak; I have seen him, and his aspect has touched me to the heart in spite of myself. Certainly, he is very unfortunate, but he can not be cruel; he will listen to the truth."

"Yes; but he will not dare to make it triumph," answered the sage De Thou. "Beware of this warmth of heart, which often draws you by sudden and dangerous movements. Do not attack a colossus like Richelieu without having measured him."

"That is just like my tutor, the Abbé Quillet. My dear and prudent friend, neither the one nor the other of you know me; you do not know how weary I am of myself, and whither I have cast my gaze. I must mount or die."

"What! already ambitious?" exclaimed De Thou, with extreme surprise.

His friend inclined his head upon his hands, abandoning the reins of his horse, and did not answer.

"What! has this selfish passion of a riper age obtained possession of you at twenty, Henri? Ambition is the saddest of all hopes."

"And yet it possesses me entirely at present, for I see only by means of it, and by it my whole heart is penetrated."

"Ah, Cinq-Mars, I no longer recognize you! how different you were formerly! I do not conceal from you that you appear to me to have degenerated. In those walks of our childhood, when the life, and, above all, the death of Socrates, caused tears of admiration and envy to flow from our eyes; when, raising ourselves to the ideal of the highest virtue, we wished that those illustrious sorrows, those sublime misfortunes, which create great men, might in the future come upon us; when we constructed for ourselves imaginary occasions of sacrifices and devotion—if the voice of a man had pronounced, between us two, the single world, 'ambition,' we should have believed that we were touching a serpent."

De Thou spoke with the heat of enthusiasm and of reproach. Cinq-Mars went on without answering, and still with his face in his hands. After an instant of silence he removed them, and allowed his eyes to be seen, full of generous tears. He pressed the hand of his friend warmly, and said to him, with a penetrating accent:

"Monsieur de Thou, you have recalled to me the most beautiful thoughts of my earliest youth. Do not believe that I have fallen; I am consumed by a secret hope which I can not confide even to you. I despise, as much as you, the ambition which will seem to possess me. All the world will believe in it; but what do I care for the world? As for you, noble friend, promise me that you will not cease to esteem me, whatever you may see me do. I swear that my thoughts are as pure as heaven itself!"

"Well," said De Thou, "I swear by heaven that I believe you blindly; you give me back my life!"

They shook hands again with effusion of heart, and then perceived that they had arrived almost before the tent of the King.

Day was nearly over; but one might have believed that a softer day was rising, for the moon issued from the sea in all her splendor. The transparent sky of the south showed not a single cloud, and it seemed like a veil of pale blue sown with silver spangles; the air, still hot, was agitated only by the rare passage of breezes from the Mediterranean; and all sounds had ceased upon the earth. The fatigued army reposed beneath their tents, the line of which was marked by the fires, and the besieged city seemed oppressed by the same slumber; upon its ramparts nothing was to be seen but the arms of the sentinels, which shone in the rays of the moon, or the wandering fire of the night-rounds. Nothing was to be heard but the gloomy and prolonged cries of its guards, who warned one another not to sleep.

It was only around the King that all things waked, but at a great distance from him. This Prince had dismissed all his suite; he walked alone before his tent, and, pausing sometimes to contemplate the beauty of the heavens, he appeared plunged in melancholy meditation. No one dared to interrupt him; and those of the nobility who had remained in the royal quarters had gathered about the Cardinal, who, at twenty paces from the King, was seated upon a little hillock of turf, fashioned into a seat by the soldiers. There he wiped his pale forehead, fatigued with the cares of the day and with the unaccustomed weight of a suit of armor; he bade adieu, in a few hurried but always attentive and polite words, to those who came to salute him as they retired. No one was near him now except Joseph, who was talking with Laubardemont. The Cardinal was looking at the King, to see whether, before reëntering, this Prince would not speak to him, when the sound of the horses of Cinq-Mars was heard. The Cardinal's guards questioned him, and allowed him to advance without followers, and only with De Thou.

"You are come too late, young man, to speak with the King," said the Cardinal-Duke with a sharp voice. "One can not make his Majesty wait."

The two friends were about to retire, when the voice of Louis XIII himself made itself heard. This Prince was at that moment in one of those false positions which constituted the misfortune of his whole life. Profoundly irritated against his minister, but not concealing from himself that he owed the success of the day to him, desiring, moreover, to announce to him his intention to quit the army and to raise the siege of Perpignan, he was torn between the desire of speaking to the Cardinal and the fear lest his anger might be weakened. The minister, upon his part, dared not be the first to speak, being uncertain as to the thoughts which occupied his master, and fearing to choose his time ill, but yet not able to decide upon retiring. Both found themselves precisely in the position of two lovers who have quarrelled and desire to have an explanation, when the King, seized with joy the first opportunity of extricating himself. The chance was fatal to the minister. See upon what trifles depend those destinies which are called great.

"Is it not Monsieur de Cinq-Mars?" said the King, in a loud voice. "Let him approach; I am waiting for him."

Young D'Effiat approached on horseback, and at some paces from the King desired to set foot to earth; but hardly had his leg touched the ground when he dropped upon his knees.

"Pardon, Sire!" said he, "I believe that I am wounded;" and the blood issued violently from his boot.

De Thou had seen him fall, and had approached to sustain him. Richelieu seized this opportunity of advancing also, with dissembled eagerness.

"Remove this spectacle from the eyes of the King," said he. "You see very well that this young man is dying."

"Not at all," said Louis, himself supporting him; "a king of France knows how to see a man die, and has no fear of the blood which flows for him. This young man interests me. Let him be carried into my tent, and let my doctors attend him. If his wound is not serious, he shall come with me to Paris, for the siege is suspended, Monsieur le Cardinal. Such is my desire; other affairs call me to the centre of the kingdom. I will leave you here to command in my absence. This is what I desired to say to you."

With these words the King went abruptly into his tent, preceded by his pages and his officers, carrying flambeaux.

The royal pavilion was closed, and Cinq-Mars was borne in by De Thou and his people, while the Duc de Richelieu, motionless and stupefied, still regarded the spot where this scene had passed. He appeared thunderstruck, and incapable of seeing or hearing those who observed him.

Laubardemont, still intimidated by his ill reception of the preceding day, dared not speak a word to him, and Joseph hardly recognized in him his former master. For an instant he regretted having given himself to him, and fancied that his star was waning; but, reflecting that he was hated by all men and had no resource save in Richelieu, he seized him by the arm, and, shaking him roughly, said to him in a low voice, but harshly:

"Come, come, Monseigneur, you are chicken-hearted; come with us."

And, appearing to sustain him by the elbow, but in fact drawing him in spite of himself, with the aid of Laubardemont, he made him enter his tent, as a schoolmaster forces a schoolboy to rest, fearing the effects of the evening mist upon him.

The prematurely aged man slowly obeyed the wishes of his two parasites, and the purple of the pavilion dropped upon him.

CHAPTER XII

THE NiGHT-WATCH

O coward conscience, how dost thou afflict me!
The lights burn blue. It is now dead midnight,
Cold, fearful drops stand on my trembling flesh.
What do I fear? Myself?
I love myself!   SHAKESPEARE.

ARDLY was the Cardinal in his tent
before he dropped, armed and cui-
rassed, into a great armchair; and
there, holding his handkerchief to
his mouth with a fixed gaze, he remained in this attitude, letting his
two dark confidants wonder whether
contemplation or annihilation main-
tained him in it.   He was deadly pale, and a cold sweat
streamed upon his brow.   In wiping it with a sudden
movement, he threw behind him his red cap, the only
ecclesiastical sign which remained upon him, and
again rested with his mouth upon his hands.   The
Capuchin on one side, and the sombre magistrate on
the other, considered him in silence, and seemed, with
their brown and black costumes like the priest and
the notary of a dying man.

The friar, drawing from the depth of his chest a
voice that seemed better suited to repeat the service

[194]

of the dead than to administer consolation, spoke first:

"If Monseigneur will recall my counsels given at Narbonne, he will confess that I had a just presentiment of the troubles which this young man would one day cause him."

The magistrate continued:

"I have learned from the old deaf abbé who dined at the house of the Maréchale d'Effiat, and who heard all, that this young Cinq-Mars exhibited more energy than one would have imagined, and that he attempted to rescue the Maréchal de Bassompierre. I have still by me the detailed report of the deaf man, who played his part very well. His Eminence the Cardinal must be sufficiently convinced by it."

"I have told Monseigneur," resumed Joseph—for these two ferocious Seyds alternated their discourse like the shepherds of Virgil—"I have told him that it would be well to get rid of this young D'Effiat, and that I would charge myself with the business, if such were his good pleasure. It would be easy to destroy him in the opinion of the King."

"It would be safer to make him die of his wound," answered Laubardemont; "if his Eminence would have the goodness to command me, I know intimately the assistant-physician, who cured me of a blow on the forehead, and is now attending to him. He is a prudent man, entirely devoted to Monseigneur the Cardinal-Duke, and whose affairs have been somewhat embarrassed by gambling."

"I believe," replied Joseph, with an air of modesty,

mingled with a touch of bitterness, "that if his Excellency proposed to employ any one in this useful project, it should be his accustomed negotiator, who has had some success in the past."

"I fancy that I could enumerate some signal instances," answered Laubardemont, "and very recent ones, of which the difficulty was great."

"Ah, no doubt," said the father, with a bow and an air of consideration and politeness, "your most bold and skilfully executed commission was the trial of Urbain Grandier, the magician. But, with Heaven's assistance, one may be enabled to do things quite as worthy and bold. It is not without merit, for instance," added he, dropping his eyes like a young girl, "to have extirpated vigorously a royal Bourbon branch."

"It was not very difficult," answered the magistrate, with bitterness, "to select a soldier from the guards to kill the Comte de Soissons; but to preside, to judge——"

"And to execute one's self," interrupted the heated Capuchin, "is certainly less difficult than to educate a man from infancy in the thought of accomplishing great things with discretion, and to bear all tortures, if necessary, for the love of heaven, rather than reveal the name of those who have armed him with their justice, or to die courageously upon the body of him that he has struck, as did one who was commissioned by me. He uttered no cry at the blow of the sword of Riquemont, the equerry of the Prince. He died like a saint; he was my pupil."

"To give orders is somewhat different from running risk one's self."

"And did I risk nothing at the siege of Rochelle?"

"Of being drowned in a sewer, no doubt," said Laubardemont.

"And you," said Joseph, "has your danger been that of catching your fingers in instruments of torture? And all this because the Abbess of the Ursulines is your niece."

"It was a good thing for your brothers of Saint Francis, who held the hammers; but I—I was struck in the forehead by this same Cinq-Mars, who was leading an enraged multitude."

"Are you quite sure of that?" cried Joseph, delighted. "Did he dare to act thus against the commands of the King?" The joy which this discovery gave him made him forget his anger.

"Fools!" exclaimed the Cardinal, suddenly breaking his long silence, and taking from his lips his handkerchief stained with blood. "I would punish your angry dispute had it not taught me many secrets of infamy on your part. You have exceeded my orders; I commanded no torture, Laubardemont. That is your second fault. You cause me to be hated for nothing; that was useless. But you, Joseph, do not neglect the details of this disturbance in which Cinq-Mars was engaged; it may be of use in the end."

"I have all the names and descriptions," said the secret judge, eagerly, bending his tall form and thin, olive-colored visage, wrinkled with a servile smile, down to the armchair.

ALFRED DE VIGNY

"It is well! it is well!" said the minister, pushing him back; "but that is not the question yet. You, Joseph, be in Paris before this young upstart, who will become a favorite, I am certain. Become his friend; make him of my party or destroy him. Let him serve me or fall. But, above all, send me every day safe persons to give me verbal accounts. I will have no more writing for the future. I am much displeased with you, Joseph. What a miserable courier you chose to send from Cologne! He could not understand me. He saw the King too soon, and here we are still in disgrace in consequence. You have just missed ruining me entirely. Go and observe what is about to be done in Paris. A conspiracy will soon be hatched against me; but it will be the last. I remain here in order to let them all act more freely. Go, both of you, and send me my valet after the lapse of two hours; I wish now to be alone."

The steps of the two men were still to be heard as Richelieu, with eyes fixed upon the entrance to the tent, pursued them with his irritated glance.

"Wretches!" he exclaimed, when he was alone, "go and accomplish some more secret work, and afterward. I will crush you, in pure instruments of my power. The King will soon succumb beneath the slow malady which consumes him. I shall then be regent; I shall be King of France myself; I shall no longer have to dread the caprices of his weakness. I will destroy the haughty races of this country. I will be alone above them all. Europe shall tremble. I——"

Here the blood, which again filled his mouth, obliged him to apply his handkerchief to it once more.

"Ah, what do I say? Unhappy victim that I am! Here am I, death-stricken! My dissolution is near; my blood flows, and my spirit desires to labor still. Why? For whom? Is it for glory? That is an empty word. Is it for men? I despise them. For whom, then, since I shall die, perhaps, in two or three years? Is it for God? What a name! I have not walked with Him! He has seen all——"

Here he let his head fall upon his breast, and his eyes met the great cross of gold which was suspended from his neck. He could not help throwing himself back in his chair; but it followed him. He took it; and considering it with fixed and devouring looks, he said in a low voice:

"Terrible sign! thou followest me! Shall I find thee elsewhere—divinity and suffering? What am I? What have I done?"

For the first time a singular and unknown terror penetrated him. He trembled, at once frozen and scorched by an invincible shudder. He dared not lift his eyes, fearing to meet some terrible vision. He dared not call, fearing to hear the sound of his own voice. He remained profoundly plunged in meditations on eternity, so terrible for him, and he murmured the following kind of prayer:

"Great God, if Thou hearest me, judge me then, but do not isolate me in judging me! Look upon me, surrounded by the men of my generation; consider the immense work I had undertaken! Was not an enormous lever wanted to bestir those masses; and if this lever in falling crushes some useless wretches, am I very culpable? I seem wicked to men; but Thou, Supreme Judge, dost thou regard me thus?

"No; Thou knowest it is boundless power which makes creature culpable against creature. It is not Armand de Richelieu who destroys; it is the Prime-Minister. It is not for his personal injuries; it is to carry out a system. But a system—what is this word? Is it permitted me to play thus with men, to regard them as numbers for working out a thought, which perhaps is false? I overturn the framework of the throne. What if, without knowing it, I sap its foundations and hasten its fall! Yes, my borrowed power has seduced me. O labyrinth! O weakness of human thought! Simple faith, why did I quit thy path? Why am I not a simple priest? If I dared to break with man and give myself to God, the ladder of Jacob would again descend in my dreams."

At this moment his ear was struck by a great noise outside—laughter of soldiers, ferocious shouts and oaths, mingled with words which were a long time sustained by a weak yet clear voice; one would have said it was the voice of an angel interrupted by the laughter of demons. He rose and opened a sort of linen window, worked in the side of his square tent. A singular spectacle presented itself to his view; he remained some instants contemplating it, attentive to the conversation which was going on.

"Listen, listen, La Valeur!" said one soldier to another. "See, she begins again to speak and to sing!

Put her in the middle of the circle, between us and the fire."

"You do not know her! You do not know her!" said another. "But here is Grand-Ferré, who says that he knows her."

"Yes, I tell you I know her; and, by Saint Peter of Loudun, I will swear that I have seen her in my village, when I had leave of absence; and it was upon an occasion at which one shuddered, but concerning which one dares not talk, especially to a Cardinalist like you."

"Eh! and pray why dare not one speak of it, you great simpleton?" said an old soldier, twisting up his moustache.

"It is not spoken of because it burns the tongue. Do you understand that?"

"No, I don't understand it."

"Well, nor I neither; but certain citizens told it to me."

Here a general laugh interrupted him.

"Ha, ha, ha! is he a fool?" said one. "He listens to what the townsfolk tell him."

"Ah, well! if you listen to their gabble, you have time to lose," said another.

"You do not know, then, what my mother said, greenhorn?" said the eldest, gravely dropping his eyes with a solemn air, to compel attention.

"Eh! how can you think that I know it, La Pipe? Your mother must have died of old age before my grandfather came into the world."

"Well, greenhorn, I will tell you! You shall know,

first of all, that my mother was a respectable Bohe-
mian, as much attached to the regiment of carabineers
of La Roque as my dog Canon there. She carried
brandy round her neck in a barrel, and drank better
than the best of us. She had fourteen husbands, all
soldiers, who died upon the field of battle."

"Ha! that was a woman!" interrupted the soldiers,
full of respect.

"And never once in her life did she speak to a
townsman, unless it was to say to him on coming to
her lodging, 'Light my candle and warm my soup.'"

"Well, and what was it that your mother said to
you?"

"If you are in such a hurry, you shall not know,
greenhorn. She said habitually in her talk, 'A soldier
is better than a dog; but a dog is better than a
bourgeois.'"

"Bravo! bravo! that was well said!" cried the soldier, filled with enthusiasm at these fine words.

"That," said Grand-Ferré, "does not prove that
the citizens who made the remark to me that it burned
the tongue were in the right; besides, they were not
altogether citizens, for they had swords, and they
were grieved at a curé being burned, and so was I."

"Eh! what was it to you that they burned your
curé, great simpleton?" said a sergeant, leaning upon
the fork of his arquebus; "after him another would
come. You might have taken one of our generals in
his stead, who are all curés at present; for me, I am
a Royalist, and I say it frankly."

"Hold your tongue!" cried La Pipe; "let the girl

speak. It is these dogs of Royalists who always disturb us in our amusements."

"What say you?" answered Grand-Ferré. "Do you even know what it is to be a Royalist?"

"Yes," said La Pipe; "I know you all very well. Go, you are for the old self-called princes of the peace, together with the wranglers against the Cardinal and the *gabelle*. Am I right or not?"

"No, old red-stocking. A Royalist is one who is for the King; that's what it is. And as my father was the King's valet, I am for the King, you see; and I have no liking for the red-stockings, I can tell you."

"Ah, you call me red-stocking, eh?" answered the old soldier. "You shall give me satisfaction to-morrow morning. If you had made war in the Valteline, you would not talk like that; and if you had seen his Eminence marching upon the dike at Rochelle, with the old Marquis de Spinola, while volleys of cannonshot were sent after him, you would have nothing to say about red-stockings."

"Come, let us amuse ourselves, instead of quarrelling," said the other soldiers.

The men who conversed thus were standing round a great fire, which illuminated them more than the moon, beautiful as it was; and in the centre of the group was the object of their gathering and their cries. The Cardinal perceived a young woman arrayed in black and covered with a long, white veil. Her feet were bare; a thick cord clasped her elegant figure; a long rosary fell from her neck almost to her feet, and her hands, delicate and white as ivory, turned its beads and made them pass rapidly beneath her fingers. The soldiers, with a barbarous joy, amused themselves with laying little brands in her way to burn her naked feet. The oldest took the smoking match of his arquebus, and, approaching it to the edge of her robe, said in a hoarse voice:

"Come, madcap, tell me your history, or I will fill you with powder and blow you up like a mine; take care, for I have already played that trick to others besides you, in the old wars of the Huguenots. Come, sing."

The young woman, looking at him gravely, made no reply, but lowered her veil.

"You don't manage her well," said Grand-Ferré, with a drunken laugh; "you will make her cry. You don't know the fine language of the court; let me speak to her." And, touching her on the chin, "My little heart," he said, "if you will please, my sweet, to resume the little story you told just now to these gentlemen, I will pray you to travel with me upon the river Du Tendre, as the great ladies of Paris say, and to take a glass of brandy with your faithful chevalier, who met you formerly at Loudun, when you played a comedy in order to burn a poor devil."

The young woman crossed her arms, and, looking around her with an imperious air, cried:

"Withdraw, in the name of the God of armies; withdraw, impious men! There is nothing in common between us. I do not understand your tongue, nor you mine. Go, sell your blood to the princes of the earth at so many oboles a day, and leave me to accomplish my mission! Conduct me to the Cardinal."

A coarse laugh interrupted her.

"Do you think," said a carabineer of Maurevert, "that his Eminence the Generalissimo will receive you with your feet naked? Go and wash them."

"The Lord has said, 'Jerusalem, lift thy robe, and pass the rivers of water,'" she answered, her arms still crossed. "Let me be conducted to the Cardinal."

Richelieu cried in a loud voice, "Bring the woman to me, and let her alone!"

All were silent; they conducted her to the minister.

"Why," said she, beholding him—"why bring me before an armed man?"

They left her alone with him without answering.

The Cardinal looked at her with a suspicious air. "Madame," said he, "what are you doing in the camp at this hour? And if your mind is not disordered, why these naked feet?"

"It is a vow; it is a vow," answered the young woman, with an air of impatience, seating herself beside him abruptly. "I have also made a vow not to eat until I have found the man I seek."

"My sister," said the Cardinal, astonished and softened, looking closely at her, "God does not exact such rigors from a weak body, and particularly from one of your age, for you seem very young."

"Young! oh, yes, I was very young a few days ago; but I have since passed two existences at least, so much have I thought and suffered. Look on my countenance."

And she discovered a face of perfect beauty. Black and very regular eyes gave life to it; but in their absence one might have thought her features were those of a phantom, she was so pale. Her lips were blue and quivering; and a strong shudder made her teeth chatter.

"You are ill, my sister," said the minister, touched, taking her hand, which he felt to be burning hot. A sort of habit of inquiring concerning his own health, and that of others, made him touch the pulse of her emaciated arm; he felt that the arteries were swollen by the beatings of a terrible fever.

"Alas!" he continued, with more of interest, "you have killed yourself with rigors beyond human strength! I have always blamed them, and especially at a tender age. What, then, has induced you to do this? Is it to confide it to me that you are come? Speak calmly, and be sure of succor."

"Confide in men!" answered the young woman; "oh, no, never! All have deceived me. I will confide myself to no one, not even to Monsieur Cinq-Mars, although he must soon die."

"What!" said Richelieu, contracting his brows, but with a bitter laugh,—"what! do you know this young man? Has he been the cause of your misfortune?"

"Oh, no! He is very good, and hates wickedness; that is what will ruin him. Besides," said she, suddenly assuming a harsh and savage air, "men are weak, and there are things which women must accomplish. When there were no more valiant men in Israel, Deborah arose."

"Ah! how came you with all this fine learning?" continued the Cardinal, still holding her hand.

"Oh, I can't explain that!" answered she, with a touching air of naïveté and a very gentle voice; "you would not understand me. It is the Devil who has taught me all, and who has destroyed me."

"Ah, my child! it is always he who destroys us; but he instructs us ill," said Richelieu, with an air of paternal protection and an increasing pity. "What have been your faults? Tell them to me; I am very powerful."

"Ah," said she, with a look of doubt, "you have much influence over warriors, brave men and generals! Beneath your cuirass must beat a noble heart; you are an old General who knows nothing of the tricks of crime."

Richelieu smiled; this mistake flattered him.

"I heard you ask for the Cardinal; do you desire to see him? Did you come here to seek him?"

The girl drew back and placed a finger upon her forehead.

"I had forgotten it," said she; "you have talked to me too much. I had overlooked this idea, and yet it is an important one; it is for that that I have condemned myself to the hunger which is killing me. I must accomplish it, or I shall die first. Ah," said she, putting her hand beneath her robe in her bosom, whence she appeared to take something, "behold it! this idea——"

She suddenly blushed, and her eyes widened extraordinarily. She continued, bending to the ear of the Cardinal:

"I will tell you; listen! Urbain Grandier, my lover Urbain, told me this night that it was Richelieu who had been the cause of his death. I took a knife from an inn, and I come here to kill him; tell me where he is."

The Cardinal, surprised and terrified, recoiled with horror. He dared not call his guards, fearing the cries of this woman and her accusations; nevertheless, a transport of this madness might be fatal to him.

"This frightful history will pursue me everywhere!" cried he, looking fixedly at her, and thinking within himself of the course he should take.

They remained in silence, face to face, in the same attitude, like two wrestlers who contemplate before attacking each other, or like the pointer and his victim petrified by the power of a look.

In the mean time, Laubardemont and Joseph had gone forth together; and ere separating they talked for a moment before the tent of the Cardinal, because they were eager mutually to deceive each other. Their hatred had acquired new force by their recent quarrel; and each had resolved to ruin his rival in the mind of his master. The judge then began the dialogue, which each of them had prepared, taking the arm of the other as by one and the same movement.

"Ah, reverend father! how you have afflicted me by seeming to take in ill part the trifling pleasantries which I said to you just now."

"*I come here to kill him!*"

[*From the Original Drawing by A. Duvivier.*]

"Heavens, no! my dear Monsieur, I am far from that. Charity, where would be charity? I have sometimes a holy warmth in conversation, for the good of the State and of Monseigneur, to whom I am entirely devoted."

"Ah, who knows it better than I, reverend father? But render me justice; you also know how completely I am attached to his Eminence the Cardinal, to whom I owe all. Alas! I have employed too much zeal in serving him, since he reproaches me with it."

"Reassure yourself," said Joseph; "he bears no ill-will toward you. I know him well; he can appreciate one's actions in favor of one's family. He, too, is a very good relative."

"Yes, there it is," answered Laubardemont; "consider my condition. My niece would have been totally ruined at her convent had Urbain triumphed; you feel that as well as I do, particularly as she did not quite comprehend us, and acted the child when she was compelled to appear."

"Is it possible? In full audience! What you tell me indeed makes me feel for you. How painful it must have been!"

"More so than you can imagine. She forgot, in her madness, all that she had been told, committed a thousand blunders in Latin, which we patched up as well as we could; and she even caused an unpleasant scene on the day of the trial, very unpleasant for me and the judges—there were swoons and shrieks. Ah, I swear that I would have scolded her well had I not been forced to quit precipitately that little town of

Loudun. But, you see, it is natural enough that I
am attached to her. She is my nearest relative; for
my son has turned out ill, and no one knows what
has become of him during the last four years. Poor
little Jeanne de Belfiel! I made her a nun, and then
abbess, in order to preserve all for that scamp. Had
I foreseen his conduct, I should have retained her
for the world."

"She is said to have great beauty," answered Joseph; "that is a precious gift for a family. She might
have been presented at court, and the King— Ah!
ah! Mademoiselle de la Fayette—eh! eh!—Mademoiselle d'Hautefort—you understand; it may be even
possible to think of it yet."

"Ah, that is like you, Monseigneur! for we know
that you have been nominated to the cardinalate; how
good you are to remember the most devoted of your
friends!"

Laubardemont was yet talking to Joseph when they
found themselves at the end of the line of the camp,
which led to the quarter of the volunteers.

"May God and his Holy Mother protect you during my absence!" said Joseph, stopping. "To-morrow I depart for Paris; and as I shall have frequent
business with this young Cinq-Mars, I shall first go to
see him, and learn news of his wound."

"Had I been listened to," said Laubardemont,
"you would not now have had this trouble."

"Alas, you are right!" answered Joseph, with a
profound sigh, and raising his eyes to heaven; "but
the Cardinal is no longer the same man. He will not

take advantage of good ideas; he will ruin us if he goes on thus."

And, making a low bow to the judge, the Capuchin took the road which he had indicated to him.

Laubardemont followed him for some time with his eyes, and, when he was quite sure of the route which he had taken, he returned, or, rather, ran back to the tent of the minister. "The Cardinal dismisses him, he tells me; that shows that he is tired of him. I know secrets which will ruin him. I will add that he is gone to pay court to the future favorite. I will replace this monk in the favor of the minister. The moment is propitious. It is midnight; he will be alone for an hour and a half yet. Let me run."

He arrived at the tent of the guards, which was before the pavilion.

"Monseigneur gives audience to some one," said the captain, hesitating; "you can not enter."

"Never mind; you saw me leave an hour ago, and things are passing of which I must give an account."

"Come in, Laubardemont," cried the minister; "come in quickly, and alone."

˙ He entered. The Cardinal, still seated, held the two hands of the nun in one of his, and with the other he imposed silence upon his stupefied agent, who remained motionless, not yet seeing the face of this woman. She spoke volubly, and the strange things she said contrasted horribly with the sweetness of her voice. Richelieu seemed moved.

"Yes, I will stab him with a knife. It is the knife which the demon Behirith gave me at the inn; but it

is the nail of Sisera. It has a handle of ivory, you see;
and I have wept much over it. Is it not singular,
my good General? I will turn it in the throat of him
who killed my friend, as he himself told me to do;
and afterward I will burn the body. There is like
for like, the punishment which God permitted to
Adam. You have an astonished air, my brave general; but you would be much more so, were I to repeat
to you his song—the song which he sang to me again
last night, at the hour of the funeral-pyre—you understand?—the hour when it rains, the hour when my
hand burns as now. He said to me: 'They are much
deceived, the magistrates, the red judges. I have
eleven demons at my command; and I shall come to
see you when the clock strikes, under a canopy of
purple velvet, with torches—torches of resin to give
us light——' Ah, that is beautiful! Listen, listen to
what he sings!"

And she sang to the air of *De Profundis:*

> "'Je vais être prince d'Enfer,
>   Mon sceptre est un manteau de fer
>   Ce sapin brulant est mon trône.
>   Est ma robe est de soufre jaune;
>   Mais je veux t'epouser demain:
>   Viens, Jeanne, donne-mois la main.'

"Is it not singular, my good General?" said she,
when she had finished; "and I—I answer him every
evening. Listen well to what I sing:

> "'Le juge a parlé dans la nuit,
>   Et dans la tombe on me conduit,
>   Pourtant j'étais ta fiancée!

Viens! la pluie est longue et glacée;
Mais tu ne dormira pas seul,
Je te prêterai mon linceul.'

Then he speaks as spirits and prophets speak. He
says: 'Woe, woe to him who has shed blood! Are the
judges of the earth gods? No, they are men who grow
old and suffer, and yet they dare to say aloud, Let
that man die! The penalty of death, the pain of
death—who has given to man the right of imposing
it on man? Is the number two? One would be an
assassin, look you! But count well, one, two, three.
Behold, they are wise and just, these grave and sal-
aried criminals! O crime, the horror of Heaven!
If you looked upon them from above as I look upon
them, you would be yet paler than I am. Flesh destroys flesh! That which lives by blood sheds blood
coldly and without anger, like a God with power to
create!'"

The cries which the unhappy girl uttered, as she
rapidly spoke these words, terrified Richelieu and
Laubardemont so much that they still remained motionless. The delirium and the fever continued to
transport her.

"'Did the judges tremble?' said Urbain Grandier
to me. 'Did they tremble at deceiving themselves?'
They work the work of the just. The question! They
bind his limbs with ropes to make him speak. His
skin cracks, tears away, and rolls up like a parchment; his nerves are naked, red, and glittering; his
bones crack; the marrow spurts out. But the judges
sleep! they dream of flowers and spring. 'How hot

the grand chamber is!' says one, awaking; 'this man has not chosen to speak! Is the torture finished?' And pitiful at last, he dooms him to death—death, the sole fear of the living! death, the unknown world! He sends before him a furious soul which will wait for him. Oh! has he never seen the vision of vengeance? Has he never seen before falling asleep the flayed prevaricator?"

Already weakened by fever, fatigue, and grief, the Cardinal, seized with horror and pity, exclaimed:

"Ah, for the love of God, let this terrible scene have an end! Take away this woman; she is mad!"

The frantic creature turned, and suddenly uttering loud cries, "Ah, the judge! the judge! the judge!" she said, recognizing Laubardemont.

The latter, clasping his hands and trembling before the Cardinal, said with terror:

"Alas, Monseigneur, pardon me! she is my niece, who has lost her reason. I was not aware of this misfortune, or she would have been shut up long ago. Jeanne! Jeanne! come, Madame, to your knees! ask forgiveness of Monseigneur the Cardinal-duc."

"It is Richelieu!" she cried; and astonishment seemed wholly to paralyze this young and unhappy beauty. The flush which had animated her at first gave place to a deadly pallor, her cries to a motionless silence, her wandering looks to a frightful fixedness of her large eyes, which constantly followed the agitated minister.

"Take away this unfortunate child quickly," said he; "she is dying, and so am I. So many horrors pursue me since that sentence that I believe all hell is loosed upon me."

He rose as he spoke; Jeanne de Belfiel, still silent and stupefied, with haggard eyes, open mouth, and head bent forward, yet remained beneath the shock of her double surprise, which seemed to have extinguished the rest of her reason and her strength. At the movement of the Cardinal, she shuddered to find herself between him and Laubardemont, looked by turns at one and the other, let the knife which she held fall from her hand, and retired slowly toward the opening of the tent, covering herself completely with her veil, and looking wildly and with terror behind her upon her uncle who followed, like an affrighted lamb, which already feels at its back the burning breath of the wolf about to seize it.

Thus they both went forth; and hardly had they reached the open air, when the furious judge caught the hands of his victim, tied them with a handkerchief, and easily led her, for she uttered no cry, not even a sigh, but followed him with her head still drooping upon her bosom, and as if plunged in profound somnambulism.

CHAPTER XIII

THE SPANIARD

Qu'un ami véritable est une douce chose!
Il cherche vos besoins au fond de votre cœur;
   Il vous épargne la pudeur
   De les lui découvrir vous-même.

LA FONTAINE.

MEANTIME, a scene of different nature was passing in the tent of Cinq-Mars; the words of the King, the first balm to his wounds, had been followed by the anxious care of the surgeons of the court. A spent ball, easily extracted, had been the only cause of his accident. He was allowed to travel; and all was ready. The invalid had received up to midnight friendly or interested visits; among the first were those of little Gondi and of Fontrailles, who were also preparing to quit Perpignan for Paris. The ex-page, Olivier d'Entraigues, joined with them in complimenting the fortunate volunteer, whom the King seemed to have distinguished. The habitual coldness of the Prince toward all who surrounded him having caused those who knew of them to regard the few words he had spoken as assured signs of high favor, all came to congratulate him.

CINQ-MARS

At length, released from visitors, he lay upon his camp-bed. De Thou sat by his side, holding his hand, and Grandchamp at his feet, still grumbling at the numerous interruptions that had fatigued his wounded master. Cinq-Mars himself tasted one of those moments of calm and hope, which so refresh the soul as well as the body. His free hand secretly pressed the gold cross that hung next to his heart, the beloved donor of which he was so soon to behold. Outwardly, he listened with kindly looks to the counsels of the young magistrate; but his inward thoughts were all turned toward the object of his journey—the object, also, of his life. The grave De Thou went on in a calm, gentle voice:

"I shall soon follow you to Paris. I am happier than you at seeing the King take you there with him. You are right in looking upon it as the beginning of a friendship which must be turned to profit. I have reflected deeply on the secret causes of your ambition, and I think I have divined your heart. Yes; that feeling of love for France, which made it beat in your earliest youth, must have gained greater strength. You would be near the King in order to serve your country, in order to put in action those golden dreams of your early years. The thought is a vast one, and worthy of you! I admire you; I bow before you. To approach the monarch with the chivalrous devotion of our fathers, with a heart full of candor, and prepared for any sacrifice; to receive the confidences of his soul; to pour into his those of his subjects; to soften the sorrows of the King by telling him the confidence his people have in him; to cure the wounds of the people by laying them open to its master, and by the intervention of your favor thus to reëstablish that intercourse of love between the father and his children which for eighteen years has been interrupted by a man whose heart is marble; for this noble enterprise, to expose yourself to all the horrors of his vengeance and, what is even worse, to brave all the perfidious calumnies which pursue the favorite to the very steps of the throne—this dream was worthy of you.

"Pursue it, my friend," De Thou continued. "Never become discouraged. Speak loudly to the King of the merit and misfortunes of his most illustrious friends who are trampled on. Tell him fearlessly that his old nobility have never conspired against him; and that from the young Montmorency to the amiable Comte de Soissons, all have opposed the minister, and never the monarch. Tell him that the old families of France were born with his race; that in striking them he affects the whole nation; and that, should he destroy them, his own race will suffer, that it will stand alone exposed to the blast of time and events, as an old oak trembling and exposed to the wind of the plain, when the forest which surrounded and supported it has been destroyed. Yes!" cried De Thou, growing animated, "this aim is a fine and noble one. Go on in your course with a resolute step; expel even that secret shame, that shyness, which a noble soul experiences before it can resolve upon flattering—upon paying what the world calls its court. Alas, kings are accustomed to these continual expressions of false admiration for them! Look upon them as a new language which must be learned—a language hitherto foreign to your lips, but which, believe me, may be nobly spoken, and which may express high and generous thoughts."

During this warm discourse of his friend, Cinq-Mars could not refrain from a sudden blush; and he turned his head on his pillow toward the tent, so that his face might not be seen. De Thou stopped:

"What is the matter, Henri? You do not answer. Am I deceived?"

Cinq-Mars gave a deep sigh and remained silent.

"Is not your heart affected by these ideas which I thought would have transported it?"

The wounded man looked more calmly at his friend and said:

"I thought, my dear De Thou, that you would not interrogate me further, and that you were willing to repose a blind confidence in me. What evil genius has moved you thus to sound my soul? I am not a stranger to these ideas which possess you. Who told you that I had not conceived them? Who told you that I had not formed the firm resolution of prosecuting them infinitely farther in action than you have put them in words? Love for France, virtuous hatred of the ambition which oppresses and shatters her ancient institutions with the axe of the executioner, the firm belief that virtue may be as skilful as crime, —these are my gods as much as yours. But when you see a man kneeling in a church, do you ask him what saint or what angel protects him and receives his prayer? What matters it to you, provided that he pray at the foot of the altars that you adore—provided that, if called upon, he fall a martyr at the foot of those altars? When our forefathers journeyed with naked feet toward the Holy Sepulchre, with pilgrims' staves in their hands, did men inquire the secret vow which led them to the Holy Land? They struck, they died; and men, perhaps God himself, asked no more. The pious captain who led them never stripped their bodies to see whether the red cross and haircloth concealed any other mysterious symbol; and in heaven, doubtless, they were not judged with any greater rigor for having aided the strength of their resolutions upon earth by some hope permitted to a Christian —some second and secret thought, more human, and nearer the mortal heart."

De Thou smiled and slightly blushed, lowering his eyes.

"My friend," he answered, gravely; "this excitement may be injurious to you. Let us not continue this subject; let us not mingle God and heaven in our discourse. It is not well; and draw the coverings over your shoulder, for the night is cold. I promise you," he added, covering his young invalid with a maternal care—"I promise not to offend you again with my counsels."

"And I," cried Cinq-Mars, despite the interdiction to speak, "swear to you by this gold cross you see, and by the Holy Mary, to die rather than renounce the plan that you first traced out! You may one day, perhaps, be forced to pray me to stop; but then it will be too late."

"Very well!" repeated the counsellor, "now sleep; if you do not stop, I will go on with you, wherever you lead me."

And, taking a prayer-book from his pocket, he began to read attentively; in a short time he looked at Cinq-Mars, who was still awake. He made a sign to Grandchamp to put the lamp out of sight of the invalid; but this new care succeeded no better. The latter, with his eyes still open, tossed restlessly on his narrow bed.

"Come, you are not calm," said De Thou, smiling; "I will read to you some pious passage which will put your mind in repose. Ah, my friend, it is here that true repose is to be found; it is in this consolatory book, for, open it where you will, you will always see, on the one hand, man in the only condition that suits his weakness—prayer, and the uncertainty as to his destiny—and, on the other, God himself speaking to him of his infirmities! What a glorious and heavenly spectacle! What a sublime bond between heaven and earth! Life, death, and eternity are there; open it at random."

"Yes!" said Cinq-Mars, rising with a vivacity which had something boyish in it; "you shall read to me, but let me open the book. You know the old superstition of our country—when the mass-book is opened with a sword, the first page on the left contains the destiny of him who reads, and the first person who enters after he has read is powerfully to influence the reader's future fate."

"What childishness! But be it as you will. Here is your sword; insert the point. Let us see."

"Let me read myself," said Cinq-Mars, taking one side of the book. Old Grandchamp gravely advanced his tawny face and his gray hair to the foot of the bed to listen. His master read, stopped at the first phrase, but with a smile, perhaps slightly forced, he went on the the end.

"I. Now it was in the city of Milan that they appeared.

"II. The high-priest said to them, 'Bow down and adore the gods.'

"III. And the people were silent, looking at their faces, which appeared as the faces of angels.

"IV. But Gervais, taking the hand of Protais, cried, looking to heaven, and filled with the Holy Ghost:

"V. Oh, my brother! I see the Son of man smiling upon us; let me die first.

"VI. For if I see thy blood, I fear I shall shed tears unworthy of the Lord our God.

"VII. Then Protais answered him in these words:

"VIII. My brother, it is just that I should perish after thee, for I am older, and have more strength to see thee suffer.

"IX. But the senators and people ground their teeth at them.

"X. And the soldiers having struck them, their heads fell together on the same stone.

"XI. Now it was in this same place that the blessed Saint Ambroise found the ashes of the two martyrs which gave sight to the blind."

"Well," said Cinq-Mars, looking at his friend when he had finished, "what do you say to that?"

"God's will be done! but we should not scrutinize it."

"Nor put off our designs for a child's play," said D'Effiat impatiently, and wrapping himself in a cloak which was thrown over him. "Remember the lines we formerly so frequently quoted, '*Justum et tenacem propositi virum*'; these iron words are stamped upon my brain. Yes; let the universe crumble around me, its wreck shall carry me away still resolute."

"Let us not compare the thoughts of man with those of Heaven; and let us be submissive," said De Thou, gravely.

"Amen!" said old Grandchamp, whose eyes had filled with tears, which he hastily brushed away.

"What hast thou to do with it, old soldier? Thou weepest," said his master.

"Amen!" said a voice, in a nasal tone, at the entrance of the tent.

"*Parbleu*, Monsieur! rather put that question to his Gray Eminence, who comes to visit you," answered the faithful servant, pointing to Joseph, who advanced with his arms crossed, making a salutation with a frowning air.

"Ah, it will be he, then!" murmured Cinq-Mars.

"Perhaps I come inopportunely," said Joseph, soothingly.

"Perhaps very opportunely," said Henri d'Effiat, smiling, with a glance at De Thou. "What can bring you here, Father, at one o'clock in the morning? It should be some good work."

Joseph saw he was ill-received; and as he had always sundry reproaches to make himself with reference to all persons whom he addressed, and as many resources in his mind for getting out of the difficulty, he fancied that they had discovered the object of his visit, and felt that he should not select a moment of ill humor for preparing the way to friendship. Therefore, seating himself near the bed, he said, coldly:

"I come, Monsieur, to speak to you on the part of the Cardinal-Generalissimo, of the two Spanish prisoners you have made; he desires to have information concerning them as soon as possible. I am to see and question them. But I did not suppose you were still awake; I merely wished to receive them from your people."

After a forced interchange of politeness, they ordered into the tent the two prisoners, whom Cinq-Mars had almost forgotten.

They appeared—the one, young and displaying an animated and rather wild countenance, was the soldier; the other, concealing his form under a brown cloak, and his gloomy features, which had something ambiguous in their expression, under his broad-brimmed hat, which he did not remove, was the officer. He spoke first:

"Why do you make me leave my straw and my sleep? Is it to deliver me or hang me?"

"Neither," said Joseph.

"What have I to do with thee, man with the long beard? I did not see thee at the breach."

It took some time after this amiable exordium to make the stranger understand the right a Capuchin had to interrogate him.

"Well," he said, "what dost thou want?"

"I would know your name and your country."

"I shall not tell my name; and as for my country,

I have the air of a Spaniard, but perhaps am not one, for a Spaniard never acknowledges his country."

Father Joseph, turning toward the two friends, said: "Unless I deceive myself, I have heard his voice somewhere. This man speaks French without an accent; but it seems he wishes to give us enigmas, as in the East."

"The East? that is it," said the prisoner. "A Spaniard is a man from the East; he is a Catholic Turk; his blood either flags or boils; he is lazy or indefatigable; indolence makes him a slave, ardor a tyrant; immovable in his ignorance, ingenious in his superstition, he needs only a religious book and a tyrannical master; he obeys the law of the pyre; he commands by that of the poniard. At night he falls asleep in his bloodthirsty misery, nurses fanaticism, and awakes to crime. Who is this gentleman? Is it the Spaniard or the Turk? Guess! Ah! you seem to think that I have wit, because I light upon analogy.

"Truly, gentlemen, you do me honor; and yet the idea may be carried much further, if desired. If I pass to the physical order, for example, may I not say to you, This man has long and serious features, a black and almond-shaped eye, rugged brows, a sad and mobile mouth, tawny, meagre, and wrinkled cheeks; his head is shaved, and he covers it with a black handkerchief in the form of a turban; he passes the whole day lying or standing under a burning sun, without motion, without utterance, smoking a pipe that intoxicates him. Is this a Turk or a Spaniard? Are you satisfied, gentlemen? Truly, it would seem so; you laugh, and at what do you laugh? I, who have presented this idea to you—I have not laughed; see, my countenance is sad. Ah! perhaps it is because the gloomy prisoner has suddenly become a gossip, and talks rapidly. That is nothing! I might tell you other things, and render you some service, my worthy friends.

"If I should relate anecdotes, for example; if I told you I knew a priest who ordered the death of some heretics before saying mass, and who, furious at being interrupted at the altar during the holy sacrifice, cried to those who asked for his orders, 'Kill them all! kill them all!'—should you all laugh, gentlemen? No, not all! This gentleman here, for instance, would bite his lips and his beard. Oh! it is true he might answer that he did wisely, and that they were wrong to interrupt his unsullied prayer. But if I added that he concealed himself for an hour behind the curtain of your tent, Monsieur de Cinq-Mars, to listen while you talked, and that he came to betray you, and not to get me, what would he say? Now, gentlemen, are you satisfied? May I retire after this display?"

The prisoner had uttered this with the rapidity of a quack vending his wares, and in so loud a voice that Joseph was quite confounded. He arose indignantly at last, and, addressing himself to Cinq-Mars, said:

"How can you suffer a prisoner who should have been hanged to speak to you thus, Monsieur?"

The Spaniard, without deigning to notice him any further, leaned toward D'Effiat, and whispered in his ear:

"I can be of no further use to you; give me my

liberty. I might ere this have taken it; but I would not do so without your consent. Give it me, or have me killed."

"Go, if you will!" said Cinq-Mars to him. "I assure you I shall be very glad;" and he told his people to retire with the soldier, whom he wished to keep in his service.

This was the affair of a moment. No one remained any longer in the tent with the two friends, except the abashed Joseph and the Spaniard. The latter, taking off his hat, showed a French but savage countenance. He laughed, and seemed to respire more air into his broad chest.

"Yes, I am a Frenchman," he said to Joseph. "But I hate France, because she gave birth to my father, who is a monster, and to me, who have become one, and who once struck him. I hate her inhabitants, because they have robbed me of my whole fortune at play, and because I have robbed them and killed them. I have been two years in Spain in order to kill more Frenchmen; but now I hate Spain still more. No one will know the reason why. Adieu! I must live henceforth without a nation; all men are my enemies. Go on, Joseph, and you will soon be as good as I. Yes, you have seen me once before," he continued, violently striking him in the breast and throwing him down. "I am Jacques de Laubardemont, the son of your worthy friend."

With these words, quickly leaving the tent, he disappeared like an apparition. De Thou and the servants, who ran to the entrance, saw him, with two bounds, spring over a surprised and disarmed soldier, and run toward the mountains with the swiftness of a deer, despite various musket-shots. Joseph took advantage of the disorder to slip away, stammering a few words of politeness, and left the two friends laughing at his adventure and his disappointment, as two schoolboys laugh at seeing the spectacles of their pedagogue fall off. At last they prepared to seek a rest of which they both stood in need, and which they soon found—the wounded man in his bed, and the young counsellor in his chair.

As for the Capuchin, he walked toward his tent, meditating how he should turn all this so as to take the greatest possible revenge, when he met Laubarde-mont dragging the young mad-woman by her two hands. They recounted to each other their mutual and horrible adventures.

Joseph had no small pleasure in turning the poniard in the wound of his friend's heart, by telling him of the fate of his son.

"You are not exactly happy in your domestic rela-tions," he added. "I advise you to shut up your niece and hang your son, if you are fortunate enough to find him."

Laubardemont replied with a hideous laugh:

"As for this idiot here, I am going to give her to an ex-secret judge, at present a smuggler in the Pyrenees at Oleron. He can do what he pleases with her— make her a servant in his *posada*, for instance. I care not, so that my lord never hears of her."

Jeanne de Belfiel, her head hanging down, gave no

sign of sensibility. Every glimmer of reason was extinguished in her; one word alone remained upon her lips, and this she continually pronounced.

"The judge! the judge! the judge!" she murmured, and was silent.

Her uncle and Joseph threw her, almost like a sack of corn, on one of the horses which were led up by two servants. Laubardemont mounted another, and prepared to leave the camp, wishing to get into the mountains before day.

"A good journey to you!" he said to Joseph. "Execute your business well in Paris. I commend to you Orestes and Pylades."

"A good journey to you!" answered the other. "I commend to you Cassandra and Œdipus."

"Oh! he has neither killed his father nor married his mother."

"But he is on the high-road to those little pleasantries."

"Adieu, my reverend Father!"

"Adieu, my venerable friend!"

Then each added aloud, but in suppressed tones:

"Adieu, assassin of the gray robe! During thy absence I shall have the ear of the Cardinal."

"Adieu, villain in the red robe! Go thyself and destroy thy cursed family. Finish shedding that portion of thy blood that is in others' veins. That share which remains in thee, I will take charge of. Ha! a well-employed night!"

CHAPTER XIV

THE RIOT

Le danger, Sire, est pressant et universel, et au delà de tous les calculs de la prudence humaine.—MIRABEAU, *Adresse au Roi.*

"THUS with imagin'd wing our swift scene flies,
  In motion of no less celerity
  Than that of thought,"

exclaims the immortal Shakespeare in the chorus of one of his tragedies.

  " Suppose that you have seen
    The well-appointed king
Embark his royalty; and his brave fleet
With silken streamers the young Phœbus fanning.

    .   .   .   .

                   . . . behold,
And follow."

With this poetic movement he traverses time and space, and transports at will the attentive assembly to the theatre of his sublime scenes.

We shall avail ourselves of the same privilege, though without the same genius. No more than he shall we seat ourselves upon the tripod of the unities, but merely casting our eyes upon Paris and the old dark palace of the Louvre, we will at once pass over the

[230]

space of two hundred leagues and the period of two years.

Two years! what changes may they not have upon men, upon their families, and, above all, in that great and so troublous family of nations, whose long alliances a single day suffices to destroy, whose wars are ended by a birth, whose peace is broken by a death! We ourselves have beheld kings returning to their dwelling on a spring day; that same day a vessel sailed for a voyage of two years. The navigator returned. The kings were seated upon their thrones; nothing seemed to have taken place in his absence, and yet God had deprived those kings of a hundred days of their reign.

But nothing was changed for France in 1642, the epoch to which we turn, except her fears and her hopes. The future alone had changed its aspect. Before again beholding our personages, we must contemplate at large the state of the kingdom.

The powerful unity of the monarchy was rendered still more imposing by the misfortunes of the neighboring States. The revolutions in England, and those in Spain and Portugal, rendered the "peace" which France enjoyed still more admired. Strafford and Olivarès, overthrown or defeated, aggrandized the immovable Richelieu.

Six formidable armies, reposing upon their triumphant weapons, served as a rampart to the kingdom. Those of the north, in league with Sweden, had put the Imperialists to flight, still pursued by the spirit of Gustavus Adolphus, those on the frontiers of Italy had in Piedmont received the keys of the towns which had been defended by Prince Thomas; and those which strengthened the chain of the Pyrenees held in check revolted Catalonia, and chafed before Perpignan, which they were not allowed to take. The interior was not happy, but tranquil. An invisible genius seemed to have maintained this calm, for the King, mortally sick, languished at St.-Germain with a young favorite; and the Cardinal was, they said, dying at Narbonne. Some deaths, however, betrayed that he yet lived; and at intervals, men falling as if struck by a poisonous blast recalled to mind the invisible power.

St.-Preuil, one of Richelieu's enemies, had just laid his "iron head" upon the scaffold without shame or fear, as he himself said on mounting it.

Meantime, France seemed to govern herself, for the prince and the minister had been separated a long time; and of these two sick men, who hated each other, one never had held the reins of State, the other no longer showed his power—he was no longer named in the public acts; he appeared no longer in the government, and seemed effaced everywhere; he slept, like the spider surrounded by his webs.

If some events and some revolutions had taken place during these two years, it must have been in hearts; it must have been some of those occult changes from which, in monarchies without firm foundation, terrible overthrows and long and bloody dissensions arise.

To enlighten ourselves, let us glance at the old black building of the unfinished Louvre, and listen to the conversation of those who inhabited it and those who surrounded it.

It was the month of December; a rigorous winter had afflicted Paris, where the misery and inquietude of the people were extreme. However, curiosity was still alive, and they were eager for the spectacles given by the court. Their poverty weighed less heavily upon them while they contemplated the agitations of the rich. Their tears were less bitter on beholding the struggles of power; and the blood of the nobles which reddened their streets, and seemed the only blood worthy of being shed, made them bless their own obscurity. Already had tumultuous scenes and conspicuous assassinations proved the monarch's weakness, the absence and approaching end of the minister, and, as a kind of prologue to the bloody comedy of the Fronde, sharpened the malice and even fired the passions of the Parisians. This confusion was not displeasing to them. Indifferent to the causes of the quarrels which were abstruse for them, they were not so with regard to individuals, and already began to regard the party chiefs with affection or hatred, not on account of the interest which they supposed them to take in the welfare of their class, but simply because as actors they pleased or displeased.

One night, especially, pistol- and gun-shots had been heard frequently in the city; the numerous patrols of the Swiss and the body-guards had even been attacked, and had met with some barricades in the tortuous streets of the Ile Nôtre-Dame; carts chained to the posts, and laden with barrels, prevented the cavaliers from advancing, and some musket-shots had wounded several men and horses. However, the town still slept, except the quarter which surrounded the Louvre, which was at this time inhabited by the Queen and M. le Duc d'Orléans. There everything announced a nocturnal expedition of a very serious nature.

It was two o'clock in the morning. It was freezing, and the darkness was intense, when a numerous assemblage stopped upon the quay, which was then hardly paved, and slowly and by degrees occupied the sandy ground that sloped down to the Seine. This troop was composed of about two hundred men; they were wrapped in large cloaks, raised by the long Spanish swords which they wore. Walking to and fro without preserving any order, they seemed to wait for events rather than to seek them. Many seated themselves, with their arms folded, upon the loose stones of the newly begun parapet; they preserved perfect silence. However, after a few minutes passed in this manner, a man, who appeared to come out of one of the vaulted doors of the Louvre, approached slowly, holding a dark-lantern, the light from which he turned upon the features of each individual, and which he blew out after finding the man he sought among them. He spoke to him in a whisper, taking him by the hand:

"Well, Olivier, what did Monsieur le Grand say to you? * Does all go well?"

* The master of the horse, Cinq-Mars, was thus named by abbreviation. This name will often occur in the course of the recital.

"Yes, I saw him yesterday at Saint-Germain. The old cat is very ill at Narbonne; he is going *ad patres*. But we must manage our affairs shrewdly, for it is not the first time that he has played the torpid. Have you people enough for this evening, my dear Fontrailles?"

"Be easy; Montrésor is coming with a hundred of Monsieur's gentlemen. You will recognize him; he will be disguised as a master-mason, with a rule in his hand. But, above all, do not forget the passwords. Do you know them all well, you and your friends?"

"Yes, all except the Abbé de Gondi, who has not yet arrived; but *Dieu me pardonne*, I think he is there himself! Who the devil would have known him?"

And here a little man without a cassock, dressed as a soldier of the French guards, and wearing a very black false moustache, slipped between them. He danced about with a joyous air, and rubbed his hands.

"*Vive Dieu!* all goes on well, my friend. Fiesco could not do better;" and rising upon his toes to tap Olivier upon the shoulder, he continued:

"Do you know that for a man who has just quitted the rank of pages, you don't manage badly, Sire Olivier d'Entraigues? and you will be among our illustrious men if we find a Plutarch. All is well organized; you arrive at the very moment, neither too soon nor too late, like a true party chief. Fontrailles, this young man will get on, I prophesy. But we must make haste; in two hours we shall have some of the archbishops of Paris, my uncle's parishioners. I have instructed them well; and they will cry, 'Long live Monsieur! Long live the Regency! No more of the Cardinal!' like madmen. They are good devotees, thanks to me, who have stirred them up. The King is very ill. Oh, all goes well, very well! I come from Saint-Germain. I have seen our friend Cinq-Mars; he is good, very good, still firm as a rock. Ah, that is what I call a man! How he has played with them with his careless and melancholy air! He is master of the court at present. The King, they say, is going to make him duke and peer. It is much talked of; but he still hesitates. We must decide that by our movement this evening. The will of the people! He must do the will of the people; we will make him hear it. It will be the death of Richelieu, you'll see. It is, above all, hatred of him which is to predominate in the cries, for that is the essential thing. That will at last decide our Gaston, who is still uncertain, is he not?"

"And how can he be anything else?" said Fontrailles. "If he were to take a resolution to-day in our favor it would be unfortunate."

"Why so?"

"Because we should be sure that to-morrow morning he would be against us."

"Never mind," replied the Abbé; "the Queen is firm."

"And she has heart also," said Olivier; "that gives me some hope for Cinq-Mars, who, it seems to me, has sometimes dared to frown when he looked at her."

"Child that you are, how little do you yet know of the court! Nothing can sustain him but the hand of the King, who loves him as a son; and as for the Queen, if her heart beats, it is for the past and not for the future. But these trifles are not to the purpose. Tell me, dear friend, are you sure of your young Advocate whom I see roaming about there? Is he all right?"

"Perfectly; he is an excellent Royalist. He would throw the Cardinal into the river in an instant. Besides, it is Fournier of Loudun; that is saying everything."

"Well, well, this is the kind of men we like. But take care of yourselves, Messieurs; some one comes from the Rue Saint-Honoré."

"Who goes there?" cried the foremost of the troop to some men who were advancing. "Royalists or Cardinalists?"

"Gaston and Le Grand," replied the newcomers, in low tones.

"It is Montrésor and Monsieur's people," said Fontrailles. "We may soon begin."

"Yes, *par la corbleu!*" said the newcomer, "for the Cardinalists will pass at three o'clock. Some one told us so just now."

"Where are they going?" said Fontrailles.

"There are more than two hundred of them to escort Monsieur de Chavigny, who is going to see the old cat at Narbonne, they say. They thought it safer to pass by the Louvre."

"Well, we will give him a velvet paw!" said the Abbé.

As he finished saying this, a noise of carriages and horses was heard. Several men in cloaks rolled an enormous stone into the middle of the street. The foremost cavaliers passed rapidly through the crowd, pistols in hand, suspecting that something unusual was going on; but the postilion, who drove the horses of the first carriage, ran upon the stone and fell.

"Whose carriage is this which thus crushes foot-passengers?" cried the cloakmen, all at once. "It is tyrannical. It can be no other than a friend of the Cardinal *de la Rochelle.*"*

"It is one who fears not the friends of the little Le Grand," exclaimed a voice from the open door, from which a man threw himself upon a horse.

"Drive these Cardinalists into the river!" cried a shrill, piercing voice.

This was a signal for the pistol-shots which were furiously exchanged on every side, and which lighted up this tumultuous and sombre scene. The clashing of swords and trampling of horses did not prevent the cries from being heard on one side: "Down with the minister! Long live the King! Long live Monsieur and Monsieur le Grand! Down with the red-stockings!" On the other: "Long live his Eminence! Long live the great Cardinal! Death to the factious! Long live the King!" For the name of the King presided over every hatred, as over every affection, at this strange time.

---

* During the long siege of La Rochelle, this name was given to Cardinal Richelieu, to ridicule his obstinacy in commanding as General-in-Chief, and claiming for himself the merit of taking that town.

The men on foot had succeeded, however, in placing the two carriages across the quay so as to make a rampart against Chavigny's horses, and from this, between the wheels, through the doors and springs, overwhelmed them with pistol-shots, and dismounted many. The tumult was frightful, but suddenly the gates of the Louvre were thrown open, and two squadrons of the body-guard came out at a trot. Most of them carried torches in their hands to light themselves and those they were about to attack. The scene changed. As the guards reached each of the men on foot, the latter was seen to stop, remove his hat, make himself known, and name himself; and the guards withdrew, sometimes saluting him, and sometimes shaking him by the hand. This succor to Chavigny's carriages was then almost useless, and only served to augment the confusion. The body-guards, as if to satisfy their consciences, rushed through the throng of duellists, saying:

"Gentlemen, gentlemen, be moderate!"

But when two gentlemen had decidedly crossed swords, and were in active conflict, the guard who beheld them stopped to judge the fight, and sometimes even to favor the one who he thought was of his opinion, for this body, like all France, had their Royalists and their Cardinalists.

The windows of the Louvre were lighted one after another, and many women's heads were seen behind the little lozenge-shaped panes, attentively watching the combat.

Numerous Swiss patrols came out with flambeaux.

These soldiers were easily distinguished by an odd uniform. The right sleeve was striped blue and red, and the silk stocking of the right leg was red; the left side was striped with blue, red, and white, and the stocking was white and red. It had, no doubt, been hoped in the royal château that this foreign troop would disperse the crowd, but they were mistaken. These impassible soldiers coldly and exactly executed, without going beyond, the orders they had received, circulating symmetrically among the armed groups, which they divided for a moment, returning before the gate with perfect precision, and resuming their ranks as on parade, without informing themselves whether the enemies among whom they had passed had rejoined or not.

But the noise, for a moment appeased, became general by reason of personal disputes. In every direction challenges, insults, and imprecations were heard. It seemed as if nothing but the destruction of one of the two parties could put an end to the combat, when loud cries, or rather frightful howls, raised the tumult to its highest pitch. The Abbé de Gondi, dragging a cavalier by his cloak to pull him down, exclaimed:

"Here are my people! Fontrailles, now you will see something worth while! Look! look already who they run! It is really charming."

And he abandoned his hold, and mounted upon a stone to contemplate the manœuvres of his troops, crossing his arms with the importance of a General of an army. Day was beginning to break, and from the end of the Ile St.-Louis a crowd of men, women, and children of the lowest dregs of the people was seen rapidly advancing, casting toward heaven and the Louvre strange vociferations. Girls carried long swords; children dragged great halberds and pikes of the time of the League; old women in rags pulled by cords old carts full of rusty and broken arms; workmen of every trade, the greater number drunk, followed, armed with clubs, forks, lances, shovels, torches, stakes, crooks, levers, sabres, and spits. They sang and howled alternately, counterfeiting with atrocious yells the cries of a cat, and carrying as a flag one of these animals suspended from a pole and wrapped in a red rag, thus representing the Cardinal, whose taste for cats was generally known. Public criers rushed about, red and breathless, throwing on the pavement and sticking up on the parapets, the posts, the walls of the houses, and even on the palace, long satires in short stanzas upon the personages of the time. Butcher-boys and scullions, carrying large cutlasses, beat the charge upon saucepans, and dragged in the mud a newly slaughtered pig, with the red cap of a chorister on its head. Young and vigorous men, dressed as women, and painted with a coarse vermilion, were yelling, "We are mothers of families ruined by Richelieu! Death to the Cardinal!" They carried in their arms figures of straw that looked like children, which they threw into the river.

When this disgusting mob overran the quays with its thousands of imps, it produced a strange effect upon the combatants, and entirely contrary to that expected by their patron. The enemies on both sides lowered their arms and separated. Those of Monsieur and Cinq-Mars were revolted at seeing themselves succored by such auxiliaries, and, themselves aiding the Cardinal's gentlemen to remount their horses and to gain their carriages, and their valets to convey the wounded to them, gave their adversaries personal rendezvous to terminate their quarrel upon a ground more secret and more worthy of them. Ashamed of the superiority of numbers and the ignoble troops which they seemed to command, foreseeing, perhaps, for the first time the fearful consequences of their political machinations, and what was the scum they were stirring up, they withdrew, drawing their large hats over their eyes, throwing their cloaks over their shoulders, and avoiding the daylight.

"You have spoiled all, my dear Abbé, with this mob," said Fontrailles, stamping his foot, to Gondi, who was already sufficiently nonplussed; "your good uncle has fine parishioners!"

"It is not my fault," replied Gondi, in a sullen tone; "these idiots came an hour too late. Had they arrived in the night, they would not have been seen, which spoils the effect somewhat, to speak the truth (for I grant that daylight is detrimental to them), and we would only have heard the voice of the people: *Vox populi, vox Dei.* Nevertheless, no great harm has been done. They will by their numbers give us the means of escaping without being known, and, after all, our task is ended; we did not wish the death of the sinner. Chavigny and his men are worthy fellows, whom I love; if he is only slightly wounded, so much the better. Adieu; I am going to see Monsieur de Bouillon, who has arrived from Italy."

"Olivier," said Fontrailles, "go at once to Saint-Germain with Fournier and Ambrosio; I will go and give an account to Monsieur, with Montrésor."

All separated, and disgust accomplished, with these high-born men, what force could not bring about.

Thus ended this fray, likely to bring forth great misfortunes. No one was killed in it. The cavaliers, having gained a few scratches and lost a few purses, resumed their route by the side of the carriages along the by-streets; the others escaped, one by one, through the populace they had attracted. The miserable wretches who composed it, deprived of the chief of the troops, still remained two hours, yelling and screaming until the effect of their wine was gone, and the cold had extinguished at once the fire of their blood and that of their enthusiasm. At the windows of the houses, on the quay of the city, and along the walls, the thoughtful and genuine people of Paris watched with a sorrowful air and in mournful silence these preludes of disorder; while the various bodies of merchants, dressed in black and preceded by their provosts, walked slowly and courageously through the populace toward the Palais de Justice, where the parliament was to assemble, to make complaint of these terrible nocturnal scenes.

The apartments of Gaston d'Orléans were in great confusion. This Prince occupied the wing of the Louvre parallel with the Tuileries; and his windows looked into the court on one side, and on the other over a mass of little houses and narrow streets which almost entirely covered the place. He had risen precipitately, awakened suddenly by the report of the firearms, had thrust his feet into large square-toed slippers with high heels, and, wrapped in a large silk dressing-gown, covered with golden ornaments embroidered in relief, walked to and fro in his bedroom, sending every minute a fresh lackey to see what was going on, and ordering them immediately to go for the Abbé de la Rivière, his general counsellor; but he was unfortunately out of Paris. At every pistol-shot this timid Prince rushed to the windows, without seeing anything but some flambeaux, which were carried quickly along. It was in vain he was told that the cries he heard were in his favor; he did not cease to walk up and down the apartments, in the greatest disorder—his long black hair dishevelled, and his blue eyes open and enlarged by disquiet and terror. He was still thus when Montrésor and Fontrailles at length arrived and found him beating his breast, and repeating a thousand times, "*Mea culpa, mea culpa!*"

"You have come at last!" he exclaimed from a distance, running to meet them. "Come! quick! What is going on? What are they doing there? Who are these assassins? What are these cries?"

"They cry, 'Long live Monsieur!' "

Gaston, without appearing to hear, and holding the door of his chamber open for an instant, that his voice might reach the galleries in which were the people of his household, continued to cry with all his strength, gesticulating violently:

"I know nothing of all this, and I have authorized nothing. I will not hear anything! I will not know anything! I will never enter into any project! These are rioters who make all this noise; do not speak to me of them, if you wish to be well received here. I am the enemy of no man; I detest such scenes!"

Fontrailles, who knew the man with whom he had to deal, said nothing, but entered with his friend, that Monsieur might have time to discharge his first fury; and when all was said, and the door carefully shut, he began to speak:

"Monseigneur," said he, "we come to ask you a thousand pardons for the impertinence of these people, who will persist in crying out that they desire the death of your enemy, and that they would even wish to make you regent should we have the misfortune to lose his Majesty. Yes, the people are always frank in their discourse; but they are so numerous that all our efforts could not restrain them. It was truly a cry from the heart—an explosion of love, which reason could not restrain, and which escaped all bounds."

"But what has happened, then?" interrupted Gaston, somewhat calmed. "What have they been doing these four hours that I have heard them?"

"That love," said Montrésor, coldly, "as Monsieur de Fontrailles had the honor of telling you, so escaped all rule and bounds that we ourselves were carried away by it, and felt seized with that enthusiasm which always transports us at the mere name of Monsieur, and which leads us on to things which we had not premeditated."

"But what, then, have you done?" said the Prince.

"Those things," replied Fontrailles, "of which Monsieur de Montrésor had the honor to speak to Monsieur are precisely those which I foresaw here yesterday evening, when I had the honor of conversing with you."

"That is not the question," interrupted Gaston. "You can not say that I have ordered or authorized anything. I meddle with nothing; I know nothing of government."

"I admit," continued Fontrailles, "that your Highness ordered nothing, but you permitted me to tell you that I foresaw that this night would be a troubled one about two o'clock, and I hoped that your astonishment would not have been too great."

The Prince, recovering himself little by little, and seeing that he did not alarm the two champions, having also upon his conscience and reading in their eyes the recollection of the consent which he had given them the evening before, sat down upon the side of his bed, crossed his arms, and, looking at them with the air of a judge, again said in a commanding tone:

"But what, then, have you done?"

"Why, hardly anything, Monseigneur," said Fontrailles. "Chance led us to meet in the crowd some of our friends who had a quarrel with Monsieur de Chavigny's coachman, who was driving over them. A few hot words ensued and rough gestures, and a few scratches, which kept Monsieur de Chavigny waiting, and that is all."

"Absolutely all," repeated Montrésor.

"What, all?" exclaimed Gaston, much moved, and tramping about the chamber. "And is it, then, nothing to stop the carriage of a friend of the Cardinal-Duke? I do not like such scenes. I have already told you so. I do not hate the Cardinal; he is certainly a great politician, a very great politician. You have compromised me horribly; it is known that Montrésor is with me. If he has been recognized, they will say that I sent him."

"Chance," said Montrésor, "threw in my way this peasant's dress, which Monsieur may see under my cloak, and which, for that reason, I preferred to any other."

Gaston breathed again.

"You are sure, then, that you have not been recognized. You understand, my dear friend, how painful it would be to me. You must admit yourself——"

"Sure of it!" exclaimed the Prince's gentleman. "I would stake my head and my share in Paradise that no one has seen my features or called my by my name."

"Well," continued Gaston, again seating himself on his bed, and assuming a calmer air, in which even a slight satisfaction was visible, "tell me, then, what has happened."

Fontrailles took upon himself the recital, in which, as we may suppose, the populace played a great part and Monsieur's people none, and in his peroration he said:

"From our windows even, Monseigneur, respectable mothers of families might have been seen, driven by despair, throwing their children into the Seine, cursing Richelieu."

"Ah, it is dreadful!" exclaimed the Prince, indignant, or feigning to be so, and to believe in these excesses. "Is it, then, true that he is so generally detested? But we must allow that he deserves it. What! his ambition and avarice have, then, reduced to this extremity the good inhabitants of Paris, whom I love so much."

"Yes, Monseigneur," replied the orator. "And it is not Paris alone, it is all France, which, with us, entreats you to decide upon delivering her from this tyrant. All is ready; nothing is wanting but a sign from your august head to annihilate this pygmy, who has attempted to assault the royal house itself."

"Alas! Heaven is my witness that I myself forgive him!" answered Gaston, raising up his eyes. "But I can no longer bear the cries of the people. Yes, I will help them; that is to say," continued the Prince, "so that my dignity is not compromised, and that my name does not appear in the matter."

"Well, but it is precisely that which we want," exclaimed Fontrailles, a little more at his ease.

"See, Monseigneur, there are already some names to put after yours, who will not fear to sign. I will tell you them immediately, if you wish it."

"But—but," said the Duc d'Orléans, timidly, "do you know that it is a conspiracy which you propose to me so coolly?"

"Fie, Monseigneur, men of honor like us! a conspiracy! Oh! not at all; a league at the utmost, a slight combination to give a direction to the unanimous wish of the nation and the court—that is all."

"But that is not so clear, for, after all, this affair will be neither general nor public; therefore, it is a conspiracy. You will not avow that you are concerned in it."

"I, Monseigneur! Excuse me to all the world, since the kingdom is already in it, and I am of the kingdom. And who would not sign his name after that of Messieurs de Bouillon and Cinq-Mars?"

"After, perhaps, not before," said Gaston, fixing his eyes upon Fontrailles more keenly than he had expected.

The latter hesitated a moment.

"Well, then, what would Monseigneur do should I tell him the names after which he could sign his?"

"Ha! ha! this is amusing," answered the Prince, laughing; "know you not that above mine there are not many? I see but one."

"And if there be one, will Monseigneur promise to sign that of Gaston beneath it?"

"Ah, *parbleu!* with all my heart. I risk nothing there, for I see none but that of the King, who surely is not of the party."

"Well, from this moment permit us," said Montrésor, "to take you at your word, and deign at present to consent to two things only: to see Monsieur de Bouillon in the Queen's apartments, and Monsieur the master of the horse at the King's palace."

ALFRED DE VIGNY

"Agreed!" said Monsieur, gayly, tapping Montrésor on the shoulder. "I will to-day wait on my sister-in-law at her toilette, and I will invite my brother to hunt the stag with me at Chambord."

The two friends asked nothing further, and were themselves surprised at their work. They never had seen so much resolution in their chief. Accordingly, fearing to lead him to a topic which might divert him from the path he had adopted, they hastened to turn the conversation upon other subjects, and retired in delight, leaving as their last words in his ear that they relied upon his keeping his promise.

CHAPTER XV

Les reines ont été vues pleurant comme de simples femmes.—
CHATEAUBRIAND.

Qu'il est doux d'être belle alors qu'on est aimée.—DELPHINE
GAY.

HILE a prince was thus reassured
with difficulty by those who sur-
rounded him, and allowed them to
see a terror which might have proved
contagious, a princess more exposed
to accidents, more isolated by the
indifference of her husband, weaker
by nature and by the timidity which
is the result of the absence of happiness, on her side
set the example of the calmest courage and the most
pious resignation, and tranquillized her terrified suite;
this was the Queen. Having slept hardly an hour,
she heard shrill cries behind the doors and the thick
tapestries of her chamber. She ordered her women
to open the door, and the Duchesse de Chevreuse, in
her night attire, and wrapped in a great cloak, fell,
nearly fainting, at the foot of her bed, followed by four
of her ladies-in-waiting and three of the women of
the bed-chamber. Her delicate feet were bare, and
bleeding from a wound she had received in running.

She cried, weeping like a child, that a pistol-shot had broken her shutters and her window-panes, and had wounded her; she entreated the Queen to send her into exile, where she would be more tranquil than in a country where they wished to assassinate her because she was the friend of her Majesty.

Her hair was in great disorder, and fell to her feet. It was her chief beauty; and the young Queen thought that this toilette was less the result of chance than might have been imagined.

"Well, my dear, what has happened?" she said to her with *sang-froid*. "You look like a Magdalen, but in her youth, and before she repented. It is probable that if they wish to harm any one here it is I; calm yourself."

"No, Madame! save me, protect me! it is Richelieu who pursues me, I am sure!"

The sound of pistols, which was then heard more distinctly, convinced the Queen that the terrors of Madame de Chevreuse were not vain.

"Come and dress me, Madame de Motteville!" cried she. But that lady had completely lost her self-possession, and, opening one of those immense ebony coffers which then answered the purpose of wardrobes, took from it a casket of the Princess's diamonds to save it, and did not listen to her. The other women had seen on a window the reflection of torches, and, imagining that the palace was on fire, threw jewels, laces, golden vases, and even the china, into sheets which they intended to lower into the street. At this moment Madame de Guémenée arrived, a little more dressed than the Duchesse de Chevreuse, but taking events still more tragically. Her terror inspired the Queen with a slight degree of fear, because of the ceremonious and placid character she was known to possess. She entered without curtseying, pale as a spectre, and said with volubility:

"Madame, it is time to make our confession. The Louvre is attacked, and all the populace are arriving from the city, I have been told."

Terror silenced and rendered motionless all the persons present.

"We shall die!" exclaimed the Duchesse de Chevreuse, still on her knees. "Ah, my God! why did I leave England? Yes, let us confess. I confess aloud. I have loved—I have been loved by——"

"Well," said the Queen, "I do not undertake to hear your confession to the end. That would not perhaps be the least of my dangers, of which, however, you think little."

The coolness of Anne of Austria, and this last severe observation, however, restored a little calm to this beautiful personage, who rose in confusion, and perceiving the disordered state of her toilet, went to repair it as she best could in a closet near by.

"Doña Stefania," said the Queen to one of her women, the only Spaniard whom she had retained, "go seek the captain of the guards. It is time that I should see men at last, and hear something reasonable."

She said this in Spanish, and the mystery of this order, spoken in a tongue which the ladies did not understand, restored those in the chamber to their senses.

The waiting-woman was telling her beads, but she rose from the corner of the alcove in which she had sought refuge, and hastened to obey her mistress.

The signs of revolt and the evidences of terror became meantime more distinct. In the great court of the Louvre was heard the trampling of the horses of the guards, the orders of the chiefs, the rolling of the Queen's carriages, which were being prepared, should it be necessary to fly. The rattling of the iron chains dragged along the pavement to form barricades in case of an attack, hurried steps in the corridor, the clash of arms, the confused cries of the people, which rose and fell, went and came again, like the noise of the waves and the winds. The door once more opened, and this time it was to admit a very charming person.

"I expected you, dear Marie," said the Queen, extending her arms to the Duchesse de Mantua. "You have been more courageous than any of us; you are attired fit to be seen by all the court."

"I was not in bed, fortunately," replied the young Princesse de Gonzaga, casting down her eyes. "I saw all these people from the windows. O Madame, Madame, fly! I implore you to escape by the secret stairway, and let us remain in your place. They might take one of us for the Queen." And she added, with tears, "I have heard cries of death. Fly, Madame! I have no throne to lose. You are the daughter, the wife, and the mother of kings. Save yourself, and leave us here!"

"You have more to lose than I, *m'amie*, in beauty, youth, and, I hope, in happiness," said the Queen, with a gracious smile, giving the Duchess her beautiful hands to kiss. "Remain in my alcove and welcome; but we will both remain there. The only service I accept from you, my sweet child, is to bring to my bed that little golden casket which my poor Motteville has left on the ground, and which contains all that I hold most precious."

Then, as she took it, she whispered in Marie's ear:

"Should any misfortune happen to me, swear that you will throw it into the Seine."

"I will obey you, Madame, as my benefactress and my second mother," Marie answered, weeping.

The sound of the conflict redoubled on the quays, and the windows reflected the flash of the firearms, of which they heard the explosion. The captain of the guards and the captain of the Swiss sent for orders from the Queen through Doña Stefania.

"I permit them to enter," said the Queen. "Stand aside, ladies. I am a man in a moment like this; and I ought to be so." Then, raising the bed-curtains, she continued, addressing the two officers:

"Gentlemen, first remember that you answer with your heads for the life of the princes, my children. You know that, Monsieur de Guitaut?"

"I sleep across their doorway, Madame; but this disturbance does not threaten either them or your Majesty."

"Very well; do not think of me until after them," interrupted the Queen, "and protect indiscriminately all who are threatened. You also hear me, Monsieur de Bassompierre; you are a gentleman. Forget that your uncle is yet in the Bastille, and do your duty by the grandsons of the dead King, his friend."

He was a young man, with a frank, open countenance.

"Your Majesty," said he, with a slight German accent, "may see that I have forgotten my family, and not yours." And he displayed his left hand despoiled of two fingers, which had just been cut off. "I have still another hand," said he, bowing and withdrawing with Guitaut.

The Queen, much moved, rose immediately, and, despite the prayers of the Princesse de Guémenée, the tears of Marie de Gonzaga, and the cries of Madame de Chevreuse, insisted upon placing herself at the window, and half opened it, leaning upon the shoulder of the Duchesse de Mantua.

"What do I hear?" she said. "They are crying, 'Long live the King! Long live the Queen!' "

The people, imagining they recognized her, redoubled their cries at this moment, and shouted louder than ever, "Down with the Cardinal! Long live Monsieur le Grand!"

Marie shuddered.

"What is the matter with you?" said the Queen, observing her. But as she did not answer, and trembled in every limb, this good and gentle Princess appeared not to perceive it; and, paying the greatest attention to the cries and movements of the populace, she even exaggerated an inquietude which she had not felt since the first name had reached her ear. An hour later, when they came to tell her that the crowd only awaited a sign from her hand to withdraw, she waved it graciously, and with an air of satisfaction. But this joy was far from being complete, for her heart was still troubled by many things, and, above all, by the presentiment of the regency. The more she leaned forward to show herself, the more she beheld the revolting scenes which the increasing light revealed. Terror took possession of her soul as it became necessary to appear calm and confiding; and her heart was saddened at the very gayety of her words and countenance. Exposed to all eyes, she felt herself a mere woman, and shuddered in looking at that people whom she would soon perhaps be called upon to govern, and who already took upon themselves to demand the death of ministers, and to call upon their Queen to appear before them.

She saluted them.

A hundred and fifty years later that salute was repeated by another princess, like herself of Austrian blood, and Queen of France. The monarchy without foundation, such as Richelieu made it, was born and died between these two salutes.

The Princess at last closed her windows, and hastened to dismiss her timid suite. The thick curtains fell again over the barred windows; and the room was no longer lighted by a day which was odious to her. Large white wax flambeaux burned in candelabra, in the form of golden arms, which stand out from the framed and flowered tapestries with which the walls were hung. She remained alone with Marie de Mantua; and reëntering with her the enclosure which was formed by the royal balustrade, she fell upon her bed, fatigued by her courage and her smiles, and burst into tears, leaning her head upon her pillow. Marie, on her knees upon a velvet footstool, held one of her hands in both hers, and without daring to speak first, leaned her head tremblingly upon it; for until that moment, tears never had been seen in the Queen's eyes.

They remained thus for some minutes. The Princess, then raising herself up by a painful effort, spoke:

"Do not afflict yourself, my child; let me weep. It is such a relief to one who reigns! If you pray to God for me, ask Him to grant me sufficient strength not to hate the enemy who pursues me everywhere, and who will destroy the royal family of France and the monarchy by his boundless ambition. I recognize him in all that has taken place; I see him in this tumultuous revolt."

"What, Madame! is he not at Narbonne?—for it is the Cardinal of whom you speak, no doubt; and have you not heard that these cries were for you, and against him?"

"Yes, *m'amie*, he is three hundred leagues away from us, but his fatal genius keeps guard at the door. If these cries have been heard, it is because he has allowed them; if these men were assembled, it is because they have not yet reached the hour which he has destined for their destruction. Believe me, I know him; and I have dearly paid for the knowledge

[258]

of that dark soul. It has cost me all the power of my rank, the pleasures of my age, the affection of my family and even the heart of my husband. He has isolated me from the whole world. He now confines me within a barrier of honors and respect; and formerly he dared, to the scandal of all France, to bring an accusation against myself. They examined my papers, they interrogated me, they made me sign myself guilty, and ask the King's pardon for a fault of which I was ignorant; and I owed to the devotion, and the perhaps eternal imprisonment of a faithful servant,* the preservation of this casket which you have saved for me. I read in your looks that you think me too fearful; but do not deceive yourself, as all the court now does. Be sure, my dear child, that this man is everywhere, and that he knows even our thoughts."

"What, Madame! does he know all that these men have cried under your windows, and the names of those who sent them?"

"Yes; no doubt he knows it, or has foreseen it. He permits it; he authorizes it, to compromise me in the King's eyes, and keep him forever separated from me. He would complete my humiliation."

"But the King has not loved him for two years; he loves another."

The Queen smiled; she gazed some time in silence upon the pure and open features of the beautiful Marie, and her look, full of candor, which was languidly

---

* His name was Laporte. Neither the fear of torture nor the hope of the Cardinal's reward could draw from him one word of the Queen's secrets.

raised toward her. She smoothed back the black curls which shaded her noble forehead, and seemed to rest her eyes and her soul in looking at the charming innocence displayed upon so lovely a face. She kissed her cheek, and resumed:

"You do not suspect, my poor child, a sad truth. It is that the King loves no one, and that those who appear the most in favor will be the soonest abandoned by him, and thrown to him who engulfs and devours all."

"Ah, *mon Dieu!* what is this you tell me?"

"Do you know how many he has destroyed?" continued the Queen, in a low voice, and looking into her eyes as if to read in them all her thoughts, and to make her own penetrate there. "Do you know the end of his favorites? Have you been told of the exile of Baradas; of that of Saint-Simon; of the convent of Mademoiselle de la Fayette, the shame of Madame d'Hautfort, the death of Chalais? All have fallen before an order from Richelieu to his master. Without this favor, which you mistake for friendship, their lives would have been peaceful. But this favor is mortal; it is a poison. Look at this tapestry, which represents Sémélé. The favorites of Louis XIII resemble that woman; his attachment devours like this fire, which dazzles and consumes her."

But the young Duchess was no longer in a condition to listen to the Queen. She continued to fix her large, dark eyes upon her, dimmed by a veil of tears; her hands trembled in those of Anne of Austria, and her lips quivered with convulsive agitation.

"I am very cruel, am I not, Marie?" continued the Queen, in an extremely sweet voice, and caressing her like a child from whom one would draw an avowal. "Oh, yes; no doubt I am very wicked! Your heart is full; you can not bear it, my child. Come, tell me; how do matters stand with you and Monsieur de Cinq-Mars?"

At this word grief found a vent, and, still on her knees at the Queen's feet, Marie in her turn shed upon the bosom of the good Princess a deluge of tears, with childish sobs and so violent an agitation of her head and her beautiful shoulders that it seemed as if her heart would break. The Queen waited a long time for the end of this first emotion, rocking her in her arms as if to appease her grief, frequently repeating, "My child, my child, do not afflict yourself thus!"

"Ah, Madame!" she exclaimed, "I have been guilty toward you; but I did not reckon upon that heart. I have done wrong, and I shall perhaps be punished severely for it. But, alas! how shall I venture to confess to you, Madame? It was not so much to open my heart to you that was difficult; it was to avow to you that I had need to read there myself."

The Queen reflected a moment, laying her finger upon her lips. "You are right," she then replied; "you are quite right. Marie, it is always the first word which is the most difficult to say; and that difficulty often destroys us. But it must be so; and without this rule one would be often wanting in dignity. Ah, how difficult it is to reign! To-day I would descend into your heart, but I come too late to do you good."

Marie de Mantua hung her head without making any reply.

"Must I encourage you to speak?" said the Queen. "Must I remind you that I have almost adopted you for my eldest daughter? that after seeking to unite you with the King's brother, I prepared for you the throne of Poland? Must I do more, Marie? Yes, I must, I will. If afterward you do not open your whole heart to me, I have misjudged you. Open this golden casket; here is the key. Open it fearlessly; do not tremble as I do."

The Duchesse de Mantua obeyed with hesitation, and beheld in this little chased coffer a knife of rude form, the handle of which was of iron, and the blade very rusty. It lay upon some letters carefully folded, upon which was the name of Buckingham. She would have lifted them; Anne of Austria stopped her.

"Seek nothing further," she said; "that is all the treasure of the Queen. And it is a treasure; for it is the blood of a man who lives no longer, but who lived for me. He was the most beautiful, the bravest, the most illustrious of the nobles of Europe. He covered himself with the diamonds of the English crown to please me. He raised up a fierce war and armed fleets, which he himself commanded, that he might have the happiness of once fighting him who was my husband. He traversed the seas to gather a flower upon which I had trodden, and ran the risk of death to kiss and bathe with his tears the foot of this bed in the presence of two of my ladies-in-waiting. Shall I say more? Yes, I will say it to you—I loved him! I love him still in the past more than I could love him in the present. He never knew it, never divined it. This face, these eyes, were marble toward him, while my heart burned and was breaking with grief; but I was the Queen of France!" Here Anne of Austria forcibly grasped Marie's arm. "Dare now to complain," she continued, "if you have not yet ventured to speak to me of your love, and dare now to be silent when I have told you these things!"

"Ah, yes, Madame, I shall dare to confide my grief to you, since you are to me——"

"A friend, a woman!" interrupted the Queen. "I was a woman in my terror, which put you in possession of a secret unknown to the whole world. I am a woman by a love which survives the man I loved. Speak; tell me! It is now time."

"It is too late, on the contrary," replied Marie, with a forced smile. "Monsieur de Cinq-Mars and I are united forever."

"Forever!" exclaimed the Queen. "Can you mean it? And your rank, your name, your future—is all lost? Do you reserve this despair for your brother, the Duc de Bethel, and all the Gonzagas?"

"For more than four years I have thought of it. I am resolved; and for ten days we have been affianced."

"Affianced!" exclaimed the Queen, clasping her hands. "You have been deceived, Marie. Who would have dared this without the King's order? It is an intrigue which I will know. I am sure that you have been misled and deceived."

Marie hesitated a moment, and then said:

"Nothing is more simple, Madame, than our attachment. I inhabited, you know, the old château of Chaumont, with the Maréchale d'Effiat, the mother of Monsieur de Cinq-Mars. I had retired there to mourn the death of my father; and it soon happened that Monsieur de Cinq-Mars had to deplore the loss of his. In this numerous afflicted family, I saw his grief only, which was as profound as mine. All that he said, I had already thought, and when we spoke of our afflictions we found them wholly alike. As I had been the first to suffer, I was better acquainted with sorrow than he; and I endeavored to console him by telling him all that I had suffered, so that in pitying me he forgot himself. This was the beginning of our love, which, as you see, had its birth, as it were, between two tombs."

"God grant, my sweet, that it may have a happy termination!" said the Queen.

"I hope so, Madame, since you pray for me," continued Marie. "Besides, everything now smiles upon me; but at that time I was very miserable. The news arrived one day at the château that the Cardinal had called Monsieur de Cinq-Mars to the army. It seemed to me that I was again deprived of one of my relatives; and yet we were strangers. But Monsieur de Bassompierre spoke without ceasing of battles and death. I retired every evening in grief, and I wept during the night. I thought at first that my tears flowed for the past, but I soon perceived that it was for the future; and I felt that they could not be the same tears, since I wished to conceal them. Some time passed in the expectation of his departure. I saw him every day; and I pitied him for having to depart, because he repeated to me every instant that he would have wished to live eternally as he then did, in his own country and with us. He was thus without ambition until the day of his departure, because he knew not whether he was—whether he was—I dare not say it to your Majesty——"

Marie blushed, cast down her humid eyes, and smiled.

"Well!" said the Queen, "whether he was beloved, —is it not so?"

"And in the evening, Madame, he left, ambitious."

"That is evident, certainly. He left," said Anne of Austria, somewhat relieved; "but he has been back two years, and you have seen him?"

"Seldom, Madame," said the young Duchess, proudly; "and always in the presence of the priest, before whom I have promised to be the wife of no other than Cinq-Mars."

"Is it really, then, a marriage? Have you dared to do it? I shall inquire. But, Heaven, what faults! how many faults in the few words I have heard! Let me reflect upon them."

And, speaking aloud to herself, the Queen continued, her eyes and head bent in the attitude of reflection:

"Reproaches are useless and cruel if the evil is done. The past is no longer ours; let us think of the future.

Cinq-Mars is brave, able, and even profound in his ideas. I have observed that he has done much in two years, and I now see that it was for Marie. He comports himself well; he is worthy of her in my eyes, but not so in the eyes of Europe. He must rise yet higher. The Princesse de Mantua can not, may not, marry less than a prince. He must become one. By myself I can do nothing; I am not the Queen, I am the neglected wife of the King. There is only the Cardinal, the eternal Cardinal, and he is his enemy; and perhaps this disturbance——"

"Alas! it is the beginning of war between them. I saw it at once."

"He is lost then!" exclaimed the Queen, embracing Marie. "Pardon me, my child, for thus afflicting you; but in times like these we must see all and say all. Yes, he is lost if he does not himself overthrow this wicked man—for the King will not renounce him; force alone——"

"He will overthrow him, Madame. He will do it, if you will assist him. You are the divinity of France. Oh, I conjure you, protect the angel against the demon! It is your cause, that of your royal family, that of all your nation."

The Queen smiled.

"It is, above all, your cause, my child; and it is as such that I will embrace it to the utmost extent of my power. That is not great, as I have told you; but such as it is, I lend it to you entirely, provided, however, that this *angel* does not stoop to commit mortal sins," added she, with a meaning look. "I heard his name pronounced this night by voices most unworthy of him."

"Oh, Madame, I would swear that he knows nothing of it!"

"Ah, my child, do not speak of State affairs. You are not yet learned enough in them. Let me sleep, if I can, before the hour of my toilette. My eyes are burning, and yours also, perhaps."

Saying these words, the amiable Queen laid her head upon the pillow which covered the casket, and soon Marie saw her fall asleep through sheer fatigue. She then rose, and, seating herself in a great, tapestried, square armchair, clasped her hands upon her knees, and began to reflect upon her painful situation. Consoled by the aspect of her gentle protectress, she often raised her eyes to watch her slumber, and sent her in secret all the blessings which love showers upon those who protect it, sometimes kissing the curls of her blond hair, as if by this kiss she could convey to her soul all the ideas favorable to the thought ever present to her mind.

The Queen's slumber was prolonged, while Marie thought and wept. However, she remembered that at ten o'clock she must appear at the royal toilette before all the court. She resolved to cast aside reflection, to dry her tears, and she took a thick folio volume placed upon a table inlaid with enamel and medallions; it was the *Astrée* of M. d'Urfé—a work *de belle galanterie* adored by the fair prudes of the court. The unsophisticated and straightforward mind of Marie could not enter into these pastoral loves. She was too simple to understand the *bergères du Lignon*, too clever to be pleased at their discourse, and too impassioned to feel their tenderness. However, the great popularity of the romance so far influenced her that she sought to compel herself to take an interest in it; and, accusing herself internally every time that she felt the *ennui* which exhaled from the pages of the book, she ran through it with impatience to find something to please and transport her. An engraving arrested her attention. It represented the shepherdess Astrée with high-heeled shoes, a corset, and an immense farthingale, standing on tiptoe to watch floating down the river the tender Celadon, drowning himself in despair at having been somewhat coldly received in the morning. Without explaining to herself the reason of the taste and accumulated fallacies of this picture, she sought, in turning over the pages, something which could fix her attention; she saw the word "Druid."

"Ah! here is a great character," said she. "I shall no doubt read of one of those mysterious sacrificers of whom Britain, I am told, still preserves the monuments; but I shall see him sacrificing men. That would be a spectacle of horror; however, let us read it."

Saying this, Marie read with repugnance, knitting her brows, and nearly trembling, the following:

"The Druid Adamas delicately called the shepherds Pimandre, Ligdamont, and Clidamant, newly arrived from Calais. 'This adventure can not terminate,' said he, 'but by the extremity of love. The soul, when it loves, transforms itself into the object

beloved; it is to represent this that my agreeable enchantments
will show you in this fountain the nymph Sylvia, whom you all
three love. The high-priest Amasis is about to come from
Montbrison, and will explain to you the delicacy of this idea.
Go, then, gentle shepherds! If your desires are well regulated,
they will not cause you any torments; and if they are not so,
you will be punished by swoonings similar to those of Celadon,
and the shepherdess Galatea, whom the inconstant Hercules
abandoned in the mountains of Auvergne, and who gave her
name to the tender country of the Gauls; or you will be stoned
by the shepherdesses of Lignon, as was the ferocious Amidor.
The great nymph of this cave has made an enchantment.'"

The enchantment of the great nymph was complete
on the Princess, who had hardly sufficient strength to
find out with a trembling hand, toward the end of the
book, that the Druid Adamas was an ingenious alle-
gory, representing the Lieutenant-General of Montbrison, of the family of the Papons. Her weary eyes
closed, and the great book slipped from her lap to the
cushion of velvet upon which her feet were placed,
and where the beautiful Astréc and the gallant Celadon
reposed luxuriously, less immovable than Marie de
Mantua, vanquished by them and by profound slumber.

CHAPTER XVI

THE CONFUSION

Il faut, en France, beaucoup de fermeté et une grande étendue d'esprit pour se passer des charges et des emplois, et consentir ainsi à demeurer chez soiàne rien faire. Personne, presque, n'a assez de mérite pour jouer ce rôle avec dignité, ni assez de fonds pour remplir le rôle du temps, sans ce que le vulgaire appelle les *affaires*.

Il ne manque cependant à l'oisiveté du sage qu'un meilleur nom, et que méditer, parler, lire et être tranquille, s'appelât travailler.—LA BRUYÈRE.

URING this same morning, the various events of which we have seen in the apartments of Gaston d'Orléans and of the Queen, the calm and silence of study reigned in a modest cabinet of a large house near the Palais de Justice. A bronze lamp, of a gothic shape, struggling with the coming day, threw its red light upon a mass of papers and books which covered a large table; it lighted the bust of L'Hôpital, that of Montaigne the essayist, the President de Thou, and of King Louis XIII.

A fireplace sufficiently large for a man to enter and sit there was occupied by a large fire burning upon enormous andirons. Upon one of these was placed the foot of the studious De Thou, who, already risen,

[270]

examined with attention the new works of Descartes and Grotius. He was writing upon his knee his notes upon these books of philosophy and politics, which were then the general subjects of conversation; but at this moment the *Méditations Metaphysiques* absorbed all his attention. The philosopher of Touraine enchanted the young counsellor. Often, in his enthusiasm, he struck the book, uttering exclamations of admiration; sometimes he took a sphere placed near him, and, turning it with his fingers, abandoned himself to the most profound reveries of science; then, led by them to a still greater elevation of mind, he would suddenly throw himself upon his knees before a crucifix, placed upon the chimney-piece, because at the limits of the human mind he had found God. At other times he buried himself in his great armchair, so as to be nearly sitting upon his shoulders, and, placing his two hands upon his eyes, followed in his head the trace of the reasoning of René Descartes, from this idea of the first meditation:

"Suppose that we are asleep, and that all these particularities —that is, that we open our eyes, move our heads, spread our arms—are nothing but false illusions."—

to this sublime conclusion of the third:

"Only one thing remains to be said; it is that like the idea of myself, that of God is born and produced with me from the time I was created. And certainly it should not be thought strange that God, in creating me, should have implanted in me this idea, to be, as it were, the mark of the workman impressed upon his work."

These thoughts entirely occupied the mind of the young counsellor, when a loud noise was heard under the windows. He thought that some house on fire excited these prolonged cries, and hastened to look toward the wing of the building occupied by his mother and sisters; but all appeared to sleep there, and the chimneys did not even send forth any smoke, to attest that its inhabitants were even awake. He blessed Heaven for it; and, running to another window, he saw the people, whose exploits we have witnessed, hastening toward the narrow streets which led to the quay.

After examining this rabble of women and children, the ridiculous flag which led them, and the rude disguises of the men: "It is some popular *fête* or some carnival comedy," said he; and again returning to the corner of the fire, he placed a large almanac upon the table, and carefully sought in it what saint was honored that day. He looked in the column of the month of December; and, finding at the fourth day of this month the name of Ste.-Barbe, he remembered that he had seen several small cannons and barrels pass, and, perfectly satisfied with the explanation which he had given himself, he hastened to drive away the interruption which had called off his attention, and resumed his quiet studies, rising only to take a book from the shelves of his library, and, after reading in it a phrase, a line, or only a word, he threw it from him upon his table or on the floor, covered in this way with books or papers which he would not trouble himself to return to their places, lest he should break the thread of his reveries.

Suddenly the door was hastily opened, and a name was announced which he had distinguished among those at the bar — a man whom his connections with the magistracy had made personally known to him.

"And by what chance, at five o'clock in the morning, do I see Monsieur Fournier?" he cried. "Are there some unfortunates to defend, some families to be supported by the fruits of his talent, some error to dissipate in us, some virtue to awaken in our hearts? for these are of his accustomed works. You come, perhaps, to inform me of some fresh humiliation of our parliament. Alas! the secret chambers of the Arsenal are more powerful than the ancient magistracy of Clovis. The parliament is on its knees; all is lost, unless it is soon filled with men like yourself."

"Monsieur, I do not merit your praise," said the Advocate, entering, accompanied by a grave and aged man, enveloped like himself in a large cloak. "I deserve, on the contrary, your censure; and I am almost a penitent, as is Monsieur le Comte du Lude, whom you see here. We come to ask an asylum for the day."

"An asylum! and against whom?" said De Thou, making them sit down.

"Against the lowest people in Paris, who wish to have us for chiefs, and from whom we fly. It is odious; the sight, the smell, the ear, and the touch, above all, are too severely wounded by it," said M. du Lude, with a comical gravity. "It is too much!"

"Ah! too much, you say?" said De Thou, very much astonished, but not willing to show it.

"Yes," answered the Advocate; "really, between ourselves, Monsieur le Grand goes too far."

"Yes, he pushes things too fast. He will render all our projects abortive," added his companion.

"Ah! and you say he goes too far?" replied M. de Thou, rubbing his chin, more and more surprised.

Three months had passed since his friend Cinq-Mars had been to see him; and he, without feeling much disquieted about it—knowing that he was at St.-Germain in high favor, and never quitting the King—was far removed from the news of the court. Absorbed in his grave studies, he never heard of public events till they were forced upon his attention. He knew nothing of current life until the last moment, and often amused his intimate friends by his naïve astonishment—the more so that from a little worldly vanity he desired to have it appear as if he were fully acquainted with the course of events, and tried to conceal the surprise he experienced at every fresh intelligence. He was now in this situation, and to this vanity was added the feeling of friendship; he would not have it supposed that Cinq-Mars had been negligent toward him, and, for his friend's honor even, would appear to be aware of his projects.

"You know very well how we stand now," continued the Advocate.

"Yes, of course. Well?"

"Intimate as you are with him, you can not be ignorant that all has been organizing for a year past."

"Certainly, all has been organizing; but proceed."

"You will admit with us that Monsieur le Grand is wrong?"

"Ah, that is as it may be; but explain yourself. I shall see."

"Well, you know upon what we had agreed at the last conference of which he informed you?"

"Ah! that is to say—pardon me, I perceive it almost; but set me a little upon the track."

"It is useless; you no doubt remember what he himself recommended us to do at Marion de Lorme's?"

"To add no one to our list," said M. du Lude.

"Ah, yes, yes! I understand," said DeThou; "that appears reasonable, very reasonable, truly."

"Well," continued Fournier, "he himself has infringed this agreement; for this morning, besides the ragamuffins whom that ferret the Abbé de Gondi brought to us, there was some vagabond captain, who during the night struck with sword and poniard gentlemen of both parties, crying out at the top of his voice, '*A moi*, D'Aubijoux! You gained three thousand ducats from me; here are three sword-thrusts for you. *A moi*, La Chapelle! I will have ten drops of your blood in exchange for my ten pistoles!' and I myself saw him attack these gentlemen and many more of both sides, loyally enough, it is true—for he struck them only in front and on their guard—but with great success, and with a most revolting impartiality."

"Yes, Monsieur, and I was about to tell him my opinion," interposed De Lude, "when I saw him escape through the crowd like a squirrel, laughing greatly with some suspicious-looking men with dark, swarthy faces; I do not doubt, however, that Monsieur de Cinq-Mars sent him, for he gave orders to that Ambrosio whom you must know—that Spanish prisoner, that rascal whom he has taken for a servant. In faith, I am disgusted with all this; and I was not born to mingle with this *canaille*."

"This, Monsieur," replied Fournier, "is very different from the affair at Loudun. There the people only rose, without actually revolting; it was the sensible and estimable part of the populace, indignant at an assassination, and not heated by wine and money. It was a cry raised against an executioner—a cry of which one could honorably be the organ—and not these howlings of factious hypocrisy, of a mass of unknown people, the dregs of the mud and sewers of Paris. I confess that I am very tired of what I see; and I have come to entreat you to speak about it to Monsieur le Grand."

De Thou was very much embarrassed during this conversation, and sought in vain to understand what Cinq-Mars could have to do with the people, who appeared to him merely merrymaking; on the other hand, he persisted in not owning his ignorance. It was, however, complete; for the last time he had seen his friend, he had spoken only of the King's horses and stables, of hawking, and of the importance of the King's huntsmen in the affairs of the State, which did not seem to announce vast projects in which the people could take a part. He at last timidly ventured to say:

"Messieurs, I promise to do your commission;

meanwhile, I offer you my table and beds as long as you please. But to give my advice in this matter is very difficult. By the way, it was not the *fête* of Sainte-Barbe I saw this morning?"

"The Sainte-Barbe!" said Fournier.

"The Sainte-Barbe!" echoed Du Lude. "They burned powder."

"Oh, yes, yes! that is what Monsieur de Thou means," said Fournier, laughing; "very good, very good indeed! Yes, I think to-day is Sainte-Barbe."

De Thou was now altogether confused and reduced to silence; as for the others, seeing that they did not understand him, nor he them, they had recourse to silence.

They were sitting thus mute, when the door opened to admit the old tutor of Cinq-Mars, the Abbé Quillet, who entered, limping slightly. He looked very gloomy, retaining none of his former gayety in his air or language; but his look was still animated, and his speech energetic.

"Pardon me, my dear De Thou, that I so early disturb you in your occupations; it is strange, is it not, in a gouty invalid? Ah, time advances; two years ago I did not limp. I was, on the contrary, nimble enough at the time of my journey to Italy; but then fear gives legs as well as wings."

Then, retiring into the recess of a window, he signed De Thou to come to him.

"I need hardly remind you, my friend, who are in their secrets, that I affianced them a fortnight ago, as they have told you."

[277]

"Ah, indeed! Whom?" exclaimed poor De Thou, fallen from the Charybdis into the Scylla of astonishment.

"Come, come, don't affect surprise; you know very well whom," continued the Abbé. "But, faith, I fear I have been too complaisant with them, though these two children are really interesting in their love. I fear for him more than for her; I doubt not he is acting very foolishly, judging from the disturbance this morning. We must consult together about it."

"But," said De Thou, very gravely, "upon my honor, I do not know what you mean. Who is acting foolishly?"

"Now, my dear Monsieur, will you still play the mysterious with me? It is really insulting," said the worthy man, beginning to be angry.

"No, indeed, I mean it not; whom have you affianced?"

"Again! fie, Monsieur!"

"And what was the disturbance this morning?"

"You are laughing at me! I take my leave," said the Abbé, rising.

"I vow that I understand not a word of all that has been told me to-day. Do you mean Monsieur de Cinq-Mars?"

"Very well, Monsieur, very well! you treat me as a Cardinalist; very well, we part," said the Abbé Quillet, now altogether furious. And he snatched up his crutch and quitted the room hastily, without listening to De Thou, who followed him to his carriage, seeking to pacify him, but without effect, because he did not wish to name his friend upon the stairs in the hearing of his servants, and could not explain the matter otherwise. He had the annoyance of seeing the old Abbé depart, still in a passion; he called out to him amicably, "To-morrow," as the coachman drove off, but got no answer.

It was, however, not uselessly that he had descended to the foot of the stairs, for he saw thence hideous groups of the mob returning from the Louvre, and was thus better able to judge of the importance of their movements in the morning; he heard rude voices exclaiming, as in triumph:

"She showed herself, however, the little Queen!"— "Long live the good Duc de Bouillon, who is coming to us! He has a hundred thousand men with him, all on rafts on the Seine. The old Cardinal de la Rochelle is dead! Long live the King! Long live Monsieur le Grand!"

The cries redoubled at the arrival of a carriage and four, with the royal livery, which stopped at the counsellor's door, and in which De Thou recognized the equipage of Cinq-Mars; Ambrosio alighted to open the ample curtains, which the carriages of that period had for doors. The people threw themselves between the carriage-steps and the door of the house, so that Cinq-Mars had an absolute struggle ere he could get out and disengage himself from the market-women, who sought to embrace him, crying:

"Here you are, then, my sweet, my dear! Here you are, my pet! Ah, how handsome he is, the love, with his big collar! Isn't he worth more than the other fellow with the white moustache? Come, my son, bring us out some good wine this morning."

Henri d'Effiat pressed, blushing deeply the while, his friend's hand, who hastened to have his doors closed.

"This popular favor is a cup one must drink," said he, as they ascended the stairs.

"It appears to me," replied De Thou, gravely, "that you drink it even to the very dregs."

"I will explain all this clamorous affair to you," answered Cinq-Mars, somewhat embarrassed. "At present, if you love me, dress yourself to accompany me to the Queen's toilette."

"I promised you blind adherence," said the counsellor; "but truly I can not keep my eyes shut much longer if——"

"Once again, I will give you a full explanation as we return from the Queen. But make haste; it is nearly ten o'clock."

"Well, I will go with you," replied De Thou, conducting him into his cabinet, where were the Comte du Lude and Fournier, while he himself passed into his dressing-room.

CHAPTER XVII

THE TOILETTE

Nous allons chercher, comme dans les abimes, les anciennes prérogatives de cette Noblesse qui, depuis onze siècles, est couverte de poussière, de sang et de sueur.—MONTESQUIEU.

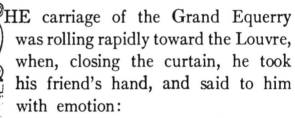

THE carriage of the Grand Equerry was rolling rapidly toward the Louvre, when, closing the curtain, he took his friend's hand, and said to him with emotion:

"Dear De Thou, I have kept great secrets in my heart, and, believe me, they have weighed heavily there; but two fears impelled me to silence—that of your danger, and—shall I say it?—that of your counsels."

"Yet well you know," replied De Thou, "that I despise the first; and I deemed that you did not despise the second."

"No, but I feared, and still fear them. I would not be stopped. Do not speak, my friend; not a word, I conjure you, before you have heard and seen all that is about to take place. I will return with you to your house on quitting the Louvre; there I will listen to you, and thence I shall depart to continue my work, for nothing will shake my resolve, I warn you. I have just said so to the gentlemen at your house.'"

In his accent Cinq-Mars had nothing of the brusqueness which clothed his words. His voice was conciliatory, his look gentle, amiable, affectionate, his air as tranquil as it was determined. There was no indication of the slightest effort at control. De Thou remarked it, and sighed.

Alighting from the carriage with him, De Thou followed him up the great staircase of the Louvre. When they entered the Queen's apartment, announced by two ushers dressed in black and bearing ebony rods, she was seated at her toilette. This was a table of black wood, inlaid with tortoise-shell, mother-of-pearl, and brass, in an infinity of designs of very bad taste, but which give to all furniture an air of grandeur which we still admire in it. A mirror, rounded at the top, which the ladies of our time would consider small and insignificant, stood in the middle of the table, whereon were scattered jewels and necklaces.

Anne of Austria, seated before it in a large armchair of crimson velvet, with long gold fringe, was as motionless and grave as on her throne, while Doña Stefania and Madame de Motteville, on either side, lightly touched her beautiful blond hair with a comb, as if finishing the Queen's coiffure, which, however, was already perfectly arranged and decorated with pearls. Her long tresses, though light, were exquisitely glossy, manifesting that to the touch they must be fine and soft as silk. The daylight fell without a shade upon her forehead, which had no reason to dread the test, itself reflecting an almost equal light from its surpassing fairness, which the Queen was pleased thus to display. Her blue eyes, blended with green, were large and regular, and her vermilion mouth had that under-lip of the princesses of Austria, somewhat prominent and slightly cleft, in the form of a cherry, which may still be marked in all the female portraits of this time, whose painters seemed to have aimed at imitating the Queen's mouth, in order to please the women of her suite, whose desire was, no doubt, to resemble her.

The black dress then adopted by the court, and of which the form was even fixed by an edict, set off the ivory of her arms, bare to the elbow, and ornamented with a profusion of lace, which flowed from her loose sleeves. Large pearls hung in her ears and from her girdle. Such was the appearance of the Queen at this moment. At her feet, upon two velvet cushions, a boy of four years old was playing with a little cannon, which he was assiduously breaking in pieces. This was the Dauphin, afterward Louis XIV. The Duchesse Marie de Mantua was seated on her right hand upon a stool. The Princesse de Guéménée, the Duchesse de Chevreuse, and Mademoiselle de Mont-bazon, Mesdemoiselles de Guise, de Rohan, and de Vendôme, all beautiful and brilliant with youth, were behind her, standing. In the recess of a window, Monsieur, his hat under his arm, was talking in a low voice with a man, stout, with a red face and a steady and daring eye. This was the Duc de Bouillon. An officer about twenty-five years of age, well-formed, and of agreeable presence, had just given several papers to the Prince, which the Duc de Bouillon appeared to be explaining to him.

De Thou, after having saluted the Queen, who said a few words to him, approached the Princesse de Gueménée, and conversed with her in an undertone, with an air of affectionate intimacy, but all the while intent upon his friend's interest. Secretly trembling lest he should have confided his destiny to a being less worthy of him than he wished, he examined the Princess Marie with the scrupulous attention, the scrutinizing eye of a mother examining the woman whom her son has selected for his bride—for he thought that Marie could not be altogether a stranger to the enterprise of Cinq-Mars. He saw with dissatisfaction that her dress, which was extremely elegant, appeared to inspire her with more vanity than became her on such an occasion. She was incessantly rearranging upon her forehead and her hair the rubies which ornamented her head, and which scarcely equalled the brilliancy and animated color of her complexion. She looked frequently at Cinq-Mars; but it was rather the look of coquetry than that of love, and her eyes often glanced toward the mirror on the toilette, in which she watched the symmetry of her beauty. These observations of the counsellor began to persuade him that he was mistaken in suspecting her to be the aim of Cinq-Mars, especially when he saw that she seemed to have a pleasure in sitting at the Queen's side, while the duchesses stood behind her, and that she often looked haughtily at them.

"In that heart of nineteen," said he, "love, were there love, would reign alone and above all to-day. It is not she!"

The Queen made an almost imperceptible movement of the head to Madame de Gueménée. After the two friends had spoken a moment with each person present, and at this sign, all the ladies, except Marie de Mantua, making profound courtesies, quitted the apartment without speaking, as if by previous arrangement. The Queen, then herself turning her chair, said to Monsieur:

"My brother, I beg you will come and sit down by me. We will consult upon what I have already told you. The Princesse Marie will not be in the way. I begged her to remain. We have no interruption to fear."

The Queen seemed more at ease in her manner and language; and no longer preserving her severe and ceremonious immobility, she signed to the other persons present to approach her.

Gaston d'Orléans, somewhat alarmed at this solemn opening, came carelessly, sat down on her right hand, and said with a half-smile and a negligent air, playing with his ruff and the chain of the Saint Esprit which hung from his neck:

"I think, Madame, that we shall fatigue the ears of so young a personage by a long conference. She would rather hear us speak of dances, and of marriage, of an elector, or of the King of Poland, for example."

Marie assumed a disdainful air; Cinq-Mars frowned.

"Pardon me," replied the Queen, looking at her;

"I assure you the politics of the present time interest her much. Do not seek to escape us, my brother," added she, smiling. "I have you to-day! It is the least we can do to listen to Monsieur de Bouillon."

The latter approached, holding by the hand the young officer of whom we have spoken.

"I must first," said he, "present to your Majesty the Baron de Beauvau, who has just arrived from Spain."

"From Spain?" said the Queen, with emotion. "There is courage in that; you have seen my family?"

"He will speak to you of them, and of the Count-Duke of Olivarès. As to courage, it is not the first time he has shown it. He commanded the cuirassiers of the Comte de Soissons."

"How? so young, sir! You must be fond of political wars."

"On the contrary, your Majesty will pardon me," replied he, "for I served with the *princes of the peace.*"

Anne of Austria smiled at this *jeu-de-mot.* The Duc de Bouillon, seizing the moment to bring forward the grand question he had in view, quitted Cinq-Mars, to whom he had just given his hand with an air of the most zealous friendship, and approaching the Queen with him, "It is miraculous, Madame," said he, "that this period still contains in its bosom some noble characters, such as these;" and he pointed to the master of the horse, to young Beauvau, and to De Thou. "It is only in them that we can place our hope for the future. Such men are indeed very rare now, for the great leveller has swung a long scythe over France."

"Is it of Time you speak," said the Queen, "or of a real personage?"

"Too real, too living, too long living, Madame!" replied the Duke, becoming more animated; "but his measureless ambition, his colossal selfishness can no longer be endured. All those who have noble hearts are indignant at this yoke; and at this moment, more than ever, we see misfortunes threatening us in the future. It must be said, Madame—yes, it is no longer time to blind ourselves to the truth, or to conceal it— the King's illness is serious. The moment for thinking and resolving has arrived, for the time to act is not far distant."

The severe and abrupt tone of M. de Bouillon did not surprise Anne of Austria; but she had always seen him more calm, and was, therefore, somewhat alarmed by the disquietude he betrayed. Quitting accordingly the tone of pleasantry which she had at first adopted, she said:

"How! what fear you, and what would you do?"

"I fear nothing for myself, Madame, for the army of Italy or Sedan will always secure my safety; but I fear for you, and perhaps for the princes, your sons."

"For my children, Monsieur le Duc, for the sons of France? Do you hear him, my brother, and do you not appear astonished?"

The Queen was deeply agitated.

"No, Madame," said Gaston d'Orléans, calmly; "you know that I am accustomed to persecution. I am prepared to expect anything from that man. He is master; we must be resigned."

"He master!" exclaimed the Queen. "And from whom does he derive his powers, if not from the King? And after the King, what hand will sustain him? Can you tell me? Who will prevent him from again returning to nothing? Will it be you or I?"

"It will be himself," interrupted M. de Bouillon, "for he seeks to be named regent; and I know that at at this moment he contemplates taking your children from you, and requiring the King to confide them to his care."

"Take them from me!" cried the mother, involuntarily seizing the Dauphin, and taking him in her arms.

The child, standing between the Queen's knees, looked at the men who surrounded him with a gravity very singular for his age, and, seeing his mother in tears, placed his hand upon the little sword he wore.

"Ah, Monseigneur," said the Duc de Bouillon, bending half down to address to him what he intended for the Princess, "it is not against us that you must draw your sword, but against him who is undermining your throne. He prepares an empire for you, no doubt. You will have an absolute sceptre; but he has scattered the fasces which indicated it. Those fasces were your ancient nobility, whom he has decimated. When you are king, you will be a great king. I foresee it; but you will have subjects only, and no friends, for friendship exists only in independence and a kind of equality which takes its rise in force. Your ancestors had their peers; you will not have yours. May God aid you then, Monseigneur, for man may not do it without institutions! Be great; but above all, around you, a great man, let there be others as strong, so that if the one stumbles, the whole monarchy may not fall."

The Duc de Bouillon had a warmth of expression and a confidence of manner which captivated those who heard him. His valor, his keen perception in the field, the profundity of his political views, his knowledge of the affairs of Europe, his reflective and decided character, all rendered him one of the most capable and imposing men of his time—the only one, indeed, whom the Cardinal-Duc really feared. The Queen always listened to him with confidence, and allowed him to acquire a sort of empire over her. She was now more deeply moved than ever.

"Ah, would to God," she exclaimed, "that my son's mind was ripe for your counsels, and his arm strong enough to profit by them! Until that time, however, I will listen, I will act for him. It is I who should be, and it is I who shall be, regent. I will not resign this right save with life. If we must make war, we will make it; for I will do everything but submit to the shame and terror of yielding up the future Louis XIV to this crowned subject. Yes," she went on, coloring and closely pressing the young Dauphin's arm, "yes, my brother, and you gentlemen, counsel me! Speak! how do we stand? Must I depart? Speak openly. As a woman, as a wife, I could have wept over so mournful a position; but now see, as a mother, I do not weep. I am ready to give you orders if it is necessary."

Never had Anne of Austria looked so beautiful as at this moment; and the enthusiasm she manifested electrified all those present, who needed but a word from her mouth to speak. The Duc de Bouillon cast a glance at Monsieur, which decided him.

"*Ma foi!*" said he, with deliberation, "if you give orders, my sister, I will be the captain of your guards, on my honor, for I too am weary of the vexations occasioned me by this knave. He continues to persecute me, seeks to break off my marriage, and still keeps my friends in the Bastille, or has them assassinated from time to time; and besides, I am indignant," said he, recollecting himself and assuming a more solemn air, "I am indignant at the misery of the people."

"My brother," returned the Princess, energetically, "I take you at your word, for with you, one must do so; and I hope that together we shall be strong enough for the purpose. Do only as Monsieur le Comte de Soissons did, but survive your victory. Side with me, as you did with Monsieur de Montmorency, but leap the ditch."

Gaston felt the point of this. He called to mind the well-known incident when the unfortunate rebel of Castelnaudary leaped almost alone a large ditch, and found on the other side seventeen wounds, a prison, and death in the sight of Monsieur, who remained motionless with his army. In the rapidity of the Queen's enunciation he had not time to examine whether she had employed this expression proverbially or with a direct reference; but at all events, he decided not to notice it, and was indeed prevented from doing so by the Queen, who continued, looking at Cinq-Mars:

"But, above all, no panic-terror! Let us know exactly where we are, Monsieur le Grand. You have just left the King. Is there fear with you?"

D'Effiat had not ceased to observe Marie de Mantua, whose expressive countenance exhibited to him all her ideas far more rapidly and more surely than words. He read there the desire that he should speak —the desire that he should confirm the Prince and the Queen. An impatient movement of her foot conveyed to him her will that the thing should be accomplished, the conspiracy arranged. His face became pale and more pensive; he pondered for a moment, realizing that his destiny was contained in that hour. De Thou looked at him and trembled, for he knew him well. He would fain have said one word to him, only one word; but Cinq-Mars had already raised his head. He spoke:

"I do not think, Madame, that the King is so ill as you suppose. God will long preserve to us this Prince. I hope so; I am even sure of it. He suffers, it is true, suffers much; but it is his soul more peculiarly that is sick, and of an evil which nothing can cure—of an evil which one would not wish to one's greatest enemy, and which would gain him the pity of the whole world if it were known. The end of his misery—that is to say, of his life—will not be granted him for a long time. His languor is entirely moral. There is in his heart a great revolution going on; he would accomplish it, and can not.

"The King has felt for many long years growing within him the seeds of a just hatred against a man to whom he thinks he owes gratitude, and it is this internal combat between his natural goodness and his anger that devours him. Every year that has passed has deposited at his feet, on one side, the great works of this man, and on the other, his crimes. It is the last which now weigh down the balance. The King sees them and is indignant; he would punish, but all at once he stops and weeps. If you could witness him thus, Madame, you would pity him. I have seen him seize the pen which was to sign his exile, dip it into the ink with a bold hand, and use it—for what? —to congratulate him on some recent success. He at once applauds himself for his goodness as a Christian, curses himself for his weakness as a sovereign judge, despises himself as a king. He seeks refuge in prayer, and plunges into meditation upon the future; then he rises terrified because he has seen in thought the tortures which this man merits, and how deeply no one knows better than he. You should hear him in these moments accuse himself of criminal weakness, and exclaim that he himself should be punished for not having known how to punish. One would say that there are spirits which order him to strike, for his arms are raised as he sleeps. In a word, Madame, the storm murmurs in his heart, but burns none but himself. The thunderbolts are chained."

"Well, then, let us loose them!" exclaimed the Duc de Bouillon.

"He who touches them may die of the contact," said Monsieur.

"But what a noble devotion!" cried the Queen.

"How I should admire the hero!" said Marie, in a half-whisper.

"I will do it," answered Cinq-Mars.

"*We* will do it," said M. de Thou, in his ear.

Young Beauvau had approached the Duc de Bouillon.

"Monsieur," said he, "do you forget what follows?"

"No, *pardieu!* I do not forget it," replied the latter, in a low voice; then, addressing the Queen, "Madame," said he, "accept the offer of Monsieur le Grand. He is more in a position to sway the King than either you or I; but hold yourself prepared, for the Cardinal is too wary to be caught sleeping. I do not believe in his illness. I have no faith in the silence and immobility of which he has sought to persuade us these two years past. I would not believe in his death even, unless I had myself thrown his head into the sea, like that of the giant in Ariosto. Hold yourself ready to meet all contingencies, and let us, meanwhile, hasten our operations. I have shown my plans to Monsieur just now; I will give you a summary of them. I offer you Sedan, Madame, for yourself, and for Messeigneurs, your sons. The army of Italy is mine; I will recall it if necessary. Monsieur le Grand is master of half the camp of Perpignan. All the old Huguenots of La Rochelle and the South are ready to come to him at the first nod. All has been organized for a year past, by my care, to meet events."

"I should not hesitate," said the Queen, "to place myself in your hands, to save my children, if any misfortune should happen to the King. But in this general plan you forget Paris."

"It is ours on every side; the people by the archbishop, without his suspecting it, and by Monsieur de Beaufort, who is its king; the troops by your guards and those of Monsieur, who shall be chief in command, if he please."

"I! I! oh, that positively can not be! I have not enough people, and I must have a retreat stronger than Sedan," said Gaston.

"It suffices for the Queen," replied M. de Bouillon.

"Ah, that may be! but my sister does not risk so much as a man who draws the sword. Do you know that these are bold measures you propose?"

"What, even if we have the King on our side?" asked Anne of Austria.

"Yes, Madame, yes; we do not know how long that may last. We must make ourselves sure; and I do nothing without the treaty with Spain."

"Do nothing, then," said the Queen, coloring deeply; "for certainly I will never hear that spoken of."

"And yet, Madame, it were more prudent, and Monsieur is right," said the Duc de Bouillon; "for the Count-Duke of San Lucra offers us seventeen thousand men, tried troops, and five hundred thousand crowns in ready money."

"What!" exclaimed the Queen, with astonishment, "have you dared to proceed so far without my consent? already treaties with foreigners!"

"Foreigners, my sister! could we imagine that a princess of Spain would use that word?" said Gaston.

Anne of Austria rose, taking the Dauphin by the hand; and, leaning upon Marie: "Yes, sir," she said, "I am a Spaniard; but I am the grand-daughter of Charles V, and I know that a queen's country is where her throne is. I leave you, gentlemen; proceed without me. I know nothing of the matter for the future."

She advanced some steps, but seeing Marie pale and bathed in tears, she returned.

"I will, however, solemnly promise you inviolable secrecy; but nothing more."

All were mentally disconcerted, except the Duc de Bouillon, who, not willing to lose the advantages he had gained, said to the Queen, bowing respectfully:

"We are grateful for this promise, Madame, and we ask no more, persuaded that after the first success you will be entirely with us."

Not wishing to engage in a war of words, the Queen courtesied somewhat less coldly, and quitted the apartment with Marie, who cast upon Cinq-Mars one of those looks which comprehend at once all the emotions of the soul. He seemed to read in her beautiful eyes the eternal and mournful devotion of a woman who has given herself up forever; and he felt that if he had once thought of withdrawing from his enterprise, he should now have considered himself the basest of men.

As soon as the two princesses had disappeared, "There, there! I told you so, Bouillon, you offended the Queen," said Monsieur; "you went too far. You can not certainly accuse me of having been hesitating this morning. I have, on the contrary, shown more resolution than I ought to have done."

"I am full of joy and gratitude toward her Majesty," said M. de Bouillon, with a triumphant air; "we are sure of the future. What will you do now, Monsieur de Cinq-Mars?"

"I have told you, Monsieur; I draw not back, whatever the consequences. I will see the King; I will run every risk to obtain his assent."

"And the treaty with Spain?"

"Yes, I——"

De Thou seized Cinq-Mars by the arm, and, advancing suddenly, said, with a solemn air:

"We have decided that it shall be only signed after the interview with the King; for should his Majesty's just severity toward the Cardinal dispense with it, we have thought it better not to expose ourselves to the discovery of so dangerous a treaty."

M. de Bouillon frowned.

"If I did not know Monsieur de Thou," said he, "I should have regarded this as a defection; but from him——"

"Monsieur," replied the counsellor, "I think I may engage myself, on my honor, to do all that Monsieur le Grand does; we are inseparable."

Cinq-Mars looked at his friend, and was astonished to see upon his mild countenance the expression of sombre despair; he was so struck with it that he had not the courage to gainsay him.

"He is right, gentlemen," he said with a cold but kindly smile; "the King will perhaps spare us much trouble. We may do good things with him. For the rest, Monseigneur, and you, Monsieur le Duc," he added with immovable firmness, "fear not that I shall ever draw back. I have burned all the bridges behind me. I must advance; the Cardinal's power shall fall, or my head."

"It is strange, very strange!" said Monsieur; "I see that every one here is farther advanced in the conspiracy than I imagined."

"Not so, Monsieur," said the Duc de Bouillon; "we prepared only that which you might please to accept. Observe that there is nothing in writing. You have but to speak, and nothing exists or ever has existed; according to your order, the whole thing shall be a dream or a volcano."

"Well, well, I am content, if it must be so," said Gaston; "let us occupy ourselves with more agreeable topics. Thank God, we have a little time before us! I confess I wish that it were all over. I am not fitted for violent emotions; they affect my health," he added, taking M. de Beauvau's arm. "Tell us if the Spanish women are still pretty, young man. It is said you are a great gallant among them. *Tudieu !* I'm sure you've got yourself talked of there. They tell me the women wear enormous petticoats. Well,

I am not at all against that; they make the foot look smaller and prettier. I'm sure the wife of Don Louis de Haro is not handsomer than Madame de Gueménée, is she? Come, be frank; I'm told she looks like a nun. Ah! you do not answer; you are embarrassed. She has then taken your fancy; or you fear to offend our friend Monsieur de Thou in comparing her with the beautiful Gueménée. Well, let's talk of the customs; the King has a charming dwarf I'm told, and they put him in a pie. He is a fortunate man, that King of Spain! I don't know another equally so. And the Queen, she is still served on bended knee, is she not? Ah! that is a good custom; we have lost it. It is very unfortunate—more unfortunate than may be supposed."

And Gaston d'Orléans had the confidence to speak in this tone nearly half an hour, with a young man whose serious character was not at all adapted to such conversation, and who, still occupied with the importance of the scene he had just witnessed and the great interests which had been discussed, made no answer to this torrent of idle words. He looked at the Duc de Bouillon with an astonished air, as if to ask him whether this was really the man whom they were going to place at the head of the most audacious enterprise that had ever been launched; while the Prince, without appearing to perceive that he remained unanswered, replied to himself, speaking with volubility, as he drew him gradually out of the room. He feared that one of the gentlemen present might recommence the terrible conversation about the treaty;

but none desired to do so, unless it were the Duc de Bouillon, who, however, preserved an angry silence. As for Cinq-Mars, he had been led away by De Thou, under cover of the chattering of Monsieur, who took care not to appear to notice their departure.

END OF VOL. I

Lightning Source UK Ltd.
Milton Keynes UK
UKHW012344061118
331891UK00010B/589/P